ASCENDING PASSION

OTHER BOOKS BY AMANDA

HEAVEN'S HEART

ASCENDING PASSION

BOOK FOUR

AMANDA PILLAR

Published by Maatkare Books
www.amandapillar.com

Editor: Pete Kemsphall

ISBN: 978-0-6480295-9-5

Cover Design: Yocla Book Cover Designs © 2018
Internal Layout: Amanda Pillar © 2019
Editor: Pete Kempshall

First Published August 2019

To all my readers. You guys rock so hard.

VALLEY OF THE KINGS

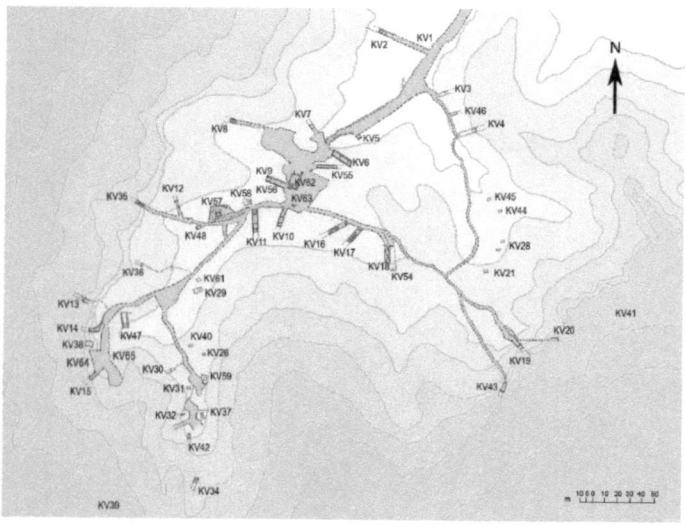

Map of the Valley of the Kings with new tombs in blue (After
https://commons.wikimedia.org/wiki/File:East_Valley_of_the_Kings_Sket
ch_Map_(Topo).png)

CHAPTER 1

Nine months earlier…

Archangels are terrifying.

Yael realized he probably shouldn't be focusing on that fact right now, considering he was sitting in front of one, but he couldn't stop the primordial fear from skittering along his spine.

And Gabriel was one of the…nicer archangels.

They were seated in a small office that had gold-veined marble walls, a glass desk and a softly carpeted floor. Yael hoped his boots weren't leaving scuff marks behind. Everything in the office was organized with the utmost precision; he had a feeling he was the untidiest thing here.

Gabriel's gold-threaded wings arched behind him as he concentrated on a scroll, tapping his fingers as he read over it.

I'm glad my wings have silver.

Yael's parents had dearly wanted him to be an

archangel, but he was happier with his warrior status. He'd grown up playing in the cloud-scudded yard of an archangel, whose gold-threaded wings soared proudly in the sky above. But he preferred to spend time with the silver-threaded warriors, rose-gold healers, and bronze scholars. Secretly though, he'd wished for pure white wings; they meant you could largely choose your destiny.

And Yael had always wanted the ability to choose.

At least I like fighting.

Finally, Gabriel glanced up. "You wished to speak to me?"

The archangel's dark hair hung messily over his forehead, his violet eyes piercing in their intensity. It was like the other angel could see into Yael's soul, right down to the sinful and jealous part of his nature.

He didn't like it.

"Yes, thank you for fitting me in to your schedule." As Heaven's spymaster, Gabriel was one of the busiest angels in all the Heavens. Yael leaned forward. "I heard you are recruiting."

Both of Gabriel's dark eyebrows rose. "You are a member of the Darts. Surely that is quite enough."

He nodded, because he couldn't lie to an archangel. Being a member of the Darts *was* prestigious, but he didn't find it satisfying. "It is important work. But I have skills that are better suited elsewhere."

His military unit was small—it only comprised six members in total—and was supposedly made up from the best of the best. And his fellow Darts *were* excellent. Dina, their captain, was almost as powerful as an archangel, while Raziel was composed, calm, and utterly focused. Azrael was perhaps one of the most skilled fighters Yael had ever met, while Zadkiel was impressive, for one so young.

And then there was Seraphina.

She was the fastest flier he'd ever met, and the inspiration for this visit: she'd been one of Gabriel's scouts, before she'd been recruited for the Darts. She'd had nothing but praise for her former master, which was vital. In a world full of powerful beings, it was rare to find one who led with compassion and integrity, even in Heaven. And if Yael was going to jump from the frying pan into the fire, he didn't want a cruel master.

His parents were bad enough.

Gabriel studied him. "You do realize the kind of work I am involved in?"

"Spying. Assassination."

The archangel's violet gaze narrowed. "Most just say spying."

"Yes, but it's the assassination I am interested in."

Does that make me a psychopath?

Maybe. Possibly?

Most likely.

Yael much preferred his favorite weapon, the garrote, to a sword. It made him unique—and unsettling—in a world full of pacifists. Swordplay was an art they could understand. You should practice it simply because it was beauty in motion. But sharp wire designed to slice and choke? No, that was too gruesome.

And, for his parents, it was a little too 'common'.

Maybe that was why he liked to get up close and personal when he killed. He never was very good at meeting his parents' expectations.

"I will review your service record," Gabriel said. "But that is no guarantee of a position with me. I expect absolute commitment, dedication, and loyalty."

"Thank you." Yael shifted uncomfortably in his seat. It was more than he could have asked for, really. But he had a suspicion that Gabriel thought he lacked the 'loyalty' element—Yael was, after all, going behind backs of the other Darts in requesting this position.

"Come back in a week."

Yael nodded and stood. "I appreciate it."

As he left Gabriel's office, he thought, *I will not be a glorified guard.*

He didn't want that for his future. For centuries, Heaven had been impervious to attack. When would he ever see battle, guarding an ancient relic that no one cared about?

That's unfair.

Lots of angels were interested in the artifact. Pilgrims came from all over the Heavens to see Heaven's Heart— but they were unlikely to steal the object. None would dare.

He was almost back at his rooms when he heard Azrael's mental shout.

Come to the sanctum, now!

Fiercely controlled panic underlaid every word.

Hand hovering over the doorknob, he shot back, *What's happened?*

�֍

Heaven has been raided.

The impossible had happened. The Celestial City had been breached by demons, the stench of their flesh polluting the air with sulfur and ozone, even after they'd escaped. The Inner Sanctum, the squat building that had sat undisturbed for centuries, had been broken open, cracked like an egg to reveal its insides.

And the insides?

Gone.

Heaven's Heart, the relic he had guarded for the past hundred years, had been stolen.

Is this a prank? A test?

Two archangels stood before them, their power and anger forcing the remaining Darts to their knees, the stone floor hard against bone. There was no sign of Dina and Zadkiel—the two squadron members who had been on guard duty—and they hadn't replied to his telepathic queries, either.

Kidnapped.

It was either that, or they'd been in on the raid. But the scattered blood and lost feathers indicated there'd been a fight. And he couldn't believe that either would betray Heaven. Betray *them.*

The archangel Michael laid a heavy hand on Azrael's shoulder, and Yael saw his fellow Dart grit his teeth. Azrael's gaze was locked on the Inner Sanctum's burned door, as if he could will it back together.

Michael spoke, fury saturating his every word. "You will *all* be punished for this."

Yael bowed his head, the other Darts doing the same.

"Do you know who breached the walls?" Raziel asked, his deep voice filling the hall.

"At this stage, it does not matter who attacked us," Michael replied, while the other archangel, Uriel, scowled. "Heaven's Heart has been stolen. Do you understand what you've all done?"

Yael clenched his jaw to keep from arguing. *What bullshit!* The identity of their attackers was the most important piece of information they could obtain; the second was what had happened to Dina and Zadkiel. The archangels *knew* that. He knew that. So why were they being so dismissive?

And why are they blaming us?

The archangels themselves had decreed that only two guards were required to patrol the Inner Sanctum, which was why there were only six Darts—they took shifts. If it had been up to the Darts themselves, there would have been bigger patrols and more soldiers.

"Sire," Raziel murmured, "if you will let us search, we will find the Heart and bring it back."

Michael's long brown hair swung over his shoulder, the braid brushing over his robes as he moved. His massive gold-threaded wings soared over his shoulders, while his pure white eyes surveyed them. "Oh, you will search for the Heart," he said. "But first, you must pay the price for your failure." A huge sword appeared in his right hand, conjured there by his power.

No.

No fucking way.

Another sword appeared in Uriel's hand, the golden metal a perfect match to the archangel's robe, his ebony skin glinting with blue highlights. A pulse of power indicated that more angels had arrived.

Gabriel. Lorath. Mirare. The latter two weren't archangels, but they were powerful in their own right, and generals in Heaven's vast army.

Yael met Gabriel's violet stare, which was filled with pity.

He swallowed against the panic, but it wouldn't abate. His pulse roared in his ears, while his fingers clenched into a fist. *I'm going to lose my wings.*

I don't deserve this.

We *don't deserve this.*

"Word of this will have reached all of Heaven before sunset," Uriel said. "Examples must be made."

"Examples?" Seraphina's voice rang out, and Yael applauded her courage.

If he ever fell in love, it would be with someone like her.

Michael stepped closer, his white gaze cold and empty. "You will all be exiled from Heaven."

Exiled.

No. He had finally taken the step toward mastering his own life, only to have it stolen away…

"You will only be allowed to return if you find all three pieces of the Heart and give them to us," Michael continued.

Wait.

"All *three* pieces?" Yael demanded.

"We guarded but one part of the Heart," Michael said. "It is time all three were rejoined and stored here for safety."

He met Gabriel's burning stare, and the archangel had the decency to look away.

Those fuckers.

They've given us an unwinnable quest.

But he would do it. No matter the cost, he would do it. There was no way he would be kept from returning to Heaven, from taking his rightful place among his peers.

"Can you give us any information on what we might seek?" Raziel asked, ever practical.

Michael shook his head. "This is a punishment. We will not help you with it."

"Then we shall leave at once, so we may find the stolen piece and its brethren." Raziel's tone was filled with purpose.

How optimistic.

But those swords hadn't been conjured just so the archangels could look like badasses.

"There is something else that must be done first," Uriel said, and Yael swore the archangel fought a smirk.

Without warning, Azrael was shoved face-down onto the blood-stained marble floor. Yael jerked as a strong hand grabbed his shoulder, pushing him forward. He turned his head, meeting the violet eyes of Gabriel. The archangel appeared sad, defeated.

"This must be done."

He stretched out one of Yael's wings then, holding it out straight, exposed the part where the tendons met the back muscles.

Breathe, just breathe, you're stronger than this.

Agony erupted through him, the pain so intense he blacked out and his heart jerked to a stop, before restarting with a vengeance. Each beat shot new pain through his every limb, and nausea threatened to empty his stomach before them all.

Breathe, just breathe.

Then it was done.

Wings shot with silver threads were thrown on the ground, just inches from his reach. Twin stumps that had once joined living flesh provided an obscene reminder of their past. Of his past. Of what he had once been.

He met Gabriel's pitying look over the top of his mutilated wings.

I will never give up.

Ever.

CHAPTER 2

The Human Realm, present day

Tears wore familiar tracks down Rowan Broome's cheeks as the coffin was lowered into the ground, the gaping maw of the earth ready to swallow its latest victim.

Death.

It wasn't pretty, nor was it welcome.

She'd begged for a cremation, but she'd been overridden. They wanted a coffin, a funeral, and a place to grieve. Rowan had wanted something safe, something that wouldn't be excavated in a few hundred years by someone like herself. To know that her loved one would be unrestricted, scattered on the wind, free to sweep through the world at will.

"You are doing well." The crackly voice was accompanied by a gentle pat on the shoulder.

Rowan turned to her gran, taking in the familiar wrinkled visage that was both welcome and unwanted simultaneously.

"Thanks." She twisted back to the grave, to the place where the man she loved was being laid to rest.

She bit back a sob.

She loved her gran, loved her family, but they all believed in magic, in what couldn't be seen, measured or studied.

In short: they were crazy.

Before, she'd been happy for them to have their delusions, to sell magic and hope to others so they could make a living. But three months ago, she'd helped her gran and suffered a head injury in the process. She'd lost memories. Lost time.

Her gran and her 'magic' hadn't been able to help her.

And when she'd gone to her gran after learning about Eric, her grandmother—'the most powerful witch in all of America'—had failed to save him. Had just let him die. Her future grandson.

Proof yet again that her magical powers were nothing more than smoke and mirrors.

Everything Gran represented was a lie, while Rowan was drowning in the truth: Eric Gunner had been the love of her life, and now he was gone.

Fatally injured in a car crash.

Fate was a cruel, fickle mistress.

A soft touch on her arm snapped her back to reality. The coffin had reached the base of the grave. Stepping forward, Rowan grabbed a handful of dirt from the damp soil piled next to the hole. Eric's mother did the same. Together, they faced the pit and threw the earth onto the wooden box below, the sound like pattering rain. The dirt sealed his fate: trapped him in the ground.

"Ashes to ashes, dust to dust..." The priest's voice droned in the background, but Rowan couldn't absorb the words.

Sobs wracked her: she had lost more than just a person with Eric's death. She'd lost the children they'd joked about, the future they'd dreamed of, the world they'd wanted to create for the two of them.

Kind hands touched her forearms as mourners streamed past her, each telling her how sorry they were, how sad it all was. It meant little. They couldn't bring him back. They couldn't take her pain away.

Their apologies were worthless.

Finally, Gran took hold of her elbow, and steered her toward the town car. "The wake is on in an hour."

Rowan dutifully climbed into the back of the Mercedes and stared straight ahead. "Take me straight there."

Gran called instructions to the driver.

A short silence ensued, one Rowan barely noticed.

"I am sorry, you know," Gran said quietly.

Rowan turned to her, dabbing at her cheeks with a handkerchief. "Not sorry enough."

"Magic can't bring the dead back to life. Some things are against the laws of nature."

"You're the most powerful witch in the Americas." She doubted that level of sarcasm had ever been directed at her gran before. "Surely such a feat would have been simple. Plus, he wasn't dead when I came to you."

"You don't believe in magic."

"You have yet to prove it's real." Rowan turned to the window, her eyes sliding over the Manhattan streetscape, as if it wasn't there.

Rowan had always felt welcome at her future in-laws. But not today. Today it was as if she were a stranger, come to perch at their son's funeral like a vulture ready to pick at the scraps.

The living room was packed with people, all dressed in black, some with drawn faces, others tear-stained and splotchy. Platters of food were passed around, while wine and liquor were at hand for those in need of something stronger.

She held a glass of water.

"Eric was such a lovely man."

Rowan turned to his aunt, Edna, and nodded mutely. Edna grabbed her free hand and rubbed it, as if she could impart warmth into Rowan's very being.

It was a kind gesture, but she didn't want it. Rather than jerk her hand away, which would be rude, she tried a wan smile, but from the widening of Aunt Edna's eyes, it wasn't a pleasant expression.

She let go of Rowan. "You should go rest, dear."

"Thank you." She didn't know what else to say.

Once she had moved on, Rowan took a sip of water, tasting nothing. A moment later, Eric's mom appeared in front of her. Her brown hair was slicked back into a bun, her oval face taut. "We need to talk."

"Okay." Placing her glass on the nearest flat surface,

Rowan followed Shannon Gunner into an empty sitting room. It was all very modern, from the sleek furniture to the large modernist paintings. What did she want to talk about? Rowan had already given back the items she thought Eric's parents would cherish the most.

In the closed room, Shannon crossed her arms over her chest. Rage flared in her brown eyes. "You aren't getting a cent."

Shock rooted Rowan to the ground. "I'm sorry?"

"You should be, you conniving gold-digger."

"Conniving *what*?"

The attack had come out of nowhere. A week ago, Eric's mom had been teasing her son about proposing to Rowan, about the redhaired grandkids she was looking forward to having.

"I don't understand." Rowan shook her head, replaying the words in her mind, but they still didn't make sense.

"You conned my son into changing his will!"

Through numb lips, she mumbled, "I didn't even know he *had* a will."

Eric hadn't owned property, not even a car. Why would he have had a will?

"Don't you lie to me." She unfolded her arms to jab a finger at her. "You know he inherited a fortune from Edward's father."

"No, I didn't."

They had never talked finances, apart from their salaries, hadn't even moved in together yet. Eric had wanted to be engaged first, and she'd been patiently waiting for him to propose.

"You're nothing but a lying wh—" Shannon's words cut off as the door opened.

"I wouldn't finish that sentence if you wish to retain the powers of speech." Rowan's gran stepped into the room, closing the door behind her.

Eric's mom scowled. "Don't you threaten me."

"Don't call my granddaughter names."

Rowan felt numb and stupid, standing between the two women. "Gran, did you know Eric was rich?"

Dark, intelligent eyes locked on Rowan. "Of course, I did. I had him investigated."

"You *what*?" Shannon screeched.

"You think I'd let any old fool date my granddaughter? You run around accusing her of being a gold-digger, when Rowan's worth is twice that of your son."

How much was Eric worth? How much am I worth?

Shannon blanched. "What?"

"I own a chain of stores across America." Gran thumped the floor with her cane. "You think I haven't set my family up for success?"

Rowan had had no idea.

She'd worked for everything she'd gotten—even paid off her college debts on her own. She'd had no idea she'd had family money. Then again, she probably wouldn't have wanted it, knowing how Gran had come by it.

"I didn't know…" Shannon muttered, her expression shuttering.

Gran leaned forward, her face intense, scary almost.

"Yes, well. That also means I can afford lawyers. Good ones. So, call my granddaughter a whore again. Do it. See your estate fall down around you."

"I—I—you misheard—"

Gran leaned back. "It is hard being old. One's hearing does fail from time to time." She turned to Rowan. "Come, let us leave this place and its misery. You will be better off surrounded by people who love you."

She nodded, then met Shannon's gaze. There was coldness there. Coldness and fear.

How unlike her son.

Eric had been loving and warm and wonderful. At least, he could be. This coldness, she'd seen it in him from time to time, but it had been fleeting. Nothing like what she was seeing now.

Leaving the room, Rowan said to her Gran, "Yes, there is nothing left for me here."

There was nothing left for her anywhere.

CHAPTER 3

Back in her small apartment, alone and dressed in her pajamas, Rowan stared down at her iPhone, and the smiling image of her and Eric on its lock screen. She couldn't bring herself to touch it.

Shannon thought she was a gold-digging whore. Had she always hated her, and simply put on a friendly face for Eric's sake? Or had she liked her, right up until the will had been read?

The thought made her heart hurt more.

All Rowan had wanted was to be part of a normal family. To have a loving husband, maybe a child or two, and to continue her career—all the while having a supportive group of in-laws, because her own family was nuts.

But it seemed that the promise of a future with a white-picket fence was a lie, too.

What in my life is real?

Her fingers were clenched around the phone, and when it rang, she jumped. She looked down at the caller

I.D.

Luke M. Starre. The incredibly handsome, incredibly rich antiquities collector she'd met three months ago.

He'd been in intermittent contact ever since he'd flown her to his Miami mansion to review his collection. It had been amazing. He owned what he claimed to be the sarcophagus of Menes, the first pharaoh of the First Dynasty of Egypt. *The* pharaoh who united the lower and upper kingdoms, creating the vast empire that had captured her imagination since she was a young child. He'd even let her take photos of it, and she'd been studying them ever since.

He had also claimed he could take her to the place where it had been found.

She'd been sorely tempted to go, but she wasn't sure she wanted to see the looted tomb. And she hadn't been able to just drop everything and leave. She had responsibilities, and work, and it felt wrong to fly away on a holiday with another man, leaving Eric behind to worry. He'd been jealous enough of Luke, even though she hadn't seen the wealthy man again.

She never told Eric that Luke had asked her on a date once, too.

Rowan had thought he was joking. When someone looked like he did—and was as rich as he was—what would he see in someone like her? Skinny, pale, redheaded and passably intelligent; not the kind of beauty queen he would be used to.

Even if she'd been single, she would have refused. She could never trust that his emotions were true, not when he had 'playboy' practically stamped on his forehead. He'd never shown romantic interest since, which had been a relief. She didn't like hurting people's feelings—or in this case, egos.

She answered the phone.

"Hi Rowan, this is Luke." His deep, dark voice punctured her melancholy. "I only have a few minutes, but I have a very interesting business proposition for you."

Straight to the point, as normal.

"Hi Luke. Just a reminder—I am not Lara Croft, Tomb Raider. I won't collect antiquities for you."

A low chuckle reached her. It was a running joke they'd established—he collected antiquities and she lectured him on his ill-gotten gains. He seemed to enjoy the debate.

"No, nothing like that," he replied. "I have sponsored an excavation in Egypt, in the Valley of the Kings. All *very* above-board. So above-board, in fact, that I've been drowning in paperwork for the past several months. I was wondering if you would be interested in working on it?"

The breath whooshed out of her.

The Valley of the Kings.

The. Valley. Of. The. Freaking. Kings.

To work there was a dream—but the permits alone were almost impossible to get.

Excitement warred with logic. "But I'd have to be approved by the authorities—"

"I may have already submitted documentation on

your behalf, in the hope you would say yes."

She closed her eyes and inhaled quickly.

Egypt. Her love, her passion...

The dig of a lifetime.

But Eric...

Her eyes snapped open. He'd want her to go. He knew it was her dream. In fact, he would have insisted, had he still been here. Not lying cold and neglected in the ground.

And what did she have left here, now?

Nothing, that's what.

Eric's mother thought the worst of her, and Rowan wasn't in the right frame of mind to deal with her own crazy family right now.

Her free hand balled into a fist so tight, her nails bit into her palm. "Yes. I'll go."

A moment's pause then Luke exhaled into the phone. "Excellent. I thought I would have to bribe you a little bit. I'll send you some paperwork to get you started. When can you leave?"

"When does the dig start?"

"In two weeks."

She gulped. "I'll see what I can do."

"Excellent." He paused. "And I am really very sorry. I heard the news about your partner. Please accept my condolences. It is always difficult to lose one we love."

"Thank you." Rowan's throat clogged, and she ended the call.

Opening her fist, she took in the angry red crescents left by her nails.

Sadness warred with elation.

Egypt. The Valley of the Kings. An excavation that could change her life—and would certainly be a great win for her career. And Eric, gone from this world for good.

Did I say yes for the right reasons?

She bit her lip.

I should call Gran, let her know.

She'd always shared major life events with her grandparent. But the anger that simmered within her wanted to deny Gran the news. To just pack up and go, leaving her none the wiser.

But she couldn't do it, no matter how much she might have wanted to. Her gran had raised her, had taken her in, and given her the life she now had. It was selfish to keep her new project a secret. And knowing Gran the way she did, the woman would just hire someone to search for her.

With a sigh, she picked up her phone. For some reason, she didn't think this conversation was going to go well.

CHAPTER 4

One week later

Yael threw a handful of glittering dust into the air, and muttered, "Halcyon Guild Headquarters, Tartarus." A heartbeat later, the dust formed into a glowing Devilsgate, big enough for him to fit through. He peered into the center of the circle: a foyer crafted from Hell's bedrock was visible—his destination.

Stepping through the portal, he exhaled as tingles of magic broke out over his skin. He doubted he'd ever get used to the sensation, and he hoped he wouldn't have to. Devilsgates were of demonic origin and he planned on being back in Heaven sooner rather than later.

After all, the Darts had already found one piece of Heaven's Heart; they only had two more to go. And Yael wasn't going to give up, no matter that their captain, Dina, had abandoned them. They'd do it without her.

Even if they did have to use the assistance of demons. *How far the mighty have fallen.*

His parents would have been horrified that Yael lived

with a Mortus demon—well, a half-Mortus demon, half-human cambion. Not that he was the idiot who'd shacked up with her. No, that honor had gone to Azrael, who Yael had once considered the coldest, most brutal of them all.

Now the fallen angel was in love, and the target of an Egyptian god of chaos.

Yael shook his head. He was still annoyed that Azrael had prevented him from killing Dru at first sight, but that was love for you. It turned people into idiots.

Glancing around the Halcyon Guild's foyer, he realized it was completely devoid of demons. Was he just meant to stand here all night? Seraphina had asked him to meet her here; and it wasn't like Yael enjoyed visiting Hell.

"Mmm, new flesh."

Yael whipped his head toward the speaker, frowning at the sight of a gray-skinned Reynard's Imp. Dru had mentioned this one before. Metcalf. He was a former colleague of hers and loved to eat the targets he was assigned. Sometimes he killed them first, sometimes he didn't.

And apparently, he had a hankering for angel-flesh.

"Try and take a bite out of me, and you'll lose your head." Yael didn't believe in giving warnings to demons, but Seraphina was now the master of the Halcyon Guild, and he didn't think she'd be happy about his killing her employees.

No matter how disgusting they were.

"Metcalf! What did I say about greeting guests?" The lilting voice filled the chamber, and, keeping most of his focus on the Imp, Yael spotted Seraphina from the corner of his eye.

He did a double take.

Seraphina's hair was gone. For close to a century, she'd worn long braids, the mass often swept up in a fancy bun or knot. But now, it had been trimmed so close to her scalp it couldn't even be classified as a pixie cut.

If anything, though, it made her even more harshly beautiful.

She raised a hand to her head. "Yes. Trick is equally horrified, amused, and in love with 'the new me'."

Trick.

Yael fought to keep the distaste from his expression. The former boss of the Halcyon Guild, Trick was now one of the most powerful beings in all three circles of Hell. Rumor had it that Lucifer and Satan were trying to work out how to assassinate him, but so far had been out of luck. No mercenary guild was willing to take on the former head of an assassin den.

At least there are some demons out there who have a brain.

Trick had signed his guild over to Seraphina, tying her to Tartarus for the foreseeable future. It was a dick move: if the Darts found the next two pieces of Heaven's Heart, then she may not be able to return to Heaven with them.

But that wasn't the worst part.

She'd become a true fallen angel.

Seraphina had been the one person he truly admired in Heaven, Hell, he may have even had a crush on her back then. And now she was ruined. Because of Trick.

Then again, Zadkiel and Azrael may also not be able to return, because they were mated to two of the most vicious Mortus demons in all the Hell realms.

It might just be Raze and me going back, now that Dina has abandoned us.

And wasn't it funny, that before falling from Heaven, he wouldn't have cared what the other Darts decided to do with their lives. Aside from Seraphina, they had been professional colleagues, nothing more, nothing less. He had admired them for their skills and intelligence, but that had been about it. Now...now he considered them friends.

A breath of air moved against his thigh, and Yael kicked out, barely missing Metcalf, who'd snuck up on him.

Damned Imp.

"Metcalf!"

The gray-skinned demon glared at Seraphina. "What?"

"Don't eat the guests. You agreed to that, remember?"

He narrowed shark-like eyes. "That doesn't sound like something I'd do."

"I have it in blood." Seraphina stared at the Imp, and power built in the room until the fine hairs on the back of Yael's forearms stood on end.

That's new.

Metcalf grumbled under his breath, then slunk from the foyer, smacking his lips and muttering about annoying snacks.

Yael rubbed his arms. "You're packing some juice now."

She raised an eyebrow. "Yes. There are some perks to being head of a guild."

He winced.

"Come now. It's not so bad." She walked away from the foyer.

He hurried to catch up. "You gave up the chance to get

back into Heaven." His brow furrowed. "Anytime soon, anyway."

"It's less about the guild than what I am. I became a true fallen by accident: I drank Lucifer's blood when I tried to decapitate him. Unless I earn my way back into Heaven through an unspecific heroic act, I'm going to stay a true fallen."

Horror seeped through him, worming into his blood and pounding through his body. *She can't get back into Heaven without completing* another *quest?*

They were already working on one almost-impossible task.

This is my fault.

Seraphina was here now because she'd decided that they needed to save Zadkiel from Trick, and Yael hadn't wanted to follow the path she'd drawn. Instead, she'd stepped up when he had refused to do so.

This could have been me.

Seraphina stopped walking, as if sensing his inner turmoil. "It's okay, Yael. I'm okay."

Yeah, but I'm not.

She was telling the truth, too. There was nothing false in her words—he'd have sensed it.

He cleared his throat. "All good."

She narrowed her eyes at his lie, but let it pass. "Thank you for coming here so quickly."

They arrived at an office, where she ushered him inside and shut the door. It was sparsely furnished, but had the appearance of someone moving in, rather than someone simply not having much stuff.

He shoved his hands in his pockets, fingers coming up against the wire of a garrote he had stashed there. "What do you need?"

"Z promised Theodora Broome a favor."

He shut his eyes. Theodora Broome. Crone, and the most powerful witch in all of the Americas. He'd met her and her granddaughter before; he preferred not to think too much about it.

"Did he specify the kind of favor?"

"No."

He opened his eyes, taking in the strong lines of her jaw, the purity of her cheekbones. "That was stupid."

"It was for Z's wings."

Now that was a sucker punch to the gut. Z had been kidnapped during the raid on Heaven, and his wings had been plucked, his organs harvested, and his body tortured by the Infernus demons who had captured him. They had had to hire Theodora Broome to heal him.

Yael took a seat in one of the spindly chairs in front of the desk. "So why isn't Z doing her the favor himself?"

Seraphina sat next to him. "He has poisonous wings and is mated to the Queen of the Mortus. He can't leave her side for long."

And Peony—the Mortus Queen—couldn't leave Hell. Not yet, anyway.

"So why are you telling me this?"

"We thought you could take on the favor for us. If you're willing."

Anger, frustration, and pride all warred within him. He didn't want to help some magical human, and he certainly wanted nothing to do with demons. But he had spent months searching for Z and been unable to find him; eventually the angel had been delivered to them by Azrael's damned demon lover.

He owed his fellow Dart. A favor was the least he could do.

"Do you know what Theodora wants?"

"She said something about bodyguard duty."

He winced. "You do realize I'm better at killing people than keeping them alive?"

"I can ask Raze if he can do it—"

"No, it's fine. I'll do it." Yael did wonder why they approached him first, but he was more used to humans than Raze. He'd spent a lot of time making contacts when they'd first arrived in the Human Realm, and he'd maintained them, even though he had wanted to bash a few heads on occasion.

Working with humans did that to a person.

"So, when do we go see Theodora?"

Seraphina stood and held out a strong hand. "Now."

CHAPTER 5

Theodora Broome was a short, elderly human woman: someone he'd normally walk right past and not give a second look. But her eyes sparkled with intelligence and cunning, and she had a bounce to her step that made Yael watch himself around her. Plus, she boasted an aura of power that made the skin on his forearms prickle.

She also seemed like she wanted to smack him. He hadn't worked out if that was in a good or a bad way, yet.

"*Him*?" Theodora jabbed a finger in his direction and glared.

Probably a bad way.

"Me." He winked, unable to help himself. Since falling, it was like the roguish part of his brain had switched into overdrive.

They were in a small room at the back of her magic shop, the incense-smell of which now clogged his nostrils, so at least the sulfur-stench of Hell hadn't lingered. As for the back room, it was utilitarian in nature—completely different to the jam-packed craziness of the storefront.

The wrinkled finger lowered. "Hmph," Theodora said, but amusement made her mouth quirk upward. She spun on Seraphina. "I made this deal with the handsome one. Not you, or him."

"The handsome one has poisonous wings. You said you needed a bodyguard, but he could accidentally kill a human with one light touch." Seraphina crossed her arms over her chest.

"I am totally more handsome than Z," Yael muttered.

"Who said I needed the bodyguard for a human?"

"You're not exactly overrun with demons here." Seraphina's voice was dry.

"What about you, then? You could pass for a human if you tried to ugly yourself up a bit."

A smile danced at the edges of Seraphina's mouth. "I am otherwise occupied now."

"I've heard about your promotion."

"Most people wouldn't say running a Hell-guild was a promotion," Yael said to himself.

"You mean most *angels* wouldn't think that," Theodora said, turning to face him. Her hearing was rather too good for a human, especially an old one. "The rest of us don't have a stick up our ass."

He barked a surprised laugh. Which was lucky, because he would have usually slit someone's throat for that insult.

"You look like you prefer to kill people rather than save them," Theodora said, studying him like he was an unusual insect.

Aren't humans meant to be the bugs?

"You'd be correct."

"At least that means you know your way around a

blade." She tapped a finger against her chin, as if she was considering his assets.

Which were numerous. Clearly.

"You could say that." Oh, the innuendo, it burned.

He was a trained assassin—had been part of Heaven's army for centuries. Sure, he was a failure to his parents, but this witch wouldn't know that. As far as she was concerned, he was the deadliest thing out there; well, aside from Seraphina, since she'd gotten her 'promotion'.

Know my way around a blade. Hah!

"What's your favorite weapon?" Theodora asked.

"My witty repartee."

She rolled her eyes.

He shoved his hand into a pocket and withdrew his favorite 'toy'. The wire slipped through his fingers as he flicked the handle into his palm. "A garrote."

"Hrm." If anything, her gaze turned more calculated as it locked onto the wire. It wasn't the standard choice, he knew. "What is your opinion on witches?"

Theodora Broome wasn't an angel, but he had the sense that she would know if he lied. He kept to the bare minimum: "Magical humans."

"Not quite true."

His statement, or their status?

"But let's move on. What do you think of humans?"

Ugh.

"Generally not worth thinking about." He could have softened the statement, sugar-coated it, but he knew she'd see through his lie. If not for the fact that the Creator wanted *all* his children preserved, then Yael wouldn't have bothered to think about humans at all.

"And what do you think about redheads?"

Seraphina's spine straightened. "You want Yael to be a bodyguard for Rowan?"

Theodora's expression turned sly. "Yes."

"But she doesn't believe in magic."

Who was Rowan? And how could she not believe in magic?

Theodora spoke, "Don't look so confused, boy. You've met her before."

How had she known he was—?

That redhead.

Months ago, he'd found her in the garden on Raze's estate. He'd thought she'd been lurking there, trying to learn their secrets; in reality, she'd just been killing time while her grandmother healed Z. He'd grabbed her by the arm—his palm still burned at the memory—and marched her to Raze's office. He'd felt like a real ass right after he'd realized what was going on.

He'd tried not to think about it since. Especially because she was the first human he'd found...pretty.

Humans weren't pretty, they weren't *anything*.

Plus, his hand had tingled for a week after touching her. That shit wasn't right.

Suddenly, he wanted to back out of this deal.

"Why does she need protection? Did her memory come back?" Seraphina asked.

Yael realized that there was a whole lot of extra information he was missing about the redhead. "Who wiped her memory?" he asked.

"Hades."

"*Hades?*" He choked on some saliva. After he finished hacking up his lungs, he glared at Seraphina. *What have you gotten me into?* he asked telepathically.

She calmly returned his stare. *Rowan helped us track down an ancient artifact that Hades had demanded we find. That's how I ended up at Lucifer's mansion. She discovered it was there.*

She went to Lucifer's mother-fucking house?

Yes. And she couldn't accept magic was real when confronted with it. Rather than cause her permanent mental damage, Hades wiped certain parts of her memory.

Yael closed his eyes. A magical human—who didn't believe in magic—had gone to Lucifer's house. *His house.* And she had walked out alive.

Alive, but not intact, his mind corrected.

Yael was pretty good in a fight, and he had a nasty temper, although he was cold and calculating when others might be prone to bursts of hotheaded stupidity. But going up against Lucifer? The guy was the *first* fallen angel. He ate children for breakfast, and demons for dinner. The fact that Seraphina had nearly taken his head off recently would only serve to make him more deadly.

I am not up to this shit.

"Are you two done talking?" Theodora drawled, tapping her temple. "It's rude to do it in front of others when they can't hear you."

She'd known they were communicating telepathically?

This woman really *was* powerful.

Yael exhaled. "Please tell me you don't need me to be a bodyguard for your granddaughter because she's caught Lucifer's attention."

Bodyguard... he really preferred the term 'close protection officer', or C.P.O.

Theodora bit her lip and had the grace to appear

slightly guilty. "Sorry, can't do that."

"What the fuck does he want with her?"

"Rowan is a conduit. The most powerful one in generations. She channels magic without even realizing it. For someone like Lucifer, that would be a serious weapon worth obtaining."

Yael's gut dropped somewhere below the floor. "How can she share the magic when she doesn't believe she has it?"

"In the past, we've asked her to just be 'open'. With family, that's enough. But with Lucifer...he'd have to build her trust."

"And how is he doing that?" Yael asked. But he could picture it. A few slow smiles from the world's prettiest former angel, a few dinners out, and the human woman would be his for the taking.

"He's organized for her to work on an archaeological dig in Egypt."

Yael blinked. That was not the answer he was expecting.

"So, he's not her lover?"

"Not yet." Theodora's mouth pinched. "But he will try to be, no doubt. Especially as Rowan's boyfriend died in a car accident a week ago."

She'd had a boyfriend?

He shook his head, that didn't matter. What mattered was that Lucifer was going to try to seduce a human woman and it was Yael's job to protect her from it. Not the type of C.P.O. duty he had expected.

What am I meant to do? Lie in between them?

"So, how I am going to stop all this?"

"Don't leave them alone for too long. Make an excuse

to be there if he's with her. And since he's shown interest, no doubt other demons will spy on her to see why. She is at risk of kidnapping, too. Satan will want her, just because Lucifer does."

"What about Hades?"

"He hasn't told me his plans." Theodora shook her head, like *he* was the idiot.

Great.

"You want me to protect your granddaughter from *two* Hell-lords, plus an untold number of demons?"

"That about sums it up."

"That's one Hell of a favor."

I am so fucked.

CHAPTER 6

Rowan stepped into the back room of Cat on a Broomstick, the scent of patchouli and neroli a comfort she hadn't expected. There, in the small serviceable room, was Gran, seated at the table and talking quietly to a man. His back was to her, so she couldn't see his face, but something about him was familiar, and it made the skin on her fingertips tingle.

The color of his hair, maybe? The shape of his broad shoulders? Maybe she'd seen him in a magazine before—he had the build to be a model.

At her entrance, they spun around to face her and her heart stuttered to a brief stop.

It was *him*.

The guy from the mansion.

Out of reflex, she rubbed her right bicep. Months ago, when she'd visited a palatial mansion in the rich part of town to help Gran 'heal' someone, the guy had grabbed her, thinking she'd been spying on his house. Her arm had ached for a week after—not from a bruise or a wound, but from something *beneath* her skin. It was like he'd branded her, somehow. The sensation had faded over time, but she hadn't forgotten it. Nor him.

Even though she'd wanted to.

It had felt like she'd cheated on Eric—this man's face popping into her thoughts when she had least expected it. Not in a naughty way, but in a daydreamy kind of way. Like if she had to imagine her perfect man, he is what she would picture: chestnut-colored hair, hazel eyes, and a face that was almost perfect, but not quite. And it was that teeny-tiny bit of imperfection that made him irresistible.

Oh, Eric had been handsome, but he didn't have the kind of unearthly beauty that this man had.

She realized she'd been standing in the doorway, still as a lump of wood. "Uhhh…"

Gran and the man stood up. He smiled in a charming way, like he knew he was hot and that it worked for him.

"Hi. I don't think we've been formally introduced." He held out his right hand. "My name is Yael."

Gingerly, she reached out, biting back a yelp when electricity zapped up her arm. It wasn't unpleasant, not like a real electrical shock, but it energized her. Her heartbeat sped up and butterflies danced in her stomach. She fought to keep her expression neutral—she couldn't let Gran see how the contact affected her. How *he* affected her.

Yael seemed to feel something as well; he jerked his hand away, wiping it on his jeans, as if she'd dirtied him. Her mouth pressed into a thin line.

You're in mourning. Who cares what he thinks of you?

She bit the inside of her cheek. How could she have forgotten about Eric, even for moment? How could she let this man—who she'd only met once before—affect her so much? As if she felt more alive from the physical contact. More…whole.

That was ridiculous.

Gran walked over to them both and prodded Rowan's foot with her cane. A warning for her to behave. "And this is Rowan, she's my granddaughter."

Heat flooded her cheeks and she cursed internally. Damn her pasty white skin and its telltale nature. She avoided Yael's gaze. "Sorry. Yes, it's nice to meet you."

He leaned back and tucked his hands into his pockets, the former smile wiped from his face. He was still handsome as hell, though.

She turned to her grandmother and opened her mouth to speak.

"Yael here will be going with you to Egypt." Gran smiled magnanimously.

"Wait, *what*?" She needed to get her ears checked. She surely couldn't have heard that right.

Gran's normally sparkling eyes darkened. "Yael is going with you to Egypt. As a bodyguard and general assistant." Steel underlined every word. This was apparently something her grandparent wouldn't budge on—not easily, at any rate.

Rowan's fists tightened and she gritted her teeth. "I don't need a bodyguard, or an assistant."

Especially not one her grandmother had picked. Or one that was quite so…disconcerting.

"Come now, it's a dangerous part of the world." Gran's voice turned soothing. She knew she'd upset her. "And having someone to help you will make things much easier."

Gah. Rowan hated it when her gran was rational. She

was at her most dangerous when she was like that. It was why Rowan had agreed to work for her in the past, even though she believed Gran's magic was nothing more than handwaving and marketing.

"I don't need anyone's help," she said, sounding like a petulant child, even to herself.

"Yael is quite experienced with history. And he comes with excellent recommendations." A small smile raised the corner of Gran's lips.

Yael snorted.

Her eyes flicked between the two of them. There was an in-joke there, but she didn't understand it.

"Come back tomorrow," Gran said to Yael. "I'll give you all the information you need."

Her 'bodyguard' nodded and strode to the door. He glanced back over his shoulder, meeting her slightly panicked stare with molten hazel eyes. "Until then."

Why did that seem like a threat?

Or worse…a promise?

He stepped through into the shop, closing the door behind him.

She rounded on her grandparent. "How could you?"

"How could I what?" Gran lowered herself onto the sofa, her joints creaking. Rowan fought the surge of worry the sound produced.

"Hire a bodyguard for me," she replied. "Interfere in my life."

"Pfft. You honestly thought I'd let you go haring off to the other side of the world without ensuring you are well cared for?"

"I'm not haring off anywhere! I am going to Egypt to *work*." Yes, it might appear like she was running away from her pain, but she'd been to Egypt before, had worked on excavations there —and elsewhere—before. It wasn't like this was a new experience.

But you hadn't done any of those things while grieving.

And she'd always had a cousin of some sort accompany her; it had been the only way Gran would let her leave the country.

Talk about controlling families.

Gran shook her head. "You aren't thinking clearly. Going to work on a dig run by some guy you don't know."

"Don't try that B.S. with me. Yes, Eric is dead. Yes, I am grieving. But don't try and say that's impairing my mental abilities. This is the opportunity of a lifetime. I am going to Egypt to work, not do anything crazy. The sponsor of the excavation has nothing to do with it."

And well, archaeological excavations were hard work. There was a lot of sweat, pain and fatigue. It wasn't like she was going off to party.

"Then if you won't change your mind, take Yael."

"I don't want Yael."

Somewhere inside, a tiny part of her screamed at the lie.

He's handsome. You're allowed to find him attractive.

But even that concession made soul-wrenching guilt flood through her. She didn't *want* to feel anything for the guy.

Rowan sighed. "If I refuse, you'll send him anyway, won't you?"

Gran smiled, her face wrinkling into the familiar expression. "Got it in one, kiddo."

Luck had never been on her side.

CHAPTER 7

With one arm, Yael scooped the pile of clean clothing off
his bed and into a suitcase. There. Packed.

Easy.

He had no idea why people went on about how
difficult it was or why several weeks of planning was
required.

He brushed his hands together and congratulated
himself on a job well done. Now, he had to decide which
weapons and what kind of spells would be best to take
with him.

"Did you bother to put any toiletries in there?"

The wry voice made him turn. He narrowed his eyes.
Dru leaned against his door frame like she owned the
whole fucking mansion.

"Why are you here?"

"I live here." She flicked long, white-blonde hair over
her shoulder and stepped into his room.

He suppressed the low growl that rose up in his chest.
"Unfortunately."

She blew him a kiss.

How could Azrael stand her?

Azrael, the toughest and coldest of them all.

She went onto her tiptoes and peered at his suitcase, like she could divine its secrets from her vantage point. "So, did you?"

"Did I what?" He grabbed the lid of the case and flipped it over his clothes. He didn't want her going through his underwear. That was just creepy.

She stared at him like he was a few bricks short of a wall. "Pack any toiletries?"

"I don't know." Had there been any in the pile?

"Then I recommend grabbing some before you zip that up. And maybe add an extra pair of boots."

He sighed. He hated it when she had a point. He walked over to the adjoining bathroom. "If you touch anything, I'll kill you."

Yael reached for an empty toiletry bag and paused, staring at his hand—the one that had betrayed him yet again with the human girl, Rowan. He shook his head and grabbed the bag. So what, that his skin had tingled, his pulse had gone crazy and he'd even— embarrassingly—gotten semi-erect at touching the human's palm? So what, that he'd never gotten that strong a physical response from any other woman he'd touched?

Maybe it was because she was a witch.

Maybe she'd put a spell on him.

Remembering the grim determination in her gaze, he dismissed the idea. No. She wasn't trying to make him fall in love with her. Even though she'd be silly not to want him.

Don't even go there.

Distracted, he shoved the first things he could find into the toiletry bag. When he returned to his room, he caught Dru playing with one of his garrotes.

"What the fuck did I just say?"

"Eh, you're all talk." She placed the garrote on his suitcase. "Plus, we all know I'd kick your ass."

At least she'd returned the weapon. The last time she'd checked out one of his toys, he'd had to go hunt it down in her room. That had led to all kinds of awkward.

She and Azrael need a better lock on their door.

"Are you two fighting again?" Azrael asked as he stalked into the room. The fallen angel was dressed to kill: black cargo pants filled with weapons and gadgets, a black T-shirt over which sat two holsters, and knives strapped to his arms and legs. His long dark hair had been done up in some kind of hippy bun.

Yael threw his hands in the air. "Yeah, everyone come in. Let's have a fucking party."

"I didn't bring any alcohol," Dru pouted.

The cambion was fucking insane. That was the only explanation. *Maybe being half-human made her crazy?* After all, humans and demons weren't meant to interbreed. When they did, well, you got oddities like the she-demon currently tormenting him.

Yael shoved his toiletries into his suitcase and then pocketed the garotte, before Dru could turn all magpie and steal it again. "So why are you two here?"

"We heard you have to do bodyguard duty," Azrael said.

"We can do it, if you don't want to," Dru added.

"What we mean," Azrael shot his lover a look, "is that we may be better suited to the job."

Why was everyone so keen to absolve him of any responsibility? Did something about him scream 'shirker'?

"I said I'd do it. And it's close protection officer, C.P.O. Not bodyguard."

"Of course," Azrael said. "But it'll be easier with a team of two."

"Plus, you're all…" Dru waved her hand.

Yael frowned. "You just pointed at all of me."

"Exactly."

"What is that supposed to mean?" Yael crossed his arms over his chest.

"You're not exactly, uh, friendly." Dru nodded to herself, as if she'd managed to say something that *wasn't* offensive.

"I am, too. Super-nice. Everyone likes me."

Azrael withdrew a knife and flicked it in the air. "You've threatened to kill Dru how many times today?"

"Only once."

The other fallen angel nodded. "Precisely."

Yael rolled his eyes. "But I am not guarding Dru."

"Pfft. Like you will be any better with a human." Dru snatched Azrael's blade out the air.

Lucky I put the garrote away.

"I will be fine." Yael could see they wanted to protest. He held up a hand. "Plus, if I need any help, I'll ask you guys."

That seemed to mollify them.

I totally won't ask them.

"Well, we're always happy to help. As long as you know you don't have to do it alone." Azrael withdrew another dagger, seeming to realize Dru wasn't going to give the first one back.

"Plus, don't you guys have an Egyptian chaos god after you?" Yael zipped up his luggage. "Not exactly good business to have an angry deity chasing you."

"Eh, Set is a pain in the ass, but he's still recovering from the whole decapitation thing." Dru paused in her knife twirling. "Which *you* did by the way. Dunno why he swore vengeance on just us."

"Maybe because he saw you two and didn't see me. I was behind him, after all."

Dru sniggered. "Did him from behind."

"Talk about the mind of a fifteen-year-old—"

"If you're all quite done here?" Raze's deep voice boomed into the room. "I need to have a quick word with Yael."

"Sure thing, boss." Dru saluted Raze, which earned her a small smile from the dark-skinned angel, then disappeared into the hall. Azrael clapped Yael on the shoulder then followed his lover.

"You needed to see me?" Yael leaned back against the bed.

"Thought you could do with a break."

"Hah."

But it wasn't just that. Raze didn't invade people's bedrooms to save them from unwanted packing advice.

"I heard that Seraphina organized for you to repay Z's favor."

And there it was.

"Yep." Yael waited for the whole 'You don't have to do it, I will' spiel.

"Thank you." Raze ran a hand over his dark hair. "She would have come to me next, and I don't tend to blend in well with humans."

"Come on now…"

But there had been no lie in Raze's words. He honestly believed that.

"I can deal with them for financial reasons, but beyond that, they start to sense there is something different about me." Of all of them, Raze was the least able to pass for a human. It wasn't his appearance, it was *him*. The vibe he gave.

"We're good. But I may need your help."

"My help?" Surprise widened Raze's eyes.

What? Was Yael such a loner that everyone was shocked when he said he needed assistance?

You know the answer to that.

Yes, fine. He didn't play well with others.

Everyone knew that, apparently.

Yael placed an arm around Raze's shoulder and steered him from the room. The other angel's bulk was a solid—and calm—warmth by his side. "Can you tell me more about conduits?"

Maybe it was Rowan's magical nature that he'd reacted to so strongly. Angels might be more susceptible to it.

"The electrical or witch kind?" Raze asked, serious.

He would have laughed, but Raze had been a scholar before a being warrior, and probably knew a lot about both. It was no doubt a valid question in his mind.

"Witch."

"Well, back in 1206 BC, Argemones the Clear stated that true conduits were only born once every four hundred years—"

"Wait. There's false and true conduits?"

"There's conduits and *conduits*. One can store magic and pass it on to others in need. The other is someone who can channel energy from the universe itself."

Yael whistled.

Now, if Rowan was the latter kind of conduit, it was no wonder Lucifer was interested in her.

I just have to work out which one she is…

Later that afternoon, Yael was back at the Cat on a Broomstick. This time, though, he was in the front of the shop, with a diffuser wafting out a strong floral scent next to his elbow. It wasn't exactly pleasant. He wondered if Theodora be annoyed if he 'accidently' knocked it over.

"Here they are." She shoved a packet of papers at Yael, who grabbed them out of reflex, thoughts of vandalism abating.

"Here what are?" He opened the yellow envelope.

"Your passport, visa, plane tickets, and permits."

He flipped open the passport's dark-blue cover and scowled. He was handsome, like, super good-looking. How the Hell had the Crone managed to find the single unflattering photo of him in existence? Then he read the name she'd given him.

"Yael Death?"

She shoved at his shoulder, as if trying to push him through the shop. "It's pronounced Deeth, as in teeth."

"People are going to think it's death."

"It's a very common name. You'll be fine."

Her shoves became more insistent. "Why are you pushing me?"

"You need to get to the airport."

"The airport? Why?" He craned his neck around to see her.

"Rowan is catching an early flight. Thought she could fool me, but I'm onto her."

"I'll just meet her in Egypt."

"Nope. Your protection starts now."

"I am not catching a plane." He dug his heels into the hardwood floor of the shop. He used to be able to fly. Climbing into a tin can and sailing through the skies was an insult.

The shoving stopped. Theodora walked around to stand in front of him, leaning on her cane. "You said you'd do the favor. Well, the favor starts now. What if someone were to sabotage the plane?"

"I don't have wings anymore, in case you haven't noticed."

She whacked him in the shin with her walking stick. It hurt. "Don't get cheeky with me, boy. You have Devilsgate spells. Oh, and yes." She reached into a hidden pocket in her dress. "Here." She handed him a locket.

"You're giving me jewelry?" He opened it. Inside was a smooth spread of gunmetal-colored powder.

"You wish. This is Clear Sight."

Both of his eyebrows rose. "There's about twenty-thousand dollars' worth here."

"I take the protection of my granddaughter very seriously. Don't stuff this up."

He shoved the yellow envelope in his pocket and tucked the Clear Sight locket in his backpack.

"Oh, and here." She thrust a gym bag at him.

"What's this?"

"A few other spells that might come in handy. I've also put a number of neutralizer charms in there—in case there are any curses in the tombs, or spells at the dig house."

"Thanks." He grabbed the handle. "If that's all?"

She jabbed him in the foot.

"What's with you and that cane?" He hopped on one leg for a few seconds, until the pain eased.

"Don't talk to your future grandmother like that. Now go."

He was striding for the door before her words registered. Spinning around, he clenched his fists. "You haven't put a love spell on me, have you?"

"Pfft. Tawdry nonsense. Now go." She flapped her hands at him. "Oh wait, you'd better call me Dora."

Wondering if he'd just been played, but not sure exactly how it had gone down, he left the store and headed for the alley behind the shop. There was no time for a taxi.

Throwing a pinch of glittering dust into the air, he whispered, "J.F.K., demon entrance."

Boy, some folks were sure going to be surprised to see him.

CHAPTER 8

"Rowan! Rowan!"

He's not really here...he can't be...

But a hand on her arm had her stopping sharply, making people in the airport lounge mutter as they had to slide around her. She shrugged off the contact before it made her whole body come alive in a tangle of sizzling nerves.

She turned to face him. "*You.*"

"Hello!" Yael gave her a casual wave and easy smile, as if they were just catching up. Like this had been pre-arranged, and she hadn't been sneaking off. He adjusted the strap on his backpack and flicked a look around the place, as if already categorizing any threats.

"What are you doing here?" She returned the smile, but it felt like a caricature. After all, she *had* been trying to get away without him. *Damnit, Gran. Have you implanted a G.P.S. tracker on me?* She wouldn't put it past her over-protective grandparent.

"Just catching a plane to Egypt. You?" Something dangerous glimmered in his eyes as they swept over her.

She liked to travel in comfort on long-haul flights, not style, but she suddenly felt self-conscious in her sweatpants and sweater.

"The same."

"Excellent. Shall we go?" He held a hand out to her side, and she started walking, if only to prevent that hand from coming into contact with her. She headed toward the lounge's exit and into the terminal. *Great. I have to spend almost eleven hours on a plane next to this oversized ass.*

That wasn't fair. He was perfectly sized: over six feet of gloriously packed muscle.

No. I didn't think that.

But she had. And what's worse, she knew she'd think it again.

What about Eric?

Her libido, it appeared, worked completely autonomously from her mind—and her heart.

"Okay. Which gate do we need to go to?" Yael peered down at his boarding pass like he'd never seen one before.

Rowan fought the urge to point to the bold text, and instead just said, "Gate B32."

"Right."

She spotted a sign with an arrow indicating they should turn right. Leading the way, she ignored the shops and other commuters with single-minded focus. She hoped it would help her ignore Yael as well, but the whole left side of her body seemed to be overly sensitized by his presence.

Ass.

"Here we are."

Passengers were already boarding the flight. A tiny

flurry of panic suffused her, before she realized there were at least ten more minutes until they closed the doors.

Hurrying through to the first-class line, she grimaced when Yael joined her. How had he managed to get a ticket so quickly? She been told there were barely a handful left when she'd booked.

Luke had paid for her upgrade.

Did Gran pay for Yael's?

It wasn't like the family couldn't afford it—Gran was loaded. And from what Gran had said at the funeral, so was Rowan.

They reached the air hostess who was scanning boarding passes. She wore a dark-blue fitted uniform with a hat set at an ever-so-slight jaunty angle. As she held out her hand for their tickets, she surveyed Yael like he was a forbidden dessert. She barely even registered Rowan's presence.

I may as well be invisible.

"Ms. Broome and Mr...Death?"

Wait. His surname was *Death*?

Forgetting her desire to avoid any and all contact, she leaned around Yael to peer at his boarding pass. Yep. There it was. *Yael Death.*

What a surname. I mean, he sure seems like he could handle himself in a fight. But Death? Arrogant much?

"It's Deeth, not Death."

"Apologies Mr. Deeth." The attendant gave him a megawatt smile that he returned, before collecting his pass.

Rowan shoved him to get him walking.

For some reason, the attendant's stare annoyed her.

You are not jealous. No. No, she totally wasn't. She just didn't like being ignored. Or being called 'Ms.' *I am a doctor, damnit. I earned that qualification.*

It said Dr. on her boarding pass.

They headed down the airbridge to the plane, and she boarded before him, leaving him behind while he tried to explain the correct pronunciation of his surname.

As she stowed her hand luggage, a hostess waited patiently nearby with a complimentary glass of champagne. Rowan didn't normally drink, but she had the feeling she might need one or two to get through the flight.

Once seated, glass of champagne in hand, she leaned her head back against the rest with a sigh. She didn't mind long-haul flights too much—they usually gave her time to catch up on work. But she didn't have any at the moment. Oh sure, there was her paper, she could continue to work on that, but she didn't think she'd be able to concentrate. And not just because of Yael's presence somewhere on the plane.

The paper had been an idea of Eric's.

"Here you go, Mr. Death."

No.

But it was happening.

"*Shokran.*" Yael sat down in the chair next to hers. She was suddenly super-thankful there was a screen that could be raised between them, and wasted no time doing just that.

How had Gran managed to wrangle this?

"You speak Masri, Mr. Death?"

He nodded, then proceeded to say something that made the attendant giggle and blush. Rowan knew a little bit of Egyptian Arabic, but she couldn't follow their conversation. She didn't need to understand the language to know he was chatting her up, though. Typical. Death was probably the only thing that would stop this guy from flirting.

Ugh.

He doesn't flirt with you.

Yeah, well, I am a client.

But something didn't sit well with her at the thought she may be the only woman alive he didn't find attractive.

You don't want him anyway.

That wasn't the point.

And...you're being childish.

She couldn't argue with that.

Once the hostess left to attend to another customer, Rowan lowered the partition to get his attention. He turned to face her, his eyes slightly wild. Was he afraid of flying? That was kind of cute.

But she wasn't going to ask him about his fear. She didn't want to know something that would make him more accessible. "Do you speak many languages?"

He stared at her, golden-flecked hazel eyes darkening.

"Never mind." She fished the in-flight menu from its pocket. *He doesn't even want to talk to you.*

"No." He held up a hand. "I am counting." A few more seconds of silence, and then, "Thirty-seven."

"Languages?"

"That's how many I speak. I can read another dozen or so but wouldn't know how to pronounce them since they're no longer spoken."

And he wasn't lying. There was something about his

expression, or the tone of his voice, but she knew he was being completely honest with her. "But *how*?"

He shrugged, then reached into the storage compartment and withdrew a book. "Like it's hard."

The best linguists in the world would struggle to remember and speak that many languages.

Who is this guy?

Was he some ex government agent who had received special language training? Maybe he couldn't speak of all them fluently.

Frowning into the menu, she realized she was in way over her head. And with that, came an even worse thought: *he's intelligent.*

If anything, that was *more* appealing than his damned good looks.

CHAPTER 9

Yael used to love to fly; soaring through the sky, nothing but the wind in his face, sun on his back, and the ground far beneath him. Losing that ability had burned almost as much as losing his place in Heaven.

As in, it had hurt like fuck.

But he was currently revising his opinion.

Why the Hell do humans do this?

Eleven hours of torture later, he had finally been able to leave the wretched tin-can of a plane. He hated flying. At least, he hated flying *now*. Even the free whiskey hadn't helped, and he'd downed enough of that for the cabin crew to give him the side-eye.

Too bad it hadn't hit the spot.

And during all of this, Rowan had ignored him.

Ignored.

Him.

There were very few people on the planet who would be capable of doing that, especially when he had *tried* to make conversation. But he'd been shut down. Nothing. Nada. Instead, he'd been left painfully aware of her presence; the brightness of her hair contrasting with the sterility of the plane, the soft lemongrass scent of her, the little movements she made when she read her book. None of which had helped to distract him from the unpleasantness of feeling like a sardine.

And since he'd only brought *War and Peace* with him—which he had finished halfway in—he had plenty of time to think. Being human would suck, he'd decided. And now, since he was pretending to *be* one while babysitting Rowan, he had to stick to their restrictions. He had to travel *their* way.

Although, this is nothing like babysitting.

No, it would be all kinds of wrong if it were.

Because yet again, she'd made the skin of his palm burn when he'd touched her, igniting a cascade reaction that had been completely inappropriate, and that didn't even consider the fact she was human.

Or thought she was human, anyway.

According to Raze, conduits were descended from primordial gods back in the hunter-gatherer days, but still. All that meant was she wasn't entirely human, even if she didn't believe in magic.

This, of course, was the tl;dr version. Raze had probably spent a good hour summing that shit up for him.

This is going to give me a migraine.

And angels didn't even get headaches.

It was time to get his mind back in the game. They were travelling in a private car to Cairo city, where they'd spend the night. There, Rowan would have dinner with her boss, who'd flown over in his private jet.

How that must hurt Lucifer.

It sure as Hell hurt Yael, so it was a fair assumption.

Rowan sat to his right, pressed into the corner of the car like that would help her avoid him in the confined space. But at least she'd talked a little bit, the excitement at arriving briefly overriding her desire to pretend he didn't exist.

This was, apparently, the first time an excavation permit had been granted in the Valley of the Kings for almost a decade. It was the most well-known burial site of Egyptian pharaohs, making it a career-changer to even be here. Rowan suspected the only reason permission had been granted at all was because Luke M. Starre had offered to build a new museum in Cairo.

What a shitty pseudonym.

Lucifer must have laughed himself silly coming up with that one. Especially since humans seemed to fall for it so easily.

The air outside the car was thick with smog, giving the city a smudged and grimy appearance, despite its vitality and vibrancy. He'd been to Cairo several times over the centuries, and he'd always enjoyed it. History was embedded in the very bedrock of the city; ancient magic and old souls haunted the modern world that thrived above it.

Plus, he liked the food.

Tomorrow, Rowan had warned him, they'd get on another plane and fly to Luxor, where they'd stay for the next several *months*.

Months.

Too bad he'd only just learned that today. Would have been nice if Dora had bothered to tell him the usual length of an archaeological excavation. His quick research into modern archaeological practice—*Time Team* and *Indiana Jones*—certainly hadn't prepared him for the truth.

He was meant to be searching for Heaven's Heart, but instead, he was going to be stuck living with a bunch of dead people. Well, surrounded by a bunch of dead people, anyway. And normally, he'd be okay with that because he would be the one causing death.

Lucky me.

They were in a luxury hotel apartment in Cairo city; the stainless steel and neutral tones reminding him of Heaven. Angels liked the whole maximum-comfort thing, even though soldiers were expected to live ascetically. The thick carpet beneath his feet made him feel guilty that he hadn't taken his boots off. Not that he was going to. He might need to spring into action at any moment, although he doubted it was likely.

Rowan just didn't seem particularly…kidnap-worthy.

Despite her status as a conduit, she appeared entirely human. Most demons would just walk right on past her. No, that wasn't fair. She was very attractive for a human; they might view her as sport of some other kind. But he seriously doubted they'd try and steal her away. Humans weren't so fun when they were being held captive. Demons got off on torture, sure, but they enjoyed it more when the person didn't realize it was happening until it was too late. You know, psychological stuff.

In the adjacent room—they shared a living area—Rowan was on the phone, and she didn't sound too happy. He had a feeling she was talking to Dora.

Shock would have been a mild way of describing her expression when they'd checked in to the hotel and she'd been told they were sharing a room. If spontaneous human combustion was possible, she would have experienced it, and he'd have had an awkward tan to explain.

Yael ambled into the small kitchenette. Maybe they'd have some cookies—or better yet, a minibar.

"Fine!" Rowan shouted. She stormed into the common space and came to a sudden stop at the sight of him hunched over the fridge. She narrowed her green eyes. "What are you doing?"

"Getting a drink. Here." He straightened and handed her a tiny bottle of vodka. "You look like you could use this."

She snatched the alcohol out of his hand. "Aren't you meant to be protecting me, rather than trying to get me drunk?"

He eyed the small bottle. "If that's all it takes to get you drunk, then we're going to have a problem."

She glowered at him and set the bottle down on the glass table with a click. "Let's get a few ground rules sorted."

He snorted and crossed his arms over his chest. This was going to be good, he knew it. "Go right ahead."

"Gran says that I can't try to ditch you, or she'll hire another three bodyguards who'll dog my every step. So, we're going to have to learn to live with each other. Rule number one, leave me alone. I work better without someone hovering over me."

"Uh, I can't leave you alone. That's kind of the point of why I'm here."

"No hovering."

He scowled. "I don't hover." He might loom in a menacing fashion, but he didn't *hover*.

"I go to work alone."

"No can do."

Clearly, she didn't understand the concept of a C.P.O. He had to have a body to guard.

"I sleep in my room alone and you *never* come in unless you knock first."

Sure, that was easy enough. "I don't plan on watching you sleep, if that's what you're scared of. I'll knock first unless I think there's something wrong. How's that?"

"And—"

"How about we work it out as we go? I am not here to stalk you. I'm here to protect you."

"Yeah, but I don't need protection."

He shrugged. "Then this is going to be an easy gig for me. Now, what time are we meeting your boss?"

"*We?*"

"Yep. I gotta eat and I can't leave you alone. Let him know you'll have an extra person at the table."

Her cheeks flushed in irritation, but she nodded. "Fine. But don't embarrass me in front of him."

"Now, why would I do that?"

CHAPTER 10

Rowan wished Yael had decided to stay back at the hotel. His presence was a burning brand against her back. After they'd left the room, the slight smirk he'd perpetually worn since offering her the vodka had died, and he'd turned professional in the blink of an eye.

And scary.

She had no doubt he'd kill anyone who tried to harm her; or mess up anyone who looked at her funny.

He was dressed in black from head to toe, and had even slid on a pair of sunglasses, which was ridiculous, since it was nighttime. *At least he isn't wearing a suit.*

But it wasn't the clothing, or the concealed weapons that told her he was dangerous—it was just *him*.

If anything, his handsomeness just added to the menace.

They entered the restaurant that Luke had picked—*Le Deck*—which happened to be on the ground floor of their hotel. *Convenient.* According to the brochure in their room, it had a Michelin-star chef.

They were hurried to the table at the back of the

restaurant, one that overlooked the Nile River. Luke was already seated there, his long brown hair tied up in a bun. He'd shaved off his small beard, so his jawline was exquisitely visible. He wore a deep-gray suit with a scarf, and his dark-blue glasses glinted in the candlelight. He stood slowly, eyes lingering on her, like she was wearing a beautiful ballgown, rather than a shapeless black dress. He reached out, grabbing both her hands, before kissing her politely on the cheek.

Over her shoulder, Yael coughed.

Luke's pale-gray gaze snapped to her bodyguard, and he scowled, the welcome in his eyes replaced by something cold. "Rowan, would you introduce me to your friend?"

She pulled out of his hold and stepped to the side, disconcerted by how quickly his mood changed. Funny how her skin didn't tingle at his touch, yet he was far more beautiful than Yael.

"This is Mr. Death." She cringed at the flush of warmth in her cheeks, the telltale sign of her embarrassment. "He was employed by my grandmother as a bodyguard."

Luke's eyebrows rose. "You need a bodyguard to work on an archaeological excavation? If I'd known, I could have hired you one myself. There will be plenty of security guards in attendance, I assure you."

His disapproval was obvious.

Had she already ruined her chance to work on the dig?

"I'm good with a shovel." Yael shrugged, removed his sunglasses and sat at the table. He draped a white linen napkin over his lap before the caramel-skinned waiter had the chance. The server's face scrunched in displeasure.

Rowan wanted to bury her head in her hands, but instead said, "My grandmother is overprotective. I believe I did mention that earlier."

Luke's attention swung back to her, warmth returning. "And so you did." He retook his seat at the table, the waiter appearing instantly at his side to deploy his napkin. Both glared at Yael as he did so.

Luke nodded his thanks and then turned to Rowan, his expression serious. "We sometimes have to make great compromises for the sake of our relatives."

Yael choked on his water.

Rowan gave him a couple of whacks on the back, and then took her own seat at the table. The server flicked out her napkin with efficient disdain, and then poured her a glass of white wine.

Rowan hadn't planned on drinking but took a cautious sip. Smooth, fruity and sweet, the wine was delicious. *I'll have to take it easy.* Last thing she needed was to be carried back to the hotel by her damned minder.

"Your food will arrive shortly." The dark-haired waiter announced, then swiftly walked away from their table.

We don't get to choose our meals?

"So, Mr. Death, have you got any experience working on an archaeological excavation?"

Yael gave a small smile. "No, but I have a certain familiarity with history."

"You do?" Rowan blurted.

Something wicked sprung to life in his hazel eyes. "Yes, you could call it a hobby of mine. Researching the past."

Maybe that was why he knew so many languages?

"And what about your experience as a bodyguard?" Luke persisted.

"I was a soldier prior to going into close protection work."

"Why did you leave the army?"

Yael met her boss' pale stare. "There was a small misunderstanding."

"You got kicked out."

"That's one way to describe it."

There was a sinister undercurrent to the conversation, and she was missing the subtext. But she didn't like how Luke was trying to undermine Yael. Sure, she hadn't asked for—nor did she want—his presence, but Gran didn't hire hacks. If she'd contracted this guy, then he was the real deal.

"But you've been working as a bodyguard since?" Rowan asked, trying to change the tone of the conversation.

"No, I've worked largely as a mercenary." He took a sip of the wine, and the look on his face challenged her to take issue with his employment history. "The pay is better. Being a C.P.O. is riskier, in some ways."

"What's a C.P.O.?" Luke asked, leaning forward, as if vastly entertained by the conversation.

"Close Protection Officer. We prefer the term to bodyguard. Don't want to remind people of Kevin Costner too much, you know?"

Luke's eyebrows lowered. "Who?"

"You don't know who Kevin Costner is?" Rowan asked with a light laugh. Sure, the movie, *The Bodyguard*, had come out the year she was born, but her gran had loved both it and Whitney Houston.

She's gone too, now.

All the good ones died young.

"Is he someone I should know?" Luke asked.

She smiled. "He's an actor. Pretty famous."

Her boss waved a dismissive hand. "Ah, hu—I mean, actors. I don't watch a lot of T.V."

"No, I don't imagine there's much time, considering your art collection."

"You really should come back and review more pieces."

Yael snorted.

"What?" Luke snapped.

"That sounds like you're asking her to come and study your etchings."

That earned a laugh from Starre, but his enjoyment didn't seem entirely honest.

It's like they're competing against each other. Sizing up who was the real alpha male here.

She hated the chest-beating stupidity.

The waiter returned, placing a bowl before each of them, the contents a soup the color of chartreuse.

"So," Rowan said, tasting the dish; artichokes, it reminded of her artichokes. "Tell me all about the excavation to date."

A flicker in the corner of her vision caught her attention, like someone had moved across the glass wall in front of them. But when she focused on the window, there was nothing there, just sodium-yellow outdoor lights and the night-dark Nile.

"Well, we've set up the site, done some ground-penetrating radar, and prepared the dig house. You're the last excavation director to arrive, so we've been waiting for you."

"There's more than one director?" Her heart sank. She'd really been hoping this was the place she could prove herself; if she had to compete with another archaeologist...

"The government wanted a local archaeologist as a director as well. So, I decided to split the role. I hope you don't mind."

"No, that's okay. It makes sense." She couldn't believe she hadn't considered this before. Most countries preferred locally trained staff working on their sites. "Who is it?"

"Dr. Ramy Mustafa."

She'd heard of him. Who hadn't? He wasn't just prolific when it came to publishing papers, he loved to be involved in T.V. documentaries about Egypt, as well. Rumor had it the government wouldn't approve filming of their antiquities without his involvement.

She took another sip of wine, the sweetness spreading through her body, making her calm, languid. "Which tomb are you looking for?"

I really should already know this information.

But she'd been in such a rush after accepting the job, she hadn't bothered asking for any details. She'd just been happy to work in the Valley of the Kings.

"I originally asked to explore the new tomb discovered adjacent to Tutankhamen's, but was declined. I believe, however, that Twosret was buried in the valley, and have a suspicion as to where."

Rowan frowned. Her specialty was the Old Kingdom, which dated from the third to the sixth dynasties.

Twosret was one of the few recorded female pharaohs to rule Egypt, and the final pharaoh of the Eighteenth Dynasty; quite a distance from the pyramid builders Rowan knew best. Then again, the Valley of the Kings had only been used from the Eighteenth Dynasty onwards; Rowan was always going to be out of her depth.

This is why someone else should really be in charge.

Oh, and there it was.

Imposter syndrome.

It didn't matter that she'd spent close to a decade studying Egypt in its entirety. That her master's degree had been on Akhenaten, an Eighteenth Dynasty reformer. No, it was because her PhD had been focused on the Old Kingdom and the early pharaohs. That's where her specialty lay.

That does not make me useless here.

No.

She could do this.

She *would* do this.

Rowan realized she'd been quiet a little too long. She gave Luke a bright smile and ignored Yael's worried glance.

"So, when do we start?"

CHAPTER 11

Lucifer was an ass.

And that scarf was fucking hilarious. Lucifer was the first fallen angel; he didn't get cold. But three months earlier, Seraphina had nearly decapitated him. Clearly, he still had a scar. Or he was hiding something else.

The weather was way too hot for the neckwear otherwise.

"I have to fly back to Miami tonight, but I will return soon to check on the excavation's progress," Luke said. He raised Rowan's hand to his mouth and pressed a kiss to the skin there.

She gave him a warm smile, one Yael thought was largely due to the enchanted wine they'd been given to drink. He'd only had a few sips, but Rowan had finished her entire glass.

She was probably meant to down the whole bottle.

Lucifer's expression turned smug; he had yet to release the human's hand.

Yeah, yeah, buddy. We know you're handsome.

The sex pheromones that Lucifer had been emanating

the entire dinner ramped up a notch—even Yael had a hard-on. He touched a hand to Rowan's lower back, urging her to start walking. She gave a little start of surprise at the contact, her emerald-green eyes growing focused. She stepped away from the Hell-lord and waved goodbye, all sweetness and fucking cotton candy.

Lucifer gave him a look that should have incinerated Yael on the spot, had he the ability.

Yael bared his teeth in a fake smile, his palm still pressed to Rowan's back. "Nice to meet you." The lie tasted like sour apples, but it was worth it to see Lucifer's nostrils flare in anger.

The Hell-lord gave Rowan a lingering smile, then turned on his heel and left.

Finally, he was gone.

I didn't think that dinner was ever going to end.

He was on edge. The paltry food portions hadn't done anything to curb his appetite, and the enchanted wine probably hadn't helped that, either. Then there'd been the demons prowling around the outside of the hotel. At one point, one of them had been so bold as to crawl over the window next to their table.

Yael didn't know if they worked for Lucifer or not, and he didn't want to find out.

Rowan shrugged off his hand, and walked toward the hotel elevator, her black dress clinging to the slender curves of her body. Halfway across the lobby, she paused, raising a hand to her head.

He hurried to catch up.

Idiot, you're meant to be watching for danger, not staring at her ass.

He was just as bad as Lucifer.

And didn't that put him in a worse mood.

"Are you okay?" He reached out to touch her shoulder, but she slid away, avoiding his palm like it was poison.

"Yeah, I was just a little dizzy, must have stood up too fast."

He didn't bother mentioning that she'd been standing for a good few minutes before her dizzy spell came on.

"Let's get back to the room. Maybe a glass of water will help."

She nodded, fingers still pressed to her temple.

Within minutes, they were back in the suite, Rowan locked in her room. The sound of water running made him picture her naked, wet, and—

What the fuck are you doing?

Maybe the enchanted wine had an aphrodisiac effect on him, too.

It would certainly explain his derailing thoughts, and the damned hard-on in his pants. He normally wasn't so easily side-tracked. Or turned on. And not by a human woman, no matter how pretty she was.

Or how strong.

During dinner, he'd been exposed to Lucifer's attempts at seduction, and they weren't the normal 'How you doin'?' kind. They were magical, imposed. Incubi were supposedly descended from the Hell-lord and Yael could see why.

But Rowan had seemed to just shrug it off, remaining ever polite and calm. She hadn't shown a single sign of attraction to Lucifer—or Yael, for that matter. Not that someone would pick him over the Hell-lord when it came to appearances. Yael was hot, but Lucifer was the poster boy for physical perfection.

Hrm. Perhaps the archangel Michael was as attractive?

He didn't know. He didn't normally check out other men.

Those pheromones must still be working on you.

It was the only explanation for why he was rating archangels based on their level of hotness.

If Dru knew, she'd be laughing her ass off at him.

The water stopped running in Rowan's room. A few minutes later, she opened the door, towel-drying her darkened red hair. She wore a dressing gown belted tight at the waist.

What a shame.

She stopped when she spotted him, as if surprised to see him in the suite. "What are you doing?"

"I was thinking about dinner and your boss."

"Right outside my door?" Her eyes narrowed, like he'd been caught perving on her or something.

"Hello? I am next to the fridge." He opened the door of the bar fridge for emphasis and withdrew a small bottle of spirits. "Closer to the alcohol this way."

"Hmph."

"Starre, do you know much about him?" Yael asked, tossing the bottle of Bacardi from hand to hand.

"He's independently wealthy, likes to collect antiques and artifacts, and is a renowned philanthropist."

What kind of charities would the Devil decide to sponsor?

Probably best that he didn't know the answer to that. It would just made him mad.

"Why?" she asked, when he didn't reply.

"I get the feeling he's hiding something."

"Him? What about you?"

"What about me?" He almost dropped the mini Bacardi in surprise.

"You haven't exactly been forthcoming about your past."

"I was hired by your grandmother," he replied, putting the little bottle on the counter. "She knows the relevant information. And you haven't asked."

Her cheeks turned rose-colored. It was kind of cute.

No, it's not anything at all.

"I am going to bed."

He shrugged. "Okay. I'll see you in the morning."

They had an early flight to catch, one he wasn't looking forward to. Apparently, the metal tube they were going to fly in was even smaller than the one they'd used to get to Egypt.

He let out a soft sigh when she stepped into her bedroom, closed—and presumably—locked the door, shutting him out. He didn't like how his body reacted to her, and there was only so much he could blame on the tainted wine Lucifer had served them. At least this way, they were separated by a door.

A flimsy door you could kick down in a second.

But a door nonetheless.

I had better go take a cold shower.

First though, he'd ward the suite, so he'd know if anything tried to break in—or if a particular redhead tried to sneak out.

CHAPTER 12

We made it.

Rowan's heart did a funny little dance at the sight of the Valley of the Kings spread out before her, a beige sea of sand and pebbles. Beneath it, limestone and shale comprised the foundation of the sixty-three known tombs. Most of them had been pillaged in the centuries since their creation.

Hopefully there'll be sixty-four tombs by the end of the dig.

Oh, it would be the archaeological find of the century. And she would have shared in the experience. Even her grandmother would have to be proud of her, she who placed little value on history if it couldn't earn decent money.

Rowan's gaze tracked over the dry river valley, taking in every detail. The spoil piles of alluvial rubble and sand from earlier excavations, the worn slopes that highlighted previous floods, the exposed tombs, and the tourists. She'd been here before—but as a visitor. She felt like she was seeing things for the first time, the analytical part of her brain going into overdrive.

She'd done it.

She was here.

Eric would be so proud of her.

Emotion choked her at the thought of her him, but she fought back the tears that threatened to turn her into a blotchy mess. He was gone, she couldn't change that. But she knew he would have been delighted with her for coming here, for taking this opportunity. Hell, he probably would have volunteered to travel with her.

I'd have Eric by my side rather than...him.

Yael.

She had ignored her bodyguard for most of the day. She knew it was childish, but she hadn't appreciated how he'd made her feel last night—like she was an idiot for working for Luke. It wasn't like Yael knew anything about the man, either. He just hadn't seemed to like him. And that shouldn't mean anything to her; she didn't know much about her bodyguard, either, so it wasn't as if she should trust his judgement over her own.

And she was usually a pretty good judge of character.

Which is why I am suspicious of Yael.

Or maybe it was because she didn't wholly trust men who were so good looking, they could attract women just by breathing?

"This place isn't great for defensive purposes," Yael said, breaking the silence between them.

She glanced over her shoulder, taking in his tall form. He was wearing sunglasses again and dressed in black like the night before. But he didn't have a speck of sweat on his face, while her cheeks were turning lobster-red in the heat.

"It's a cemetery site. Why would they have thought

about defensive purposes when building it?" This was a place of rest, a place where the ancient Egyptians had buried their dead so that they could live their second lives—well, mythical second lives.

"Considering the majority of the tombs here have been looted, it's probably something they should have spent some time on."

She hated to admit he was correct, so she decided to say nothing at all.

"Do you know where we'll be staying? Do we have to camp here?" He rubbed his chin.

"No, there's a dig house about five minutes away by car." It had been built by Luke opposite Howard Carter House—they'd passed the mostly demountable structure on the way to the valley.

"We should go check out our accommodation, then."

She nodded. Her bags were no doubt baking in the back of the car they'd hired at Luxor. They strode back through the valley, passing the entrance to the resting place of Tutankhamen, the boy king who'd become famous beyond belief, all because his tomb had been discovered intact. No one ever really talked about his father, Akhenaten, who was far more interesting, at least in her opinion.

Yael shoved his hands in his pockets. "So, I hear most of the people who found Tutankhamen died horribly."

What a way to make conversation.

"Approximately ten people died shortly after the tomb was opened, but Howard Carter, the archaeologist who discovered the tomb, lived for another sixteen years. That's hardly everyone, considering there were around sixty people on site at the time."

"But ten people died."

"Of malaria, or arsenic poisoning, or assassination. I think there was a suicide or two, as well. They are hardly the results of a curse."

Of course, Gran probably had a thing or two to say about that, but since Gran's magic was mostly nonsense, Rowan doubted it had anything to do with reality.

"Curses aren't always obvious things."

"Oh really?" A thought occurred to her. She stopped walking, even though they were almost back at the visitor's carpark. "You think they're *real*."

Yael paused. "I think there's a lot of things out there that can't be easily explained through science, and I think they deserve some respect and wariness."

He's being honest.

She didn't know how she knew that, just that it was so. He seriously thought that science couldn't account for everything. "You're not a conspiracy theorist, are you?"

If he tried to tell her that the pyramids were built by aliens...

He laughed and started walking again. "No. Do you know how hard it would be to pull off some of those conspiracies? It would take teams of people working around the clock to keep the truth from people."

"You sound like you've thought about that a lot."

"Just a little bit."

Funny, she hadn't picked Yael as the introspective type. He seemed all brash and bluster—like his every thought would soon emerge uncensored from his mouth.

They reached the Renault, and Yael motioned for her to drive. She thought it was a nice change, that he let her take charge. Most of her male colleagues insisted on being behind the wheel, even if they could barely keep the car between the lines. She'd thought it was a guy thing—an inbuilt chauvinism—but Yael proved that wasn't the case. It was just a 'them' thing; their egos were too fragile to let the woman drive, since she might be better.

It took a bare five minutes for them to reach the dig house—or more accurate, compound—and she pulled into the parking area. They were met by a short woman with shiny brown hair, a delicate nose complete with glittering stud, and an easy smile.

"Dr. Broome?"

Rowan straightened, pulling her laptop bag's strap higher on her shoulder. "Hello, yes, that's me." She smiled—smiling always seemed to help with these things.

The brunette returned a dazzling grin, transforming her from pretty into lovely. "Excellent. I'm Kayla Perkins, well, Dr. Perkins. But call me Kayla. I'm an archaeologist, too." She thrust out a hand, which Rowan shook. Her accent was strange—a little Egyptian, a little American, with a dash of British.

Kayla's eyes widened when Yael turned around, backpack on, gym bag slung over one shoulder, and a suitcase in each hand. "Who is *that*?"

"That is my...uh...assistant. Mr. Death." She deliberately mispronounced it.

Rowan swore she could hear Yael's teeth grinding from the other side of the Renault.

Kayla's eyes widened. "Death? Your surname is Death? That is so cool."

Yael shook his head. "It's pronounced Deeth, like teeth."

"Oh." Her expression fell, like she was disappointed that his surname wasn't macabre.

"But it's spelled death," Rowan murmured.

Kayla's smile returned. "I'll take that as a good omen."

"Omen?"

"We're going to need all the help we can get. We did some G.P.R. scanning, which shows there are some subterranean chambers, but we don't know if it Twosret's tomb or not."

A tall, stick-thin man strode into view, a pair of glasses perched on his beaklike nose. "It's not Twosret."

"You don't know that." Kayla scowled.

"Her mummy has already been found."

"Pfft. That is just a theory, one that isn't supported by the D.N.A. or any other evidence."

"We know that her tomb was stolen and reused by Setnakhte, her successor, and that she was reburied elsewhere."

"Yes, but her husband, Seti II, was reburied in KV15, and Twosret wasn't. Her followers could have moved her body to a new tomb after Setnakhte rose to power. It's been done before."

Yael's brow furrowed. "KV15?"

"KV stands for Kings Valley, and the number is the numeral assigned to the tomb," Rowan explained.

"Right." He removed his sunglasses, his hazel gaze direct. "So what number are we searching for?"

"Sixty-four."

"Well then, let's get to it."

Kayla clapped her hands. "I like your attitude. Now, come inside. Don't mind the stork-man there, he's a stick in the mud."

"I heard that." The stranger held out a hand. "I'm Dr. Colin Murdoch."

Rowan shook it. His grip was firm but not overbearing, like he had nothing to prove. It made her like him instantly. "Dr. Broome."

"Nice to meet you. I heard you were doing research on the sarcophagus of Menes…"

She smiled. Yes, this was going to be wonderful. Surrounded by like-minded colleagues, and in a place that spoke to her soul. It would be good to be here. Even with Yael hovering over her like a worried parent.

I'll just keep ignoring him.

Why did she get the feeling that that would be easier said than done?

CHAPTER 13

Time Team and *Indiana Jones* had it all wrong.

There were no instant finds, no out-of-control boulders, and certainly no Nazis. Enthusiasm was high, but that was about it. Yael had spent the morning following Rowan as she walked over the site, studying some papers and an iPad, while talking in hushed tones to her co-director. The co-director had, in turn, ignored all her suggestions and decided where they were going to excavate without her input.

Their brief argument had proved entertaining, but Rowan had backed down quickly. It disappointed him. He'd thought she had more spark.

The rest of the day had been boring. Yael adjusted his hat and scanned the site again. *Nada. Nichts.* Nothing. Just a bunch of tourists crammed up against the portable fencing that marked the start of their dig site. The barrier was patrolled by the Egyptian police. Turns out that the government really didn't want this tomb looted, if it was found to be intact.

Made his job easier.

Not that he thought humans would be the problem.

As for the archaeologists, there were currently five on site, all underneath a marquee that had been set up as a sort of headquarters. The Lara Croft wannabes all peered at a map of the valley, like it was the key to Heaven. Meanwhile, a hundred yards away, a group of workmen had begun clearing soil from the area targeted for excavation. They were working at the end of the valley, in the shoulders of the old riverbank. A small cliff rose above them, providing a little shade from the sun. Stone doorways marked the presence of other tombs, and a staircase led the way to the workmen's area.

That's where the real effort is happening.

Yael frowned at the group under the marquee, which had been set up adjacent to the sidewalk. Of the five archaeologists, only two were human: Rowan and the Egyptian co-director, Dr. Mostafa. Dr. Perkins, Dr. Murdoch and Dr. Campbell were demons of some kind, but he had no idea what their species was. They looked human, but there were plenty of demons who could pass for humans with minor cloaking spells, and then there were the ones who could physically shift into a human form. These doctors could be either. And considering Lucifer was their boss, he could have given them stronger spells to change their appearance—they could be *anything*.

Hell, one of them could be an Infernus for all I know.

Those winged bastards were some of the most dangerous demons in all three circles of Hell, and had been responsible for the raid on Heaven that had resulted in his fall. He'd gladly kill every last one of them, if he could. But he doubted Rowan would appreciate him decapitating one of her colleagues.

Humans were funny about the whole death thing.

Dr. Perkins spun around and gave him a jaunty wave, as if she could sense his attention on her. He scowled. She grinned and went back to the paperwork.

Succubus. Or something like that.

He couldn't imagine a demon being so blasé about his presence, otherwise. Because even though he was fallen, the demons should have been able to sense what he was. And it should have made them uneasy.

Then again, their boss is a fallen angel, too.

Yeah, but Lucifer was a true fallen, and evil to boot.

Yael still had a chance of redemption.

Then again, Murdoch and Campbell didn't seem too bothered by him, either. *Maybe they think I'm on a leash, because I'm here as Rowan's C.P.O.*

How wrong they were.

But he wouldn't kill them if they didn't try to kill him first. Or touch Rowan.

Eventually, the archaeologists' meeting broke up, and Rowan turned briefly toward him. He ambled over. Better that he act nonchalant rather than bored.

"So, solved world peace and all that?" He came to a stop under the marquee. In the shade, it felt like the temperature had dropped by ten degrees. Despite that, beads of sweat had formed on Rowan's forehead, and her cheeks were pink, like she was blushing.

"Hah." She rolled her eyes. "Just had to work out the logistics. The other doctors want to dig a dirty great big pit in order to find the tomb's doorway, but they know it's not best practice."

He could understand why demons would want to

rush things—patience was not a virtue they cultivated. "Mostafa agreed to that?"

"No, thankfully. He agrees with me. We open three trenches and target the most likely location from the G.P.R."

G.P.R.? Wait, that was radar or something. Right.

"So how long do you think that will take?"

She wiped the back of her hand against her forehead. "A month, maybe? There's a lot of alluvial wash here, although not as bad as it is in the bottom of the valley."

She stared down at the map.

"What is it?"

"I just think we're digging in the wrong place."

"But you said the radar showed a tomb was there."

"Yes, but I have this gut feeling...it's not Twosret's."

A gut feeling?

Normally, he'd dismiss someone's intuition. But this woman was a conduit and had been around magic-users her whole life, no matter that she didn't believe in magic herself. Her gut feelings probably had a little more weight to them.

Plus, she'd managed to find an artifact for Seraphina—one that had been guarded by Lucifer for millennia—in a single day.

"So, why do you think it's not Twosret's tomb?" he asked. Because why the Hell not? There wasn't much else to do here.

She stared at him for a moment. "Do you really want to know?"

"I wouldn't have bothered asking otherwise."

Rowan stabbed a finger down at the map. "KV14 was her original tomb—for her and her husband, Seti II. But her successor usurped the tomb, reburying Seti II in KV15. We don't know where she was reburied."

There was about ninety feet between the two tombs she indicated. He waved a hand. "Yes, you said this before."

She gave him a surprised glance, like she hadn't expected him to remember.

Do I look stupid?

No.

Maybe she just assumed he was, because...*I have no fucking idea why. Cos I'm a C.P.O.?* Well, if she thought he wasn't too clever due to his job choice, then she was a snob.

Just like all the other asshole angels back home.

Or, more accurately, like his parents.

She shook her head slightly, then said, "Right. Well, they want to excavate next to KV15. And from what the G.P.R. shows, well, it's a big tomb."

"Twosret was the pharaoh's wife—why wouldn't she get a big tomb?"

"She wasn't just the pharaoh's wife. She *was* pharaoh. She took the throne for herself after Seti's death. And her successor, Setnakhte, stole her tomb. Setnakhte's son, Ramesses III, even removed her from the king list. She was delegitimized. Setnakhte would never have buried her in an elaborate tomb."

Burn. To have your name erased from history, that was one of the harshest punishments he'd heard of. Aside from torture and all that.

"If that's the case, he could have just dumped her body anywhere. Why bother reburying it at all?"

Rowan tapped her chin. "He reburied Seti II, her

husband. Some believe—like Dr. Mustafa, and the others here—that her loyal followers took her body before Setnakhte could get to it, and reburied her in another vacant tomb."

"And you think they wouldn't have had time to bury her in a large tomb."

"Not one designed just for her, no. The Egyptian kings didn't tend to have empty tombs lying about. They began building one during their lifetime. She's either in another pharaoh's tomb, if it's a big one, or she is on her own, in a small chamber that could have been built quickly."

He could see her logic.

"But we think that her followers opened up the next-closest tomb and put her there," Dr. Kayla said, suddenly in the marquee with them.

She moves fast.

She'd been with the others bare seconds ago.

Can Succubae move that quickly?

He'd have to ask Dru—or, preferably, Raze.

Rowan shook her head. "It's a good theory, but I think she was buried in her own small tomb."

"But nothing showed up on the G.P.R. where you want to dig. There is no tomb where you're suggesting." Dr. Kayla pointed at a position directly opposite where the excavation crew was working. Yael turned to that part of the valley and frowned. He got the sense of old magic from there, but then, the whole valley was like walking through a supermarket of ancient spells.

Kayla sidled up to him, giving him puppy dog eyes. "Would you like to come with me and see where we're digging?"

"Thanks, but I'll stick with Rowan."

"Are you sure?" She touched his arm, and he swore her eyes turned an electric green for a moment, before reverting to their normal color.

"Very." He bared his teeth in the simile of a smile.

She grinned and disappeared.

"I think you have a fan, there." Rowan's tone was cool to the point of iciness.

He turned back to the redhead. "Yeah, it happens."

She snorted.

Now, as long as it doesn't happen to you too, we're all good.

Because women had a habit of liking him—and well, he didn't particularly like anyone.

CHAPTER 14

Their first day on site was complete.

The workers had already managed to remove an impressive amount from the first excavation trench, and Rowan had had them set up sieves and a wash trough in order to start testing the spoil for any miscellaneous artifacts.

Dr. Mustafa thought she was wasting her time, but Rowan had learned the hard way that there could be hidden gems in soil located outside of tombs, especially since most burial chambers in the valley had been looted prior to any real archaeological investigation. Dropped finds could be anywhere.

Plus, if the ground right outside was packed with artifacts, then they'd know the tomb was likely to have been disturbed previously.

Now all she had to do was finish packing up the marquee and they'd be ready to head back to the compound.

Yael had been a largely silent presence the entire day. He roamed the site—always within twenty yards of her—

and had been quite a distraction for her co-workers. Dr. Mustafa hadn't approved of the 'unnecessary disruption', while Drs. Perkins, Murdoch and Campbell had seemed simultaneously fascinated and appalled by him. Dr. Perkins more fascinated than appalled.

Rowan thought Kayla may have a crush on the big bodyguard.

Who wouldn't?

Me.

That's who.

Although she could certainly see his appeal. And whenever they touched...well, it was better that they didn't. She didn't like the way her body responded to his, and she certainly wasn't ready to move on after Eric. He'd only been gone two weeks.

Having sex isn't moving on.

Yeah, well, she wasn't that kind of person. Not that she and Eric had had an amazing sex life, since they hadn't lived together. But still.

It felt like a betrayal to even consider it.

Rubbing her chest, she fought back the sudden cascade of grief. Gone, he was gone forever. No more laughter, or late-night texts, no more holidays, plans, dinners, or *anything*. It was the simple things she missed: like giggling on the phone, holding hands, or laying on the couch snuggled up together while they watched a movie.

"Are you okay?" Kayla paused while packing up the maps.

Rowan swallowed a couple of times, trying to shift the lump in her throat. "Yeah."

No.

The small woman pursed her lips. "You don't look it."

I just lost my best friend. The man I thought I'd spend the rest of my life with. And even though it's only been two weeks, it's getting harder to reminder the exact shape of his face...

"My partner died a couple weeks ago. I just had a moment."

"I'm sorry." Kayla glanced down and patted Rowan on the hand. "Losing loved ones can be difficult."

It was an odd way to phrase it, but she appreciated the sentiment.

"There! All done." Kayla held up the last cardboard tube and grinned. "You ready?"

Rowan nodded. She hadn't actually done all that much tidying in the marquee, but then it had hardly been trashed. "Let's go." She turned to Yael and waved. He nodded to indicate he'd seen her.

"He's so hot."

Rowan glanced back at Kayla, who had an armful of map tubes and an eyeful of bodyguard. She decided it was best not to comment.

"It's the whole 'I'm-gonna-slit-your-throat' vibe he's got going, you know?"

A surprised laugh emerged from Rowan, washing away the pain of Eric's loss. "No, I can't say that I do."

Kayla sent her a sly grin. "More for me then!"

"More what for who?" Yael asked.

Of course, he has to join us now.

If she could have sunk through the former riverbed, she would have.

"Don't worry your pretty little head over it," Kayla said.

"Pretty little head?" A glossy chestnut eyebrow

twitched.

Kayla stopped walking and adjusted her map tubes. "You're right. Don't worry your big head about it. I bet you have quite the…ego."

Rowan felt the evil glance Yael gave her, concealed as it was by his dark Aviator sunglasses. "I'm as modest as I am humble."

She smirked despite herself. Yael and Kayla continued their banter through the lingering tourist crowd to the cars, and then thankfully decided to call a truce at the minivan. They crammed into the vehicle together, Kayla's maps jabbing Rowan in the side, after Yael somehow called shotgun before anyone realized it was up for grabs. Dr. Mustafa claimed the driver's position, and they were off.

Of course, he has to drive.

He was a local, but still. He hadn't even asked anyone else if they would have liked the privilege.

You're not really angry about him driving.

No, she wasn't.

She wasn't angry with him at all.

Liar.

So what, that he'd ignored all her suggestions for the excavation?

They reached the compound, Kayla springing from the van like she hadn't spent a day in the heat. Dr. Murdoch followed in a more sedate fashion, his long wiry limbs easing from the car like a spider clambering from its web. Dr. Campbell followed, leaving Rowan last.

She didn't think Dr. Campbell had spoken more than two words to her since she'd met him yesterday. Short, and built like a weightlifter, he had an imposing nose and beady eyes that seemed to assess everything and anything in his path. He mostly talked to the lanky Dr. Murdoch, even ignoring Kayla, who was hard to ignore considering her irrepressible nature.

Outside the van, Rowan nodded to Kayla and then walked toward the sleeping quarters. They reminded her of school camps—a long cabin-like building comprising a set number of doors, each leading to a bedroom. In this case, however, it was a fancy trailer, and she didn't have to share a room with anyone. And the porch was enclosed, to prevent mosquitoes and other creepy crawlies from finding their bedrooms easily, which was a relief. Scorpions and snakes weren't really her thing. Especially not in her bed.

Tonight would be her first official night here as excavation director.

Yael followed her onto the porch, the trailer squeaking with their weight. "What now?"

"What do you mean?" She wiped sweat from her forehead with her sleeve.

Ugh. She forgot how gross she got in the heat.

Yael, of course, looked like he'd just spent the day sitting in air-conditioned comfort. *How does he do that?*

Worse, she'd been under the marquee for half the day, whereas he'd been out in the sun, wandering the site and staring menacingly at the tourists.

He took off his sunglasses and leaned his shoulder against the wall next to her door. "I need to work out your routine so I can establish any safety protocols required."

She wanted to lie, and say she was going to go into Luxor and party all night, but she wasn't an idiot. She needed sleep to fight the jet lag. "I'm going to have a shower, then debrief, then eat. Probably work some, and then bed. It will probably continue like that the whole excavation."

"Fine. I'll wait here."

"Wait here?" She frowned.

"Yes, but first, let me check your room."

"Check my room?" She knew she sounded like a parrot, but what?

He withdrew a small locket from his pocket, opened it, and then dabbed some powder on his eyelids.

"What are you doing?"

"Putting on makeup."

She glared.

He tucked the jewelry away. "It helps me see better."

"Okay."

Eyeshadow helps him see better?

But his words rang with the truth. Maybe he had skin irritation or something—not that he appeared like he'd had eczema a day in his life—and it was a medicated powder.

Yael pushed off the wall and motioned for her to step aside. She did, worried he might pick her up and simply move her out of the way. She didn't want to know what that would feel like, and she certainly didn't want his hands on her. She knew how *that* felt.

He opened the door to her room and stepped inside.

It was bigger than she'd thought it would be.

There was a small desk near the door, a double bed with two nightstands, a small chair that could almost pretend to be a couch, and a T.V. There was even an attached bathroom.

Yes! No communal showers for me.

How had Luke managed to arrange all this?

He's rich as Croesus, that's how.

Yael moved around the room, poking at her bed, lifting her mattress, and even going through the drawers, which were all empty. Her bags had been placed inside the doorway, but other than that, the room was as clean and vacant as if it had never been used before. It even had a fresh smell; like that of a new car.

Wait.

"Did you just put glitter on my sheets?"

Yael straightened from his squat next to her bed. "No."

She glanced down, but there was nothing there. She swore she'd seen him flick a handful of shiny dust over her bedspread. She glanced around the room. No sign of sparkles—and everyone knew once glitter made it into your house, it was never leaving.

He disappeared inside her bathroom.

She decided not to follow him into the confined space.

He was muttering to himself when he emerged a few minutes later, wiping his hands together like he was cleaning them. But there was no sign of glitter there, either.

Maybe I was seeing things.

It had been a long day, and a headache was pounding its way across her forehead.

Yael clapped his hands together, drawing her attention back to him. "Okay. All good. I'll wait outside." He quickly left, closing the door behind him.

She sagged back against the wall, sudden tears threatening to spill.

Taking a deep breath, she rubbed her eyes, her hands coming away wet.

I miss you, Eric.

CHAPTER 15

Yael stood on the porch, enclosed by flyscreens, and stared out across the compound. There were two rooms on this particular trailer; one was empty. He assumed the spare was for Lucifer when he deigned to visit. The remainder of the compound was just dust and quiet. All the archaeologists had disappeared inside their rooms, while the staff that worked here—cooks, cleaners, security guards, and assistants—were busy doing whatever it was they did.

Yael's accommodation was on the other side of the compound, next to one of the cooks. He hadn't even rated his own bathroom; he had to share a communal one. *My room is about half the size of Rowan's.* Maybe less. But it did have an air conditioner, at least.

Not that I'll be spending much time there.

Considering he had to guard Rowan 24-7, he wasn't going to have a lot of downtime. *I may have to call in help at some stage.*

It galled him to think that, but even he needed to sleep.

At least *his* bed hadn't been covered in spells.

Rowan's had lit up like a Las Vegas casino when he'd stepped into her bedroom. The Clear Sight powder was certainly effective, he'd give it that. The glow from the enchantments in her bedroom had almost blinded him.

Lucifer really wants her to like him.

There were basic things, like listening spells, but there were also other more sinister magics, such as the complicated dream-weave that had been laid on her bed. Every time Rowan touched it, she'd start thinking about whoever the spell had targeted. In this case, Yael suspected it was Lucifer.

Raze would have loved to study it.

The other Dart found non-angelic magic fascinating, and something as complicated as the dream-weave would have left him pondering for days. As it was, Yael only had time to throw a handful of neutralizer at the spell and hope it worked. The glow had certainly dimmed, but hadn't completely disappeared, before he'd stepped out of her room.

Footsteps approached from inside the apartment, and then Rowan's door opened. She stopped when she spotted him, her mouth open in a little 'o'.

She's cute like that.

No.

Don't even go there.

Her damp, dark-red hair was tied back in a bun, and she was wearing a pair of loose jeans and a long-sleeved blouse. She looked fresh.

While I'm standing here with sand in odd places.

It was like he'd been to the beach, even though he'd been standing around a graveyard all day, fully dressed.

Rowan collected herself and stepped onto the porch

next to him, closing her door behind her. "Have you even left?"

"No."

"Are you going to be stalking me now?"

"I don't stalk people." *Much.* He'd stalked Dina, but that didn't count. "I'm your C.P.O. I need to know where you are and be close by in case something happens."

She rolled her eyes. "Nothing is going to happen."

"Your grandmother hired me for a reason."

She shook her head. "Yeah, well, Gran is overprotective to a fault. You'll learn that the hard way."

At first, he would have agreed with Rowan, but not so much anymore. Demons had been at the hotel, and he could sense more outside the compound, which, thankfully, was warded up the wazoo and guarded by Lucifer's lackeys. The other archaeologists were also demons, although he doubted they'd be a problem—they were Lucifer's employees. As for the other demons, the ones outside the compound, they may be Lucifer's, or they could belong to Satan or Hades.

If they didn't answer to Rowan's boss, and he had to guess who sent them, Yael would pick Satan. The Hell-lord was known to be the jealous type: whatever someone else had, he wanted. And if Rowan was as powerful a conduit as he was beginning to think she was, then Satan would love to get his hands on her. Just as much as Lucifer would.

Rowan walked away from him when he didn't reply, heading toward the mess area. He caught up to her quickly, his longer legs making short work of her head start. The compound glittered with magical spells, visible courtesy of his Clear Sight powder. *Lucifer is on point.* The compound's boundary was bright as a 7-11, and other spells—anti-fire, anti-violence and others—glimmered on the buildings and communal areas.

"Have you heard of these other archaeologists before?" Yael asked.

"I'd heard of Dr. Mustafa—everyone who knows anything about Egypt has." She was quiet for a moment, thoughtful. "You know, I don't think I have heard of the others before."

Well, didn't that say something?

"Doesn't everyone know everyone?" Like, how many archaeologists could there be?

"In some cases, yes. But in others, the world is a big place. Unless you go to lots of international conferences, you might never meet some people."

"They don't exactly look Egyptian." Well, Campbell might pass, except for his surname. But Murdoch appeared to have Scandinavian ancestry and Kayla, British. Although, considering they were demons wearing flesh-suits, it probably didn't mean a thing anyway.

"No, you're right. Kayla said she got her PhD from Oxford, and Colin from Leiden University. Dr. Campbell would have to actually speak for me to learn about his history."

Degrees could be forged. Look at the passport and paperwork that Dora had put together for him. But Yael wasn't going to point out to her that her colleagues could be frauds. They certainly seemed to know enough of the right jargon to fool Rowan.

Who knows, there might be some demons who are actually qualified archaeologists. Given that Lucifer liked to collect antiquities, the possibility was real.

They reached the mess hall, finding the other archaeologists already there, along with a group of Egyptian men and women whom he hadn't met. The assembly was clustered around one of the three long tables that stretched down the center of the room.

"Who are they?" he asked.

"Students, they're meant to help."

Wonderful.

Even more people he would have to keep an eye on.

None of them showed any signs of magic, however. Curious, he turned to the three demon archaeologists. Campbell's true form was partially visible under the illusion he wore—red skin, coal-black eyes and fur. A Cornak demon, if he guessed right—they specialized in curses. Specifically, in making them; but he supposed they could theoretically break them as well.

Interesting choice.

Dr. Murdoch hid a large, insect like form, covered in scales. He was an Anguis demon, which were *extremely* rare. That meant he had no idea what Murdoch was capable of. As for Kayla…she was exactly the same. She turned back toward them, pointing at Rowan and smiling. Her eyes flashed neon green.

He was sure now. *Succubus.*

He would have to be careful around her, because even though he was a fallen angel, he was still susceptible to her charms. Anyone with a pulse was.

Rowan left his side to go to the group. Seeing she was surrounded—and in a safe place—he quickly grabbed some food from the chef and headed outside. He hadn't had a chance to go over the compound with a fine-tooth comb, since they'd stayed in Luxor the night before. Supposedly it was because their rooms weren't ready, but Yael thought it was more likely that Lucifer wanted to finish lacing Rowan's with spells.

He prowled the perimeter—a tall wire fence—coming face to face with an Envio demon: huge, horned, and purple skinned, they largely worked as mercenaries. This one was dressed in a security guard's uniform.

"Yo, angel-boy, what are you doing here?" The demon deliberately blocked Yael's path. Two more were closing in.

"I am a C.P.O. for one of the archaeologists."

The demon snorted. "In case you hadn't noticed, they're demons."

"Not the one I'm guarding."

The demon sniffed the air. "Ah yes, there are some humans here. Well, worry not featherless one. We'll protect the camp from any bad guys."

Ugh.

Demons.

"Good. Means I have less work to do."

That earned him a laugh, and a slap on the shoulder— why the fuck was the Envio being friendly?

"You're not too bad for a halo. Now remember, stay out of our way, and you'll stay alive."

Yael withdrew a dagger and played with it, tossing it in the air. "Ditto."

"Aw, he thinks he's scary." The three Envio demons laughed.

"I've decapitated gods. You guys aren't too much of a challenge."

"Oh yeah, which god?" the speaker taunted.

"Set."

That earned a low whistle. "He's a nasty one."

"Sure is. But he was also headless for a while." He gave them a lazy grin. "Can you guys grow yours back?"

They muttered something in the negative and moved aside, allowing him to walk past.

After he'd finished his rounds, he took a quick shower and checked out his sleeping quarters again—his room only had a listening spell on it, which he decided to leave active. He then walked back to the mess, to find Rowan eating dinner next to Kayla.

Rowan glanced up at him. "Where have you been?"

"Oh, here and there." He gave her a wolfish smile.

Kayla snorted. "My, what big teeth you have."

"Aren't you a bit old for nursery rhymes?" he asked.

She laughed, and so did Rowan, the latter appearing startled by the fact she could.

Yeah, well, her partner just died. So maybe it is surprising.

"Okay, I am done. See you later." Rowan stood, then took her plate to the kitchen. She met him at the doorway, where he followed her back to her room. "Good night."

"Night."

She went inside, shutting the door with a decisive click. Figuring that was it for the evening, he settled back against the wall. Her room had two windows—one in her bathroom, and one next to him. There was only one door. If she wanted to leave, she'd have to walk past him. And if someone wanted to attack, they'd have a lot of trouble coming in through the bathroom; the window was barely a foot square.

The temperature dropped rapidly with the fall of darkness, and after a couple of hours he was just pondering grabbing a jacket when the door jerked open. Rowan stood there, illuminated from behind. She wore a navy-blue tank top and a pair of shorts with unicorns on them.

Unicorns?

"You're going to stand there all night, aren't you?"

"Sure am."

She glared. "Why are you smirking?"

"Your shorts have unicorns on them."

"So what?" She crossed her arms over her chest, which only emphasized her breasts.

Eyes up. Eyes up.

"I didn't think you believed in magic."

"I don't. They're just cute."

"Right." His smirk grew.

"Oh, for crying out loud. Come inside."

His mirth vanished. "Say what now?"

"I'll feel bad if you insist on standing outside all night. You can sleep on the floor."

"I don't need to sleep, it's fine."

She shot him an incredulous look. "Are you on drugs or something?"

"No. I've just been trained to stay awake for long periods of time." He assumed the human military would do something similar. From the acceptance on her face, his guess was correct.

"Well, we're not in any danger. Won't hurt you to rest your eyes."

"I'll stay out here."

"Fine." She shut the door again.

It really was getting cool out. Never mind, he could deal with it. He'd had to put up with worse.

An hour later, the door opened again. Rowan was disheveled, her red hair a wild nimbus around her face.

"Do you need something?" he asked when she didn't say anything.

Dried tears had left salty trails on her cheeks.

"Come inside."

Seeing her upset did weird things to his insides. Wanting to protest, but unable to argue against the evidence of her sadness, he stepped through the door and closed it behind him. "Why are you crying?"

She scrubbed at her cheeks. "Eric."

For a blinding second, he didn't know who she meant—and then it sank in. Her boyfriend. The dead one.

"It will get easier."

She threw a blanket at his chest.

He caught it. "I'm not saying your pain is invalid, just that it will get easier."

Her expression softened. "Thank you."

She climbed into her bed, wrapping a blanket around herself like a cocoon.

Yael glanced at the floor. It was definitely warmer in here. And there was enough space for him to stretch out, unlike the bed in his room, which was about a foot too short.

Shrugging, he lay on the carpeted floor, using his hands behind his head as a makeshift pillow. "Sleep well."

Strangely, the sound of her rustling in bed, her soft breaths, it was comforting. Like this was a perfectly normal situation, him listening to her fall asleep.

CHAPTER 16

They'd formed a truce, over the past three weeks. Rowan would get out of bed first, tiptoeing across to the bathroom, where she would sneak inside and lock the door, to get ready for the day. By the time she emerged, Yael was up and dressed—not that he was ever *un*dressed—his blanket folded neatly and stashed away in the wardrobe.

They'd get breakfast together, head off to site with the others, and he would patrol the archaeological excavation the entire day, always close by, and always at hand in case she needed help. He'd even assisted some of the workers when they'd hit a tough patch of soil; the man could dig like a machine.

They'd then record everything at the end of the day, pack up, fight their way through the dispersing tourists, and head back to the compound for the night. Have a shower—separately, of course—then eat dinner. Go to bed.

Rinse and repeat.

It had gotten to the point where Rowan expected his

presence, even felt a little lonely if he had to duck away in the evenings to grab some new clothes or something. It was silly, and she hated herself for it, but she had never lived with another adult before—not one who wasn't related to her, anyway.

It was nice.

Eric loved his personal space too much for us to move in together.

It felt like a traitorous thought, but it was true. He'd said he would only sacrifice his independence for the woman he'd marry. *Which I assumed would be me.*

But...had that been a fair assumption? Wouldn't Eric have wanted to spend as much time with her as he could? He'd been her first serious relationship—her family had scared off all the others—so maybe she hadn't had the right expectations.

Yael's presence was silent and steady—when he wasn't being a smartass—and she enjoyed his company. Liked having him around, even when he was being rude-ish.

The worst part of him being there were the dreams, though. They'd start out featuring Luke: Rowan and her boss would be on a romantic date somewhere, but once they grew intimate, the dream would morph, Luke changing into Yael. Her brain always took a few moments to catch up, and she'd wake, sweating, the feel of Yael's mouth on hers embarrassingly real.

But it never was.

He was always in his position on the floor, or sitting next to the door, reading. Sometimes he was even eating a bowl of cereal; he refused to tell her where he'd stashed the box.

This morning was particularly awkward. In her dream, they'd been naked and entwined together, not having sex, but almost. *His body can't really be that amazing.* It had been all sharp planes, an eight-pack, and a huge...

"Yo! What's taking you so long? I'm hungry."

Rowan dropped her toothbrush in the sink.

She'd been daydreaming. Heat burned in her cheeks, but thankfully Yael couldn't see her, as she was locked in the bathroom.

"I'll be five minutes!" she shouted back.

She picked up her toothbrush, brushed her teeth, straightened her hair, and wiped her face clean in record time. She opened the door just as Yael was about to knock again, his fist raised in mid-air.

His hazel eyes swept over her. "Good, you're ready."

"Let's go." She slipped past him and out the door.

He locked up behind her. "You feeling okay? You're a bit flushed."

"I'm fine."

"Humans get sick." He frowned. "Are you sick?"

Humans? Like what? He's an alien or something?

"No." Hoping her curt tone would forbid any further questions, she shoved open the mess hall's door. Kayla was already inside, the plate before her filled with falafel, eggs and pita bread. Three coffee mugs were also in the melee.

Woman likes her coffee.

If Rowan had three cups before noon, she was jittery for the rest of the day. Kayla had three cups before she left for site.

Standing in front of the small buffet, Rowan eyed the

offerings. At the start, she had enjoyed the Egyptian cuisine, but after three weeks she longed for a bowl of granola. Grabbing some bread and eggs, she figured that would do.

"That's all you're eating? No wonder you're so skinny." Yael gestured at her plate, then proceeded to heap a bit of everything on his.

"I'm not skinny." She didn't think she was overweight; but she wasn't model-thin. And she was okay with that. Plus, she didn't have much of an appetite after her dream this morning. She still felt embarrassed to look at her bodyguard.

"Fine. You do you. Means more for me."

"Like you were going to leave anything, anyway," Rowan muttered, heading over to Kayla's table.

"Ah, you know me too well." The familiar smirk was back.

She was so grumpy that she wanted to smack it off his face. Instead, she dug into her eggs and pita.

"What are you two bickering about this time?" Kayla downed the last of her coffee.

"Food." Yael jerked his chin in her direction. "She doesn't eat enough."

"What are you, my dad?" Rowan snapped.

He appeared horrified at the suggestion.

Kayla snort-laughed. "You guys crack me up. You're like an old married couple."

"Glad someone enjoys it," Rowan growled then quickly shoved her mouth full of food so she couldn't say anything else stupid.

Old married couple? The idea wasn't quite as horrifying as it should be.

"Colin reckons we're about to find the entrance to the tomb in his trench," Kayla said, then glanced at the bottom of her coffee cup, amazed it was empty.

"Do you run on that stuff?" Yael asked, pointing at the cup with his fork.

Kayla slapped his utensil away. "Don't they teach you manners in He—wherever you're from?"

He bared his teeth. "No."

Rowan finished her mouthful, ignoring their exchange. "Well, since we couldn't find the entrance with the other three trenches, let's hope he's right."

The G.P.R. had shown that the tomb terminated at each of the four trenches. The only problem? It didn't show where the door was. G.P.R. only indicated changes in soil that occurred from voids, or the presence of stone, and since most of the tombs had stairwells leading into them, well, it showed up simply as a room.

I still think we're digging in the wrong spot.

She couldn't pinpoint the exact cause of her doubt, just that she knew this new tomb wasn't Twosret's. But it shouldn't matter. Discovering a new tomb in the Valley of the Kings was an immense achievement, regardless of whether it was the 'right one'.

"I went through the sieve finds yesterday from Colin's trench," Kayla said, turning the empty coffee cup in her hands. "There were a number of small gold objects, even a broken *ushabti*."

Ushabtis were small figurines said to come to life to serve the tomb's owner—it meant that actual servants didn't have to be killed and buried with their former masters. The figurines weren't left outside tombs, not unless they had been dumped there by grave robbers.

"That isn't a good sign that the tomb is intact."

"No. Colin seems to think it could be debris left over from KV15."

Rowan made a non-committal sound, while Yael finished his mound of food.

"Let's go."

Four dusty hours later, they unearthed a staircase.

KV64, here we go!

"This is it!" Dr. Murdoch rubbed his hands together in glee, while Dr. Mustafa and Dr. Campbell stood stone-faced at the top of the stairs. Rowan crouched down four stairs away, using her trowel to scrape at the compact alluvial soil that covered the remainder of the staircase. The shiny golden back of an ornamental scarab appeared, and her heart sank. As she worked, broken shards of pottery also emerged.

Dr. Mustafa came to crouch down next to her. "What is it?"

"There are artifacts all through this. I don't think it bodes well."

While the pottery fragments and scarab should have been left *in situ*—so they could be recorded first—Dr. Mustafa pried up the scarab with care. He flipped it over, the dusky skin of his palm contrasting against the warm gold. His hand clenched on the item. *"Maatkare."*

Excitement made Rowan's skin tingle and she fought the urge to pry apart his fingers and steal the object. "Can I see?"

Slowly, he opened his hand, letting her pick up the

scarab. There, on its back, was ⌐ 𓁹𓏏 𝖫. *Neter Nefer Maatkare.* Translated, it meant the God Good Maatkare. This referred to Hatshepsut, one of the other female pharaohs form the Eighteenth Dynasty.

"They've found her body," Rowan murmured. It had been the talk of the community a few years ago. Her mummy had been identified from D.N.A. — all from a tooth found in a box labelled with her name. Like Twosret, her mummy had been moved from the original burial chamber. Unlike Twosret, they'd found Hatshepsut's body — on the floor of her wet-nurse's tomb.

"So they think." Mustafa squinted down at the sand that buried the remainder of the stairs. "But this could be her daughter's tomb."

"Neferure? I thought Howard Carter found that."

"It was mostly empty. She was the only daughter of Maatkare. She would have been entitled to a grand tomb."

"Let's see if any of the other finds mention her cartouche." Rowan placed the scarab back where it had been found and motioned to Kayla to record the artifacts. She then climbed the exposed stairs and headed to the marquee, where all the washed artifacts had been left out for cataloguing, a task assigned to some of the university students.

There was nothing that referenced any other pharaohs.

"This could have just been coincidence then," Rowan said to Dr. Mustafa. Over the past three weeks, he had warmed to her slightly.

"Possibly. Or maybe Twosret had kept artifacts from

the other female kings."

It was feasible, she supposed. The Eighteenth Dynasty had boasted Hatshepsut and Nefertiti as pharaohs, with the possibility that Smenkhkare had also been a woman. Excellent precedents for someone who wanted to rule without a male king by their side.

When she didn't say any more, Dr. Mustafa turned back to the towering spoil mound and Colin's trench. "We shall keep digging through the night. Now we are close, we cannot leave the site unattended. Even the security guards will not be enough; we need as many people on site as possible, to prevent thieves from taking advantage. I will tell Mr. Starre that KV64 will be ready for opening tomorrow."

"Tomorrow?"

So soon?

She didn't think she was ready.

CHAPTER 17

Casa de los Condenados, Sheol

Raze was a patient man. In fact, he felt like he'd spent his entire life waiting for *something*. He wasn't entirely sure what he was waiting for, but that didn't seem to bother him, and he was beginning to find that strange. At first, almost a millennia ago, he'd believed it was because he was going to be the Head Scholar at the Celestial Library. Then, four hundred years later, when the silver had bloomed in his wings, he'd thought he would become leader of the Darts.

Now, he was thankful it had been neither of those things.

It meant that he still had *potential*. That losing his wings wasn't the end of his achievements, that he would still live on to become someone to remember.

What he was to be remembered for…well, the fun was in learning that.

He'd always been a believer that it wasn't about the finish line, it was about the race.

"Hey, you want another drink?" One of the *Casa de los Condenados* bartenders, a Foraci demon, had come up to his shady corner. Most of the bar was open space, filled with tables, and with a counter running the length of one wall. A staircase was located behind him, and he guessed that's where the offices and accommodation were located.

As the Foraci turned to shout something back at the bar, her cheek tattoos became visible. She had the markings of a Scryer, indicating she was one of the most powerful of their kind. It was rare to see one outside the Foraci sects.

Why is she working in a bar?

Then again, why had he decided to open a mercenary business in the Human Realm?

Maybe she just likes mixing drinks.

And maybe I don't collect other people's secrets as a hobby.

Realizing he had been quiet a little too long, he said, "I'll have a Dark and Stormy, please."

"Sure thing." She paused, taking in the books on his table. He'd brought a couple of tomes with him to read until Z arrived. "You waiting for anyone?"

"Actually, yes."

She nodded and headed back to the bar.

Z had wanted to meet him here, rather than back at the house. Raze had thought about dissuading him but had decided it would be good to leave the mansion. He spent most of his time holed up in the library—or any other library he could get access to—trying to find a hint about the remaining two pieces of Heaven's Heart.

Getting some 'fresh air' was good for him.

Plus, he enjoyed visiting Hell—not that he'd admit

that to the others. Despite the sulfuric stink, it was so...alive. Vibrant. Hungry.

And chock-full of secrets to be pried open and studied.

A moment later, the reason Z picked this meeting place became clear. The angel entered the bar with a male Mortus at his side. The demon had his black hair done up in a ponytail, and his cold gray gaze surveyed the room. At the sight of his olive-green skin, half the bar stampeded to get out of his way.

One stroke of a Mortus' skin would result in death.

And a painful one at that.

There was no known cure to their toxin. You were either immune, or you were dead. And if you were immune, well, that either meant you were an angel, or you were said Mortus' mate. Most people probably wouldn't be too happy to learn they were the latter.

Raze allowed a small smile to lift the corners of his mouth at the sight of the scattering demons. Too bad the patrons didn't realize that Z's wings were just as fatal as the Mortus' skin. The poisonous green filaments had appeared soon after Z had become the mate of the Mortus Queen. Forever changed, his future was now with his lover, not Heaven.

In a way, Raze envied him: to know your place in the realms, to understand your purpose.

That would be idyllic.

Z spotted Raze and made a beeline for him, with the Mortus following in his wake. By the time they arrived, half the patrons had either left the bar, or were huddling together on the opposite side, whispering among themselves. As if that would save them from the Mortus, should he decide to attack.

They weren't the most feared of all demons for no reason.

Raze studied the newcomer, tilting his head in welcome. "You are Dru's cousin, yes?"

The Mortus' chilly eyes widened a fraction. "And you are?"

"This is Raze," Z said. "We used to work together in Heaven."

"Ah, you are one of the fallen." The Mortus sneered slightly.

Raze wasn't offended; he had the feeling this expression was normal for the demon.

Z sighed, as if the demon's lack of manners was a personal affront. "Raze, this is Godric."

"Why have you brought a Mortus demon to Sheol?" Raze asked.

He, too, lacked manners.

Z pulled out a chair, spun it around, and sat. "We're meeting Seraphina here after."

He frowned. "Why?"

"Trick organized with Peony for one of the Mortus to work at the Halcyon Guild. As the new Guild Master, she has inherited the agreement."

The Mortus were highly insular—for one to go and work for a mercenary guild was almost a miracle. The Mortus only served the Mortus.

"You wish to be an assassin?" Raze asked.

Godric lifted an eyebrow. "You could say I have a natural talent for it."

"Indeed."

The Foraci bartender returned, clunking his beverage on the table so that some of the liquid spilled. She jerked her head at Godric. "That going to stay long?"

Raze shrugged. "He isn't *my* guest."

She turned slit-pupiled eyes on Z. "Yo, wing-man, he staying long?"

"You could ask me yourself," Godric murmured.

"Unless you're ordering a drink, I don't have to talk to you."

Challenge burst to life on the Mortus' face. "In that case, I'll have a glass of wine."

"Wine." Disbelief turned the Foraci demon's mouth slack.

"Yes. Do you have any red?"

The Foraci walked back to the bar, Godric close behind her.

"He is a top-level psychopath," Z murmured.

Raze gave a dry chuckle. "He will fit in perfectly with some of Seraphina's employees, then."

With Dru a former Halcyon Guild member, Raze thought the male Mortus would fit in perfectly. She wasn't exactly the welcoming—or completely sane—kind.

"I have these for you." Z reached into his leather jacket and withdrew a yellow envelope.

Raze took it, opened it. He pulled out some photos, flicked through them.

"You didn't say those pictures were for him." Godric had returned, a glass of red wine in his hand. The smell of rust caught the air currents. Blood wine.

"He is the scholar I was referring to," Z replied.

"Hmph."

Raze turned the prints so they caught the light. His pulse sped up. "This is ancient angelic." He scanned the document. It spoke of an amazing hubris on behalf of the author: they claimed sole responsibility for the creation of Hell.

"Peony says that the Mortus were formed from a union between an angel and Satan," Z said. "The walls of the den are covered in ancient angelic writings. I think this section may be what you're looking for."

"Thank you." There were dozens of pictures here.

"This is just the first batch. We can give you more."

"Thank you."

At that moment, Seraphina appeared behind Z, tapping him on the shoulder, careful to avoid his wings. Z spun around and gave her a careful hug. Raze ignored them, focused on the photographs.

I am the Angel of Death and Doom. I will bring about the End of Days, and my Children will be the most Feared in all the Realms...

CHAPTER 18

Valley of the Kings, Egypt

"Wait, we have to stay here all night?" Yael gazed out over the archaeological dig. A group of students and workers were huddled in the discovered stairwell, arguing over the best way to remove the soil that still clogged the tomb.

Funny that the tomb went *down* into the cliff wall, while the others around it were straight in or upward. *These grave diggers were a bit smarter.*

Rowan stood beside him under the marquee, which was growing darker from the setting sun. "We're so close now, Dr. Mustafa says we can't leave. Too risky for grave robbers."

Fucking Hell.

Yael had been awake for three weeks straight. Sure, he pretended to sleep when he was trapped in the room with Rowan, because he didn't want her to think he was a creeper, staring at her all night long. Which he only sometimes did.

Yeah, you're a creep. But she was so innocent when she slept.

Yael hadn't felt innocent ever.

Even as a child, he'd known he was a failure. Doomed to forever disappoint his parents. As an adult, he'd tried to carve out his own future, but see where he'd ended up?

He plucked his cell from a pocket and stared at the screen.

You said you'd ask for help.

With a sigh, he sent a text message to Azrael. He could go a month without sleep if he had to, but why do it if it wasn't necessary? He was already beginning to feel the effects of heightened tension, and he was worried he'd miss something as a result.

"So, are you looking forward to Luke's arrival tomorrow?" Kayla sidled up to him.

"I've already met him. There's not much to anticipate."

Her neon-green eyes widened. He'd taken to wearing the Clear Sight spell constantly. Better to be prepared and all that. When it wore off, it was almost strange to see her in her human face.

"But you're..." She flapped her hands at him.

"You just indicated all of me."

"Exactly."

He grimaced.

She stood on her tiptoes and whispered, "You're a fallen *angel*, wouldn't you want to meet the first one of your kind?"

Astonishment kept him quiet. For the past few weeks, he and the archaeologists had very carefully avoided discussing the fact that he was an angel and they were demons. It was like they had politely agreed they were all going to pretend everyone was human.

"Well?" Kayla demanded, settling back onto her feet.

"He's your lord and master. You really think I'm going to give you my honest opinion?"

"You can't lie."

He leaned down, his mouth so close he could see her hair flutter when he spoke. "That's where you're wrong. Angels can lie, it just doesn't feel good when we do."

Shock made her eyes flare.

"But Lucifer always said—"

"He is the King of Liars. Don't forget that."

"That's Satan."

"Satan is the King of Deceit. They aren't the same thing."

The demon pursed her lips. "What about Hades, then?"

Yael straightened. "We never gave him a title. He is just Hades, God of Death. Dude apparently doesn't like nicknames, and he's someone you don't want to fuck with."

"Yeah, my kind learned that the hard way." Her expression turned somber.

What kind of Succubus *was* she?

"Look, for a demon, you're not too bad. Try not to get too mixed up in the Hell-lord's shit and you should survive."

"Lucifer plucked me out of obscurity, he sent me to university in the Human Realm, he *helped* me. I'd do anything for him."

"Famous last words."

Rowan approached them, a tentative smile on her face,

but her eyes were strangely cool. "What are you guys talking about?"

"Theology," Kayla replied smoothly. "Lucifer, Hades, Satan and all that."

"Really?" Rowan quirked her head to the side, studying him. "I didn't think you'd be interested in theology."

"Oh, I have a great interest in theology. I just don't talk about it much. Too much jibber-jabber about one's personal beliefs can be off-putting, you know?"

"Did he just say 'jibber-jabber'?" Kayla snorted.

"He watches a lot of Netflix."

"And how do you know that?" The demon waggled her eyebrows at Rowan who turned a deep scarlet.

Deciding the conversation had dropped to a level even he didn't like, Yael strode away to check the perimeter. He had no problem making dirty jokes—Hell, he excelled at it—but he didn't like the insinuation that he would Netflix and chill with Rowan.

Why?

Well, for starters, she's human. She doesn't believe in magic, and well, because she's sad. Most nights, he could sense it in her, a deep melancholy that chipped away at her soul. He'd known her boyfriend had died, but he hadn't realized how deeply humans could feel.

How deeply *she* could feel.

He reached the edge of the guarded area, eyesight piercing the burgeoning darkness. Demons patrolled the edges of the valley with military precision. He'd easily marked them as Lucifer's men. Down near the tourist entrance, local authorities monitored any comings and goings, as well as regularly dispatching sentries of their own. This place was probably as safe as back at the compound. Plus, there were plenty of spells to ward people away from the tombs, and their excavation site.

He glowered.

The protection spells were new.

Behind him, gravel crunched underfoot. He flicked a knife into one hand, and spun, ready to slam the blade home. He pulled back at the last instant, almost stumbling in his attempt to change direction.

"What the hell?" Rowan's hand hovered over her throat, and her eyes were wide in shock.

He straightened and shoved the knife back into its sheath. "Sorry. You shouldn't sneak up on people."

She glowered. "I was trying to be quiet. And you shouldn't try and stab everyone who comes by."

"It's my job to stab people."

That didn't come out quite right. But he wasn't about to apologize for it, either.

Her mouth tightened.

At least she isn't sad or annoyed.

Two emotions he didn't particularly enjoy dealing with. But angry, he didn't mind that at all. He could deal with her being pissy.

"Yael! Yael! Yay-eeeelllll!"

Oh no.

No.

Now was not a good time.

"Yaaaaaayy-elllll!"

With a wince, Yael pivoted to see Dru bounding down over the cliff, Azrael hard on her heels. Two demon guards were chasing them in the distance. How far had they come?

Dru skidded to a stop in front of him and shot a triumphant grin over her shoulder. Her white blonde hair whipped around her face, and she wore an almost identical outfit to his own—black shirt, black cargo pants, military-grade boots. He wanted to complain that she'd stolen his style, and was about to say something when—

"I won!"

Azrael's blue eyes glinted with amusement. "You cheated."

Dru's expression turned feral. "You bet I did. Best way to win."

Yael cleared his throat. "Hi, Dru. Azrael."

"Yo, Yael. We got your message. Or, well, Az got your message, but I know you meant to send it to both of us. Since I gave you packing advice and all."

"Uh." Rowan stepped forward and tugged on his sleeve, careful to avoid any direct physical contact. "Who are they? Have they got clearance to be here?" Then she scowled. "Packing advice?"

Yael thought frantically for a moment. How was he going to explain this? He really should have put more information in the SMS. NEED TO SLEEP. COME VISIT, probably wasn't the best choice of phrasing.

"Azrael is my brother." Funny, how that didn't taste like a lie. And from Azrael's startled expression, it didn't sound like one, either. "Dru is his partner," he added, as her gray gaze narrowed menacingly. The cambion had a temper when she thought she was being slighted.

Dru sniffed. "I prefer the term 'Master'."

Azrael rolled his eyes. Rowan issued a startled laugh.

Then Rowan turned on *him*, and not the crazy woman across from her. "You have a family?"

"I wasn't born through immaculate conception, so yes." Again, all truth…

"I didn't mean that. You just never said anything. And you certainly didn't mention that they were in Egypt."

Dru and Azrael were watching them like they were at some sporting event.

"Well, you didn't ask. And they only just arrived."

Rowan's jaw snapped shut. They'd spent days and days together, and she'd never really asked anything about him. Tried to ignore him, except for when her boredom or sadness got too great for her. It was a shame because he kind of enjoyed spending time with her, prickly as she was.

"We're here so Yael can sleep."

"Like he doesn't do that every night."

"You sleep every night?" Azrael asked, brows raised.

"No, I don't."

"You don't?" Rowan turned her big eyes on him. "When was the last time you slept?"

"A while ago."

Guilt turned her expression dark. "I didn't realize."

"There's only me out here, and well, people like to kidnap other people when it's dark."

Rowan turned on her heel and marched back toward the marquee. "I'm going to kill Gran!"

"Why does she want to kill her grandmother?" Dru asked, peering after her. "Is it a witch tradition thing?"

"No, it's a Rowan thing." He sighed.

"Cool." Dru nodded. "I think we'll get along."

He didn't really have anything to say to that.

CHAPTER 19

Yael's brother and sister-in-law were decidedly… strange. Well, maybe his brother Azrael was okay, but Dru had actually believed Rowan wanted to kill her Gran.

It had taken a bit of explaining to convince her otherwise.

The scary part was that Dru didn't seem troubled by the idea of murder at all. She was just curious why Rowan would want to murder her grandparent, in particular.

"Is it a witch thing?" Dru asked.

"What? No!" Rowan glanced around quickly.

So, Yael had already told them about her Gran's beliefs.

Great.

"Please don't mention the witch thing again," she said. "I don't want the others thinking I come from a crazy family."

Dru appeared thoughtful. "You know, not everything can be explained through science."

"Yes, it can."

"You sound like my sister. And she was proven wrong, too." Dru brushed her hands together.

"Okay then."

I am not getting into this conversation with her.

Rowan glanced over to the marquee, where Yael and Azrael were with Dr. Mustafa and Dr. Campbell, filling out the paperwork that had resulted from their arrival. *It would have been nice if he'd warned me they were coming.* It had been a bit of a shock.

The sudden jealously especially so.

When Dru had run across to them, yelling Yael's name in that playful way, Rowan had an awful sinking feeling. Was this woman Yael's wife? His lover?

And worse, why did it even matter if she was?

Yael was not someone she would ever date. And it wasn't like she was ready, either.

Kayla bumped shoulders with her suddenly. Although, given their height different, it was more like banging her side against Rowan's elbow.

"The new guy's even hotter."

"Really?"

Azrael was of a similar height to Yael, but he had shoulder-length black hair and crystalline blue eyes. To be fair, his body was amazing. But then, so was Yael's. It was clear the two of them kept in shape; their job surely required it. Azrael's handsomeness, however, was almost too perfect, a bit like Luke's. You could look at it all day, but it was something you could appreciate aesthetically, not physically.

She couldn't even picture him getting dirty, not with that pristine appearance.

"If your eyes are on the tall dark and handsome one,

then you better turn your attention elsewhere." Dru had appeared next to Kayla, silent as a shadow. "He's mine."

How did she move so fast?

Kayla turned, her mouth opening and closing like a fish out of water.

"Kayla?" Rowan asked.

"Sorry." She seemed to gather her thoughts. "I was just caught by surprise."

Dru smirked, like she knew exactly what had shocked the archaeologist…and it wasn't the way she'd appeared like a ninja.

There's definitely something else going on here.

Ever since Rowan had arrived with Yael, there had been an undercurrent of insider jokes between him and the other archaeologists. And nobody had seen fit to let her in on the secret. Now, well, there seemed to be a whole different set of insider information she wasn't aware of, because Dru made Kayla nervous, and there wasn't anything particularly scary about her: white blonde hair, serious gray eyes, and beautiful golden skin. She wasn't exactly Jason from *Friday the 13th*. In fact, she didn't seem too intimidating at all, if you ignored the knife that had suddenly appeared in her hand.

Wait, she has a knife?

Where had that come from?

No wonder Kayla had gone a little pale.

"Now, Dru, honey, what did I say about knives and strangers?" Azrael said as he came to stand beside his partner.

Dru appeared crestfallen, like he'd told her to kick a puppy. "That I shouldn't use one to stab them."

"Exactly."

Maybe Dru is scarier than I thought.

A lot scarier.

"But she was ogling you," Dru protested, pointing at Kayla with the blade.

Kayla straightened. "I don't ogle."

Yael smirked. "Yeah, you do. Like, all the time."

"She does?" Dru frowned and the knife disappeared. "Well, that's different. Means she isn't singling Az out."

"People are allowed to look at him, Dru." Yael rolled his eyes.

"Not with intent, they're not."

"How do you define 'intent'?" Yael asked.

She glared. "By whether or not I've stabbed you."

Oh god. I think she might actually be serious.

Azrael tsked. "Come now, you two haven't seen each other in weeks and you're already arguing. And in front of strangers, no less."

Yael narrowed his eyes, but didn't make a snarky reply. Dru simply shrugged, as if to say, 'You know me'.

That seemed to ease the growing tension, and Dru and Azrael wandered off to check out the rest of the site. Rowan thought she heard Dru mutter about collecting 'goodies', but Azrael shook his head at whatever she was saying.

Kayla decided she needed to go check on the excavation, leaving Rowan and Yael alone. He closed the distance between them, the marquee suddenly feeling crowded, even though it was just the two of them. "I'm going back to the compound and getting some sleep."

"Okay, but I have to stay—"

"I know. Azrael and Dru will keep an eye on you. Dru is crazy, but she knows how to fight. You'll be safe with them."

She was beginning to agree with him, at least as far as Dru was concerned. "When will you be back?"

"Before that tomb is opened."

Then he was gone, his long stride eating up the distance as he walked back to the visitor's parking lot.

For the first time in almost a month, Rowan was free of her bodyguard.

Too bad it made her feel lonely.

"Are you all right?"

Rowan looked up from where she rested her head on her forearms, her knees drawn up to her chest. Fatigue had settled deep in her bones. She wasn't up to spending thirty-six hours awake, but she couldn't bear to leave site and sleep, just in case they opened the tomb without her. Dr. Mustafa had done the smart thing and gone to nap in the van.

Kayla, on the other hand, was wide awake and cheery.

Maybe it's all the coffee she drinks. Has her permanently wired.

Drs. Murdoch and Campbell were squirreled away somewhere, poring over maps and iconography books.

"She looks tired." That was Dru.

Is it my haggard appearance that gives it away? "I am."

"But it's only six in the morning," Kayla protested. A stainless-steel mug of coffee was in her hand.

Rowan shook her head, tempted to snatch the coffee from her and down it like a woman dying of dehydration. "I haven't slept all night."

"So?" Kayla asked.

Dru squatted next to Rowan. "Humans need sleep."

What is with them and saying 'humans'?

Like, none of them seemed to be extra-terrestrials.

Dru poked her in the arm.

"Hey!" Rowan protested.

"Did you want some coffee?" Kayla asked.

"Yes, please." Rowan held out her hand.

Kayla gripped her mug like it was the last source of caffeine on earth. "You can't have mine."

"Then why'd you offer it to me?" Rowan demanded.

Rowan was seriously considering theft when one of the students ran up to them, sweat dripping down his face, and his expression triumphant. "We've found the door!"

It was time.

CHAPTER 20

Tower of Tortures, Sheol

"They have reached the end of the stairs, Your Excellency," Seneschal said. "No doubt the door will be uncovered soon. They are completing the excavation and will wait for you arrival before it is opened."

Glancing up, Lucifer realized he was awaiting a reply. "That is excellent news."

And truly, it was. It was the best bit of news he'd heard since the lovely Rowan had lost her boyfriend in that car crash.

Seneschal nodded regally. Lucifer had worked with him for millennia and had long since forgotten his real name. Petty nonsense like that was meaningless in the grand scheme of things.

Well, his grand scheme, anyway.

The tall Tortas demon backed out of the library, his horns dipping to ensure his passage under the door frame. With patterned skin and wide eyes, Tortas demons were perhaps the least scary of them all, but they excelled at detail-oriented tasks. They had survived the eons through being useful to other, more powerful demons.

It was a handy evolutionary trick.

Hell, how Lucifer hated that word now.

Trick.

His eyes narrowed. A fallen angel who was now a full archangel, Trick was the only real threat to Lucifer's power. For Sheol could only be ruled by another archangel, or by one of Lucifer's children. And he had no living children; he'd ensured that. He'd personally eliminated any and all threats, no matter how old or young.

As if that wasn't bad enough, Trick was in a relationship with Seraphina, the fallen abomination who had nearly killed him. Him. The Prince of Darkness, King of Lies. She'd almost severed his head, and in doing so had inadvertently become true fallen, and so even more powerful.

Once I find the artifact, she will pay.

So would Heaven. So would everyone.

And Dr. Rowan Broome was the key to it all.

CHAPTER 21

Valley of the Kings, Egypt

This was it.

The door to the tomb.

Luke had arrived on site around midday, and Rowan was so tired she was seeing stars. But it would be worth it, even if her gut said the tomb wasn't intact. More broken artifacts had been found in the soil near the door, which was itself cracked. Hieroglyphs had been carved into the surface, but she hadn't been given the chance to translate them, Dr. Campbell taking the honor.

The stocky Campbell approached Luke, beetle brows lowered. Luke stood in the center of the marquee, surveying plans, wearing khaki-colored pants, a light blue shirt and a white scarf. It was hot enough that the scarf was weird, but Rowan wasn't about to criticize his fashion sense, considering his outfit probably cost more than her mortgage. She sidled up, listening in.

"There are the typical warnings, my lo—Sir, but there are cracks in the stone slab over most of the curses,"

Campbell said.

Luke murmured something back, too low for her to hear.

"Yes, I believe so."

Luke straightened. "Excellent. Let us open the tomb."

But Yael isn't here.

It was a silly, irrational thought. She didn't need him to open the tomb.

Let's do this.

She strode from the marquee to the excavated staircase. Students and workers lined the sides of the trench, an honor guard, and Dr. Mustafa stood proudly in front of the broken slab, a crowbar in hand.

"Stand aside," Luke said.

Dr. Mustafa blinked. "Excuse me?"

"Dr. Campbell here will open the tomb, with assistance from Dr. Murdoch."

"But I am the Director—"

"You are the *Co*-Director," Luke snapped. "And I sponsored this dig. They will open the door."

Dr. Mustafa cheeks darkened, but he handed the crowbar to the spindly Murdoch.

"He looks pissed."

She jumped at the low whisper, her heart pounding in surprise and delight.

Yael!

He came back.

Of course he did, he's being paid to watch over you.

"Did you hear him say he was the *Director*?" she asked.

"Yes. Ass." Yael's hazel eyes glimmered.

Dr. Campbell and Dr. Murdoch muttered to

themselves as they angled the crowbar into the gaps in the stone. Surely it would take more than the two of them to open the tomb. That piece of rock had to weigh almost a ton.

Yael leaned down to speak in her ear, his breath tickling the fine hairs on her nape. "This tomb has been robbed."

She froze, trying to ignore her pulse that raced from the slight contact. "How do you know?"

He was silent for a few heartbeats, then murmured, "Instinct."

Luke turned to them. "So, what are you two gossiping about during this momentous occasion?"

Like a chastised schoolgirl, she lowered her head in humiliation. Yael straightened and leveled a glacial gaze on her boss. "Whether or not the tomb is intact."

"And what does your extensive archaeological experience tell you?" Luke asked, viper-quick.

"That it isn't."

"We shall see."

Dr. Campbell gave a shout of effort, and the stone slab crashed to the floor, throwing dust up into the air.

Rowan coughed as the fine particles hit her face, and by the time her vision cleared, the doorway was exposed. The scent of old, old things reached her, a strange musty smell that was hard to define.

Dr. Campbell and Dr. Murdoch strode inside the tomb, flashlights on and illuminating painted walls that bore scratches and cuts.

It's a passageway.

Excitement rushed through her as she took in the walls; they were the first people to see these designs in thousands of years. The colors were still bright: rich reds, brilliant blues and dusky greens.

The passageway continued for another thirty feet or so, from what she could tell.

Twosret could be here, she thought, although, her gut still told her she wasn't.

Rubble was strewn inside the tomb, but not fresh broken rock, like the door. No, this was old. *The tomb really has been robbed.* She spotted a burned cartouche, the paint melted into a black stain covering the carving. She stood, hand hovering over the barely visible markings: *Nfr nfrw itn.*

Neferneferuaten.

Oh my god.

"Guys!" she called out.

As Dr. Campbell turned toward her voice, his flashlight briefly blinded her. Holding up one hand to shield her eyes, she pointed at the burned writing with the other. "This says Neferneferuaten."

"Isn't that the royal name of Nefertiti?" Yael asked quietly.

She shot him a sharp glance.

He shrugged. "I've been reading."

"Neferneferuaten was also the name of Akhenaten's daughter," Luke said, coming back to study the cartouche.

He touched the stain. He shouldn't be touching anything, especially not with his bare hands, but she had the feeling he wouldn't respond well to a reprimand. Instead, she said, "It is also the accepted pharaonic name of the female king who ruled after Akhenaten."

Kayla came closer, phone out. "Hold the light better

so I can see it." She took a picture of the cartouche, then continued down the passage, sweeping her cell around and videoing everything.

"If this is what I think it is..." Rowan tilted her head back and stared at the intricate painted roof.

"What do you think it is?"

Not Twosret's resting place, that's for sure.

"I think this is Nefertiti's tomb. Or the tomb of the pharaoh who ruled as Neferneferuaten. A recent paper says Neferneferuaten was two of Nefertiti's daughters, but we shall see."

As they walked on down the passageway, more evidence of disturbance was clear. Discarded pieces of gold and silver, and broken pieces of timber; small fragments, like they'd fallen out of bags or from armfuls of loot.

After about forty yards, and deep into the cliff above them, a chamber branched off the main passage. Her skin tingled with excitement...until she poked her head inside.

Her heart sank as she took in the almost empty room, populated only with broken fragments and debris. The walls here were painted, but they too were damaged. Dr. Murdoch was inside, taking photographs and murmuring to himself.

"Nothing?" she asked, even though she already knew the answer. Some things needed to be said aloud, though.

"Nothing. Campbell went ahead with lo—Mr. Starre."

Funny, how the other archaeologists never called Luke by his first name. Even Dr. Mustafa didn't, although she had the feeling that was more out of disrespect than anything else—an effort to keep the sponsor at a distance.

Returning to the hall, she took a deep breath of stale air. *Don't get too excited. You know the tomb has been robbed. It's been cleared already.*

It was just difficult not to hope, not to wish that this could be the find of the millennium.

Ten yards later, there was another chamber, this one half-full of timber equipment. She thought she saw the wheel of a chariot, and the prow of a small boat. There could even be a wooden coffin in there, but it was hard to distinguish anything in particular by her flashlight's narrow beam. But from what she could see, each item was damaged, and objects had been shoved into a pile, presumably to make room while the looters had gone through the rest of the treasure.

"Careful." Yael shuffled her to the left slightly.

"Why?" There wasn't anything on the ground that she could see.

"Let's go to the next chamber."

"But—"

"Don't you want to see if there is a mummy anywhere?"

"Good point."

Normally she would argue that it wasn't about the grave goods, that it wasn't about finding mummies. But to hell with it, that was totally what this dig was about. It was about finding the body of Twosret, but in this case, she'd settle for the Nefertiti.

They passed two more chambers, before the corridor terminated in a large open area. Both of the side-rooms had been looted, although there were still some items left intact. Little gold though, and certainly no precious stones, that she'd been able to see.

By the time she reached the open chamber, Dr. Campbell had already set up his flashlight—and several spares—to try and illuminate as much of the room as possible. Eight large stone pillars stood proudly in the center of the room, surrounding a stone sarcophagus.

On the edge of the room were another three sarcophagi, as if they'd been shoved aside.

If Neferneferuaten was two women, then surely there would be two sarcophagi here.

She approached the nearest pillar, gaze running over the hieroglyphs.

"It's the Book of the Dead." Yael's voice made her jump.

"How do you know that?"

"'My name is known in Upper Egypt'," he read, "'and my name will be remembered in all of Lower Egypt, on this day'…" His voice trailed away.

"You read hieroglyphic?"

"I told you I knew several languages."

Damnit, he had. And she'd never asked what those languages were.

She turned back to the pillar and scanned for the cartouche that would indicate the spell-caster's name, but there was none.

Time to look at the sarcophagus.

She was two steps away from the stone coffin when Dr. Campbell appeared in front of her. "Dr. Broome, just a moment." He threw a handful of sand onto the floor between her and the coffin.

"What are you doing? You shouldn't be introducing foreign matter into the tomb, it's bad enough that we are in here—"

"It's okay. You can go now." Then he scuttled away, over to where Luke stood studying the three other sarcophagi.

She turned to Yael, who was watching everything with laser precision. "Did you see what he did?"

"Yes."

"The audacity!"

"Mmmm."

She glared at him. "Are you humoring me?"

He smiled, and the expression made her breath catch in her throat. He was always handsome, to the point where she had almost grown used to it. But his smile, his *real* smile, not the perpetual smirk or the fake lascivious grin, that was something new. And it was devastating.

"I would never dare. Now, let's see who this bad boy belongs to."

CHAPTER 22

Yael could see why Lucifer had ensured a Cornak demon was on hand for the tomb opening. There were curses upon curses here, although many had already been triggered and were simply echoes of their former glory. But for the active ones…well, it appeared Cornak demons were as good at destroying them as they were at making them. There had been at least four that the demon had disabled before Rowan had reached them.

And, thanks to his Clear Sight spell, Yael had been able to prevent Rowan from stepping into some other nasty bits of magic, as well.

Lucifer should really have had her working by Campbell's side.

Or kept her by his, if she was really that important to him.

But no, Lucifer had been following the Cornak demon from object to object, demanding to know if a certain something—he hadn't said what—was there.

So, he's searching for an artifact in particular.

Yael had thought that the entire dig was perhaps an

elaborate hoax to get closer to Rowan, to seduce her into his circle, but since the Hell-lord had only been here a total of two days, he was beginning to realize that Lucifer really was interested in the dig itself.

Dude does love to collect antiques.

After listening to Rowan and the others for the past few weeks, Yael knew that the Hell-lord wasn't going to be able to just sneak an artifact out the door, however. Not unless he was the first one to find it, and then evade discovery by Mustafa or Rowan.

He could just rewrite their memories. It shouldn't be too difficult for an archangel to do.

Maybe that's what he's been planning all along.

Yael scanned the tomb for more spells, but there were even fewer than before. Campbell was methodically neutralizing them as he went. He'd focused on curses first, then regular spells after that. By tomorrow, it would probably be safe. *How many humans have died in these things, because they didn't know any better?*

Although, according to Rowan, curses didn't exist.

"It says this belongs to Neferneferuaten. This could be Nefertiti." Rowan pointed down at the sarcophagus, her eyes sparkling with excitement.

Damn.

That expression was like a punch to the gut.

I want her to look at me like that.

Wait, no he fucking didn't.

Clearly, he needed to get his head checked or something.

Kayla paused her videoing. "We won't be able to open the coffin for days."

"If ever." Rowan's expression turned rueful. "There's

so much to translate."

There was. The walls and ceiling were covered in hieroglyphics and art. And from what he'd read, there was a lot dedicated to the remembering of the pharaoh's name. Like they knew they it was going to be forgotten and were trying to stave off the inevitable.

He was about to wander over and eavesdrop on Lucifer's conversation when Rowan swayed, unsteady on her feet. Leaping forward, he grabbed her arms, clenching his teeth against the pulse of awareness that speared through him at the contact. "Are you okay?"

She tried to pull away from his grip, but it was a token effort. "I'm tired."

"Did you sleep at all, last night?"

She shook her head, red curls bouncing.

Fuck.

Yael looked over his shoulder at Kayla. "I'm going to take her back to the compound."

"Right."

Then he swept the protesting Rowan into his arms, and strode down the long passageway, into the fresh air. Hot sand, sizzling sun and *life*. That's what the Human Realm smelled like outside the tomb. It seemed to revive her slightly, and she struggled against him.

"What happened? Anyone die?" Dru was at his side in an instant.

"No one died." He rolled his eyes.

"Pity. There are at least two assholes in there."

He fought a grin. "Yeah, well, I'm still alive, thanks."

Yael didn't particularly like Dru most of the time, but now and again he did find her amusing.

"Can you let me go?" Rowan asked.

Shit, he'd forgotten he was still holding on to her. And the close proximity was doing things to him. Unwelcome things.

How can one tiny human make me so hard?

It was fucking embarrassing. At least she seemed to have no clue.

He put her down.

Dru gave him a curious stare, then turned to Rowan. "Let's go." The two women walked toward the parking lot, and he was surprised to note they were almost the same height. Rowan just seemed more fragile than Dru. Like he could snap her if he held her too tight.

Azrael suddenly appeared at his side.

Yael glared. "Where have you been?"

"Checking out the site. Where's Lucifer?"

"In the tomb right now."

Azrael gave a slight shudder. He and Dru had stayed clear of Starre since his arrival, probably the smartest thing Dru had done for a while. Yael expected Azrael to be sensible about it, though. Except for Dru, the guy was shrewd, and had cunning down to a fine art.

At the parking lot, Dru and Rowan were arguing over who should drive.

"There's something not right about this whole set up," Azrael said.

"I agree completely. Can Dru even drive?"

"No idea. Not that that would stop her." Azrael strode toward the cambion. "Dru!"

Deciding to take the passenger seat before anyone was the wiser, Yael was mildly surprised when Rowan got in the driver's side.

"Should you be doing that?" She'd almost collapsed

from fatigue ten minutes prior; driving probably wasn't the best idea.

"I can make it the five minutes." And she did. Hunched over the steering wheel, grimly focused, she drove with more precision than Mustafa managed on a good day.

He followed her to her room, noting how she took exaggerated steps in her efforts to walk straight. *It's like she's drunk.* Except she hadn't touched alcohol after their first night in Cairo.

Once inside, she handed him a towel and headed for the bathroom.

Yael stared down at the material then back at Rowan. Panic clawed at him. Was she inviting him to...? "Why did you give me this?"

Her cheeks flushed. "I meant to give you a blanket." She plucked the towel from his hands. "This was meant to be for me."

"Right. I don't need a blanket."

She stopped outside the bathroom door, her lips pursed in confusion. "Why not?"

"I'm not staying. Dru and Azrael will be here to watch over you."

Her expression turned shuttered. "Oh."

"I'll be back later. I have a few errands to run."

"Fine."

Was she angry at him?

The sharp click of the bathroom door seemed to indicate she was.

But I didn't do anything.

Confused, he stepped out onto the porch. He paused at the sight of Lucifer leaning against the wall. He'd taken his glasses off, and his brown hair was loose around his face. "I see you and Rowan are well acquainted." Something dangerous glittered in the Hell-lord's eyes.

"Yeah. We're B.F.F.s."

"You're *what*?"

"Never mind." Would it hurt the guy to use the Internet every once in a while?

"Don't get too comfortable with your situation. It will be over soon."

"Really?" Yael supposed he should be frightened by Lucifer; he could feel the Hell-lord's power emanating from across the porch. But he'd never really done what was expected of him. Plus, he'd kind of gotten over his terror of archangels when they'd cut his wings off.

"The dig will be over soon, and so will your usefulness."

He grinned. "I wouldn't be too sure of that." Then he sauntered off the porch.

Lucifer appeared in front of him. Teleportation. Yael drew up short. "Rowan Broome is mine, angel. Keep your hands and dick to yourself, and I'll let you live. Touch her, and I'll kill you."

Yael just lifted an eyebrow.

The Hell-lord vanished.

Yael moved to a shadowed area behind the back of Rowan's rooms and prepared to open a Devilsgate. Azrael found him there. "You leaving?"

"I need to grab a few supplies and get some sleep."

"Didn't you do that earlier?"

"I had trouble." He didn't want to mention that he'd had one great, big, long sex dream about Rowan. He'd woken irritated and unrested. He was going to go to her grandmother and get some 'help' to fall asleep.

Azrael clapped him on the shoulder. "Get some rest. Dru and I will take care of the human."

"Thanks."

Yael threw a handful of dust into the air, and muttered, "Cat on a Broomstick, Manhattan." The back alley behind the magic store appeared in the center of the glowing circle, and he stepped through, not bothering to look back.

Azrael had this.

The alley was dark and poorly lit—deliberately so, he thought—and it smelled like piss and garbage. The back door to the Cat opened, spilling yellow light onto the stoop. Dora stood framed in the doorway, the light behind her creating a kind of whacked halo.

The elderly woman eyed him up and down. "You're late."

He checked his watch before he could help himself. "I didn't have an appointment."

"Hmph. Here." She thrust a hessian bag at him.

He closed the distance between them and took it. "What's this?"

"Extra neutralizing spells. A few more Devilsgates. And I added a bit of sleeping powder as well."

Narrowing his eyes, he opened the sack. Sure enough, there were spells galore in there, plus a little plastic bag of green dust.

"How did you know?" Was she spying on them?

"I am the most powerful witch—"

He cut her off. "In all of the Americas. Right."

Yeah, she's totally spying on us. How, he didn't know. But he'd work that out later.

"Now, go get some rest so you can return to my granddaughter." She made shooing motions at him.

"Thanks."

The door had already closed behind her.

Turning back to the alley, he threw another handful of gate dust into the air and spoke the mansion's address. A moment later, he'd stepped through into the foyer. If he'd been a regular Joe trying to get in, the Devilsgate would have spewed him elsewhere in the world, but since he was keyed to the ward Raze had placed on the mansion, he got free access to the inside.

He strode straight for the library, Raze's favorite hangout. *Bingo.* The dark-skinned angel was at his desk, hunched beside a pile of documents that looked like an attempt at the record for the world's tallest paper tower.

"Raze?"

The other angel's head snapped up. "Ah, Yael. You're back."

"Just for a few hours."

"Yes, Azrael mentioned you needed some sleep. Enjoy." Raze's head was already dipping back to his desk. The guy was seriously addicted to studying.

Perhaps—

"Do you have any idea why Lucifer would be specifically interested in finding the tomb of an Egyptian pharaoh named Twosret?"

Raze didn't even look up. "It rings a faint bell, but…" The sentence tailed off as the angel went back to searching through a stack of photographs.

Realizing that he wasn't going to get anything further out of the distracted angel, Yael turned and headed for his room. Hopefully the sleep powder Dora had given him would work. He needed to stay sharp, because he had the feeling things were only just starting to get interesting.

CHAPTER 23

I can't believe I actually was happy when he came back.

Rowan kicked the side of the bed, cracking her toe. Pain burst up her leg, making her hop around the room like a crazed rabbit. "Damnit." She sat on the edge of the mattress, rubbing her throbbing foot. Why was she being such an idiot?

I can't believe I kind of miss him.

They'd only spent the last three weeks together, but it had felt almost like a lifetime. And that made her feel guilty as hell, because Eric had only been gone a month

It's just because you're tired. You know you're more emotional then.

She didn't know how all the others had been able to stay awake so easily over the past two days; she was so tired she was seeing things. She kept getting flashes of white in the corner of her vision, like things were glowing in her bedroom. It was likely the aura of an impending migraine.

Time for sleep. If I rest now, I might be able to beat the headache before it kicks in.

She climbed into bed, all too aware that the room felt empty without Yael. She punched her pillow a few times, just because, then she curled up on her side, pretending her bodyguard was in the room, that she was safe, and that she wasn't alone with her thoughts. With her pain.

Luke's voice drifted to her. "Rowan, you are so beautiful, you put the blooms to shame."

She started awake, to see a field of wildflowers. Pink, blue, purple and yellow, they formed a sea of colors so intense, so unreal, that she knew she had to be dreaming. The edges of the field were shrouded in mist, and it felt isolated, this little place of wonder.

For a dream, everything felt real, like she was actually sitting in the field, the ground firm and slightly cool underneath her. She wore a loose white dress and a sunhat; Luke sat opposite her, dressed in a light shirt and tan pants. His long hair was unbound, framing his face, making him all the more handsome. He wore a careful expression, and had one knee raised, an elbow resting on it.

"Where are you glasses?" she asked. He was different without them, the gray of his eyes almost white, the perfection of his face a little too relentless.

"I don't need them here."

"Okay." She smiled to cover her unease. Something about this dream was off. Like it was coming from outside her mind, not within it.

That's crazy.

Yes, but she *was* dreaming.

Stuff didn't have to make sense.

That thought calmed her.

"You really are magnificent." He leaned closer, smiling.

She met his stare and froze. His eyes were cold now, colder than snow. He might smile and praise her, but there was something calculating in his gaze. Realizing he was waiting for a response, she mumbled, "Thank you."

He drew back, as if surprised by her reply.

Isn't that what most women say when they're uncomfortable around a guy?

He reached out and clasped one of her hands in his own. *He's persistent.* The touch was meant to be reassuring, but she found the heat of his grip confining.

"Am I making you uncomfortable?" he asked.

Why do guys ask that when they know they are? Like by acknowledging it, it made it okay.

"I don't know what I've done to earn such praise from you." Her answer was pathetic, she knew, but she didn't want a confrontation, even in her dreams. In fact, she wanted the dream over and done with so she could get some rest. Her body and brain needed it.

Something like pity flickered through his expression, before it settled on earnestness. "You are remarkable."

A little devil came to life in her. Clearly Dream Luke wasn't the giving-up kind of guy. "In what way?"

He wasn't expecting that.

The fact he didn't have a ready answer made it clear his words were just empty fawning.

"Come now," she urged. "Surely there is something about me that has earned your regard."

"You are intelligent." His voice deepened. "And you

are beautiful."

She pulled her hand out of his clasp, disappointed. "I am not beautiful."

So even my subconscious doesn't appreciate lies.

You'd think this would be the one place she'd fall for it, the fantasy. An amazingly hot guy thinking she was his sun and moon. But no. Even in her sleep she was too pragmatic for that.

Lucky me.

"Don't be ridiculous," Luke said.

"I might pass for pretty, but I am not beautiful. Don't waste your time on meaningless flattery."

He leaned back, as if she'd slapped him. "I—"

The dream warped. One moment she was in the field, and the next, she was spinning through space, nothing but stars and velvety darkness surrounding her. Her stomach lurched at the sudden change, then she landed on the ground with a thump, her body throbbing from the impact.

What kind of a dream does that?

Her lip stung. She licked it, surprised at the iron taste. Wiping the blood away with her white sleeve, she checked herself for more injuries. Nope, just the split lip, although she'd have some bruises. Pushing herself up, she scanned her new environment: polished marble floors and cloud-colored marble columns soaring to a powder-blue ceiling above. In the middle of the expanse, a stone chamber squatted, its architectural lines reminding her of a mausoleum.

"Where am I?" she muttered to herself, as she shoved herself up on her knees.

"Heaven."

Yelping, she spun around. Yael was behind her. He wore a white robe, belted at the waist with silver rope, like some Grecian god. His eyes were locked on the mausoleum.

"Why am I here?"

He turned to her and swallowed, like being here was so painful that he struggled to talk. "I don't know."

"Why are *you* here?"

He sighed, like she was the nosiest person alive. Reaching out a hand, he helped her stand. His grip sent sparks through her, her whole body coming to life. He let go as soon as she was on her feet.

"I used to live here."

Her eyes widened. "You used to live in Heaven?"

"Yep. Worked here, too."

"As what?"

"An angel."

She snickered. "What?"

"You think it's funny? That I was once an angel?"

"Oh." Her eyes widened. "You're serious."

Dream Yael really was offended.

"Yes, I'm serious. Come." He strode toward the squat building, and she trailed along behind him.

"Where are your wings?" she asked, taking in the finely hewn muscle of his back.

He didn't answer.

I bet the real Heaven looks different to this. It was so austere. Not that she actually believed in Heaven and Hell, but she figured that Heaven would be all green fields and lush paradise. Not some sterile hall with a tomb in the middle.

The door of the mausoleum had been blasted away.

"It's broken," she said. Scorch marks marred the gray stone within, an empty pedestal standing forlornly in the center of the space.

"This used to house one of our most precious artifacts: Heaven's Heart. Ten months ago, it was stolen. I was part of a special military unit designed to protect it. After it was taken, we were banished. Our wings cut off."

Now I feel like an asshole.

He was watching her like she was meant to reply. Why was this dream so odd? Normally things just happened, and she rolled with it. She didn't have to actually *think* about stuff. "Can you get back into Heaven?"

"Yes, if I find the artifact, and the two other pieces that were once part of it."

"Were all three stored here?"

"No. The other two have been lost to Heaven for eons."

"A bit of an impossible quest, then."

"Yep." He glanced down at his watch, checking the time. He opened his mouth to say something, but she cut him off.

"So why aren't you flattering me?" she blurted.

"I—*What*?"

"I was dreaming I was with Luke. He was being overly nice. Then I come here and you're all business."

Yael stepped close to her, his body barely a hair's breadth away, and leaned down, his hazel eyes intense. "I am *always* business."

Why did that sound more seductive than anything Luke had said?

The angel straightened slowly, his gaze sweeping over her, making her body heat. "Plus, I don't need to flatter you. You know what you're worth."

Rowan awoke with a gasp.

CHAPTER 24

Lucifer slammed a fist on the table, shattering it into a thousand pieces.

How did she do that?

While she'd been at the valley this morning, he'd had a sorcerer re-do all the spells her bodyguard had neutralized in her room. The most important was the dream-weave spell on her bed. It was designed to make her dream of him, and to enable him to reach her while she was sleeping; to slip into her subconscious and control the flow of her dream. It was amazing what a few well-placed nighttime fantasies could do, even with the most stubborn of people.

But somehow, he'd lost control of her while she slept. They were in the Field of Fancy—as he liked to call it— and he had been slowly but surely wooing her. Women loved flattery. He'd used the field numerous times over the years; the flowers emitted a subtle aphrodisiac that worked on the subconscious mind.

However, she hadn't reacted typically. Her pulse hadn't raced with latent lust, her skin had remained creamy, with no telltale flush of excitement. It was as if the flowers hadn't had any impact on her at all. And she'd been skeptical of his compliments. He was willing to forgive that, however. It served to highlight how intelligent she was, that she would not fall prey to a few kind words.

It made him appreciate her more; and worry less about that other fallen angel. Yael did not have the physical perfection he had, and his attitude was abrasive. No, even if he did say a few pretty words to Rowan, she would not succumb.

But Luke needed Rowan.

At the end of the day, however, he didn't need her to be willing. It would make life easier for her, but it was not necessary for his plans. If she would not succumb to his charm soon, he would be required to use more forceful measures…

CHAPTER 25

Yael was back in Luxor the next afternoon, feeling refreshed but a little edgy. While he hadn't had any sex dreams of Rowan this time, he'd had a doozy nonetheless. He'd been in Heaven, showing her the Sanctum and the missing Heaven's Heart. Not only was it sacrilege to show a human the Celestial City, it was also beyond comprehension he'd tell her about his fall and the artifact.

Thank God it was just a dream.

Although it certainly had felt real.

Knocking on her door back at the compound, he waited impatiently for her to answer. Azrael and Dru had checked in earlier via SMS to say she'd been fine, but he didn't like being away from her for so long. What if Lucifer had tried to seduce her? He couldn't picture Azrael throwing himself between them, not with Dru around.

Although it would have been fucking hilarious if Dru had decided to take on the Hell-lord.

He raised his fist to knock again when the door swung

inward. Rowan stood on the other side, in the black gown she'd worn to dinner in Cairo. The dress was shapeless, but it accentuated her long legs. Her red hair was out, and she even wore a faint smattering of makeup. His eyes were drawn to her lips where—

"What the Hell happened?" He barged into the room and dragged her under the light, angling her face so he could see better. "Who did this to you?"

Carefully, he raised a finger and her split lip. She hissed in discomfort, but he couldn't see any other bruises or wounds that would indicate she'd been attacked.

Her lip was split on her arrival in Heaven...

But that was just a dream.

Rowan stepped out of his hold. He was surprised she'd allowed him to manhandle her for that long. "I woke up with it."

He frowned. "You woke up with it?"

"Yes. I went to bed, no injury. Woke up to blood all over my pillow and a split lip. I figure I must have bitten it or something."

The vertical line of the wound was in completely the wrong direction for it to have been caused by her teeth, but he didn't bother setting her straight. Because telling her the truth wasn't an option: that she might have done it during a dream, where she landed face-first on the floor of the Inner Sanctum.

Can humans even visit other people's dreams?

But then, she wasn't entirely human, and he had ingested some magical sleep powder from her grandmother. Maybe *he* had reached out to *her*.

Better not have any more of that stuff.

She was scowling at him; he'd been looming over her a little too long.

Time to change the subject.

"So why are you dressed up?" he asked.

"This?" She ran her hands over her slender body. *Kill me. Why did she have to do that?* "We're going out."

"We are?"

She rolled her eyes. "Not us."

"Right." He wasn't following.

"Well, you can come, obviously. But Luke is taking the archaeologists out to dinner, to celebrate the tomb opening."

She crossed the short distance to the desk and grabbed her purse. "Let's go then."

"Sure."

"Actually, let me check my makeup." She touched her wounded lip and headed for the bathroom. It was the only time he'd ever seen her care about her appearance. It was strange, that she was nervous about it.

He much preferred her confidence.

After she'd left the room, he quickly withdrew the Clear Sight powder and applied it. He should have done it before heading to the mansion, but he'd been more concerned about getting some sleep.

Opening his eyes, he was nearly blinded by the glowing spells.

Damn.

Someone had been busy in the past day.

Every spell he'd neutralized over that past three weeks was back, and then some. Her bed was like a fucking eighties dance party.

A knock sounded and he opened the door to see

Azrael and Dru there.

"Whoa!" Azrael blinked rapidly.

"You can see these without the Clear Sight powder?"

Azrael rubbed his eyes. "Yeah. Can't you?"

"No."

Azrael was only a century older than him, why could he do it and Yael couldn't? "Have you always been able to?"

"Yes, I thought all of us Darts could. Seems like that isn't the case." He put on a pair of sunglasses. "That's better."

"What kind of spells are there?" Dru asked. "Tell me, tell me!"

"Lots. Mostly listening," Azrael replied. "There's a badass dream-weave one, too."

Dru gave a low whistle, impressed.

Rowan emerged from the bathroom. "Oh! You're all here. Great. Let's go."

Something dark and green filtered through Yael's mind at her ready acceptance of Dru and Azrael. *No need to get jealous, asshole. Those two are devoted to one another.* And they were. It was the only good thing he could say about Dru: she clearly loved the shit out of Azrael.

The four of them headed for the parking lot, where they met Kayla, Campbell and Murdoch. Lucifer was nowhere to be seen. *Thank fuck.* They all piled into the minivan—Yael in shotgun, the driver's seat vacant.

"Where's Dr. Mustafa?" Rowan asked.

"He's not coming," Kayla replied, attention locked on the gravel yard outside the car window.

"Then who's driving?"

Murdoch shifted in his seat, long limbs protesting

their confinement. "One of the guards."

A demon dressed entirely in black climbed into the driver's seat. Yael figured he could only see the guy's true form because of the Clear Sight, because Rowan didn't let out a scream at the appearance of a bright-pink horned monstrosity.

The guard pulled out of the lot and guided the van out onto Wadi Al Melok Road. As he drove, Kayla chattered in the back with Rowan, winning the occasional quip from Dru. The men were largely silent, but that could be because Murdoch seemed to be permanently cramped, and Campbell looked like he was about to leap out the van door whenever Azrael glanced his way.

Why is he scared of Azrael and not me?

Best not to dig too deep into that one.

Almost half an hour later they reached the Nile River. Washes of ancient magic broke over his skin as they crossed the waterway, but he couldn't see any spells. In the back of the van, everyone was rubbing their arms, even Rowan.

He had no idea what it signified.

They then drove *back* over the Nile again, onto an island, but this time there was only a faint tingle of electricity. Apparently, the western bank of the river was significant for some reason. *I should ask Raze to check that out after he finishes with Twosret.*

The guard parked the vehicle, and they climbed out into the road. Yael scanned the area, but it would be impossible to defend Rowan against attackers here. It was an open street, with a mosque to their left, and gardens to their right and ahead. Even with Dru and Azrael, they were short-staffed.

At least there's a guard and the other archaeologists. He doubted they'd let anything happen to Rowan, either. Their boss would have their heads. Despite that, he still felt uneasy as they walked the thirty feet to the restaurant.

Lucifer was waiting for them, already seated at a round table. Demons patrolled the foyer, and Yael could sense more outside.

Rowan paused. "Why are there only five chairs?"

Lucifer flicked open the menu, although Yael doubted he was actually reading it. "Because there are five of us."

"There's eight."

Lucifer lowered the menu. "It is your bodyguard's job to watch over you, not sit at the table and share your food."

"I can't eat while they stand there hungry."

It was a nice sentiment, although her concern was unnecessary. Yael could go days without food. And Lucifer knew it.

"It's their *job*."

"To starve?" Rowan looked incredulous.

"To stand guard." Lucifer was glaring at her over his glasses, but she didn't seem to care.

The woman has the balls of a giant.

"I'll go somewhere else, then. I won't eat otherwise." She turned to leave.

"Fine." Lucifer jerked his head and a waiter appeared at his side. Anger simmered from the fallen angel. "Get some more chairs."

Rowan smiled, but it wasn't triumphant, just pleased, like she was proud of Lucifer for coming to the right decision. "Thank you."

The irritation vanished from Lucifer, as if it had never been. "You're welcome. Now, come sit next to me."

Great. Now I have to watch the King of Jerks flirt with Rowan all night.

CHAPTER 26

Rowan knew she'd annoyed Luke by insisting the others sit with them, but she honestly didn't think she could eat while Yael, Azrael and Dru watched. She understood their job was to protect her, but they were out to dinner. And she wasn't about to get kidnapped while eating French cuisine in Luxor.

Not with so many people in attendance.

God, I'm becoming paranoid like Gran.

But her gut was telling her there was something *different* about the people surrounding her. She couldn't put her finger on it, aside from the fact that Azrael, Yael and Luke were far too good-looking to be real. They put Chris Hemsworth to shame, and that man had a god-like beauty. Dru was also super-attractive, but in a lethal kind of way. And then there were the other archaeologists. They weren't unbelievably hot, but she'd overheard Colin talking to Dr. Campbell the other day about curses—they'd been discussing them as if they were *real*.

She'd thought only her family talked like that.

Luke raised a glass of red wine, drawing her back to

reality. He was seated to her right, and Kayla to her left. Azrael, Dru and Yael had been placed on the opposite side of the table.

"To discovering a tomb!" Luke took a sip of his wine, and everyone followed suit.

After all the glasses were returned to the table, people started talking amongst themselves. Rowan kept her voice calm. "I thought you might be disappointed the tomb doesn't belong to Twosret."

Luke turned to her, his eyes intense behind his blue-framed glasses. "There were more bodies in that tomb than just the pharaoh's."

"True."

"You do not think any of the mummies in the tomb could belong to Twosret?" Luke asked, leaning closer to her. The scent of sandalwood reached her. He smiled, his movie-star handsomeness overwhelming.

Rowan clenched her fingers on the linen napkin in her lap, begging her brain to *work*.

"No, I don't think so, but that's only a gut feeling. I'm probably wrong."

She hadn't had a chance to read the text on the other sarcophagi, so hadn't gleaned any clues as to who was inside. But she wasn't wrong.

Despite her utter disbelief in superstitious nonsense, Rowan had always trusted her gut. It had yet to be mistaken—she'd even managed to discover a lost Japanese artifact through following a hunch. As far as she was concerned, Twosret was not in that tomb.

She forced her fingers to relax on the napkin, smoothing it out over knees. *Just because he's handsome as sin doesn't mean you have to lose your brain when he smiles.*

But her composure was a hard-won thing. It wasn't that she wanted to jump his bones, or kiss him, or anything like that. It was as if her mind froze at the sheer inhuman beauty of him, like it had reached the maximum capacity for processing visual stimuli.

"Well, time will tell us if Twosret is there or not. I have doubled my personal guard on the site, and the Egyptian government has also provided more guards. We want nothing to happen to our find of the century." His expression was magnanimous generosity, but something felt off about it all.

Why would a self-confessed antiquities hoarder care about preserving a site for the Egyptian public?

It was the one nagging doubt she hadn't been able to erase about Luke, no matter his assurances that his purchases were done in a legitimate fashion. It was illegal to buy artifacts in most countries—hell, Egypt had a standing policy that anything privately owned should be returned to the government.

As the dinner progressed, however, Rowan found herself having fun. Luke was witty, Kayla funny in a sly way, and Yael would occasionally interject with the odd smartass comment that had her fighting back laughter. She was careful to keep her alcohol intake to a minimum as well. She didn't need a hangover; not with so much text to translate over the next few weeks.

"So, Azrael. Your parents gave you an interesting name."

The dark-haired minder paused, his dessert-filled spoon halfway to his mouth. "They did."

"It means 'help from god'." Luke gave him a slight sneer.

It's happening again. A conversation with a subtext she didn't understand.

Azrael finished his spoonful and smiled, his blue eyes almost glowing in the dimly lit restaurant. "In Islamic lore it also means 'angel of death'."

Luke sat back in his chair. "Rather foreboding, isn't it?"

"For you, maybe." Azrael placed a hand on Dru's wrist. Her knuckles white as she gripped her butter knife. "For me, it is just a name."

Luke tilted his head, the sneer still firmly in place. He turned to Yael, as if ready to pick apart his name next, but a waiter appeared. "Would anyone like tea or coffee?"

Rowan swore Kayla's gaze turned lustful at the mention of coffee. Feeling slightly remorseful, Rowan said, "I'm rather tired, do you mind if we head home soon?"

Luke's smirk disappeared. "Of course. Let us leave."

The other archaeologists stood up immediately, their desserts largely finished, except for Colin's. He cast a regretful look down at the half-eaten pudding.

"We don't have to go right away —"

"Nonsense." Luke flicked a hand through the air dismissively. "We should all get some rest."

Yael, Dru and Azrael also stood, their plates empty on the table. Rowan studied Yael's face, and was surprised at the coldness there.

Maybe Luke had been right in insisting she let him do his job.

Worry gnawed at her, and she bit the inside of her cheek to keep from asking Yael if she'd done something wrong. *We are not in a relationship. It doesn't matter if I've offended him somehow. He's only here because he's paid to be.*

While the logic was true, it didn't feel that way anymore. She thought they'd become friends of a sort.

Outside, the night air was brisk and cool, the watery scent of the Nile strong. They were bare steps from the car when Luke stopped, his head tilted to one side, like he was listening to something. Even Kayla, Colin and Dr. Campbell looked like they could hear some distant sound. Rowan rubbed her ears—now what was she missing?

Luke turned back to face them, his eyes nearly glowing in the moonlight. "I have to go. I will be back soon."

Then he strode off to the gardens, disappearing from sight.

What the hell?

He just…vanished.

Maybe he's standing behind a tree.

Yes, that was probably it. He no doubt needed to take a private call and didn't want everyone listening in.

She unlocked the van's sliding door, only to be shoved violently against the paneling.

"What—?" The intense shock of electricity told her who was touching her.

Yael.

A scream shattered the air.

Her bodyguard cursed. "Get down on your knees. And don't turn around."

She dropped to the ground, confused but not stupid. Her knees protested the impact, pain shooting through her legs, making her hiss. Peering over her shoulder, her jaw dropped at the site of large, shadowy figures attacking Dr. Campbell and Colin. The assailants were *huge* with bulky, oddly shaped heads.

Are they wearing masks?

One of them got close to Colin, and the archaeologist jabbed out with the blade of his hand, striking the man in the throat. The attacker crumpled, hands clutching at his neck, but another two took his place, one pinning Colin's arm behind him. A whoop sounded to her right, and something spun through the air, glinting silver in the moonlight. It landed with a thud, an agonized scream coming from one of Colin's assailants, making Rowan clasp her hands over her ears.

A knife. It was a knife.

She glanced up at the sound of crumpling metal. A large figure stood crouched on the top of the van, the roof buckling under his weight. A long arm, complete with dark claws reached for her. She inched back, bumping into Yael's legs. He spun around.

I don't understand—

"Duck!" Yael yelled.

She ducked.

The air whistled over her head, and a wet fleshly thud followed. Warmth sprayed over her face, and she touched it, terrified because she knew what it was. Smeared on her fingertips, the liquid glinted black in the poor light.

Blood.

I have blood on my face.

Bile rose in her throat and she vomited, her stomach cramping; her whole being directed to emptying herself out.

Focus on what's happening around you. But she couldn't.

She wiped her mouth before she remembered she had blood on her hand, and gagged reflexively.

What if I got it in my mouth?

She desperately searched to see if there was anything she could use to clean her face. Then she spotted it.

The severed limb.

Blood oozed sluggishly from the disembodied arm, its skin a gray-purple hue. She hadn't thought flesh would turn that color after being amputated. Long, black nails curled from the fingertips, and strange markings were carved into the skin.

I don't—

"Get her out of here!" Yael shouted, his voice strained.

He fought three cowled attackers, wielding a gleaming sword that was licked with white fire. *Where had he gotten that from?*

A hand was shoved in her face.

She jerked back.

"It's me. Grab my hand." Dru pushed Rowan closer to the road, and lashed out with a leg, catching another shadowy figure in the face. Her white hair flicked out behind her, her ponytail sweeping through the air.

Obeying out of instinct, Rowan reached up and grabbed Dru's hand.

"See you back at the compound," Dru shouted.

Darkness descended, and she couldn't *see* anything. A heartbeat later, she blinked open her eyes, to find herself in the compound's familiar parking lot.

"What—?"

Then, for the first time in her life, she fainted.

CHAPTER 27

It's like a fucking parade of Envio demons.

Yael had never seen so many in one place before. The species was normally buried deep in Hell or working as mercenaries for some rival guild. They didn't tend to spend much time in the Human Realm. Now, however, they were emerging from the surrounding gardens like psychotic gnomes on the warpath.

Yael slashed out with his sword—he'd fucking *conjured* a sword!—slicing through the chest of a purple-skinned Envio that had tried to decapitate him with a clawed hand. Black blood spewed from the wound, and the demon stared down at his torso in surprise, before toppling over, dead.

Seemed like his new kickass blade could slice clean through armor. *Sweet.*

He lashed out with a back kick, taking the demon behind him in the throat. Gagging noises followed him as he moved on to the next group of attackers.

More demons poured into the area, and it was all they could do to hold them off. They were outnumbered three-to-one, but with the incoming flood of new demons, that would soon change.

Thank the skies Dru had managed to get Rowan out of here with her damned teleportation ring.

At least the compound has wards and guards. The wards being the most important thing. Nothing could get in that wasn't already approved. And he seriously doubted these bastards were on the invite list.

"We need to get out of here!" Azrael shouted, cutting a deathly swathe through the demons, coming to stand back-to-back with Yael. The angel was even more lethal, if anything, since his fall.

Maybe Dru's bloodthirsty nature is a good thing for Azrael. No, I didn't just think that.

Yael scanned the area. Everyone in their team was still alive, with Campbell and Murdoch holding their own. But it was Kayla who shocked him. Her eyes glowing like emerald flames, she seemed to simply suck the life right out of anyone she could touch. Desiccated Envio corpses lay in her wake, and the demons were now avoiding her at all costs, almost tripping over themselves to get out of her way.

He'd never heard of a Succubus who could do that, but damn, now he was worried about all those times the archaeologist had teasingly tried to grope him.

However, he was more worried about how the Hell were they going to get a Devilsgate open in time, to get out of here? He didn't have a spare hand to throw the spell, and he doubted any of the archaeologists had one stashed in their pockets.

He and Azrael ducked as a blast of heat whooshed over their heads—a wave of raw burning power scorching the night. A piercing whistle made Yael's eardrums ache, as magic built up in a blistering crescendo. Around them, the attacking Envio demons exploded in a gory shower of blood and viscera. Yael raised an arm over his face to protect his eyes from the debris, holding his sword at the ready with his other hand. But nothing further happened.

The tide of furious magic receded.

Dead.

They were all dead.

Almost fifty Envio demons, turned into a rain of flesh.

Their enemy annihilated, Yael's weapon vanished with an electrical sizzle.

He groaned; he was covered Envio bits. *Great.* He didn't think one shower alone was going to be enough to get rid of it all. And he was going to have to throw out the clothes.

Now I am going to have to wear the slightly less-black pair of cargo pants I brought with me.

"My lord, thank you!" Kayla bowed from the waist, her eyes locked on the ground.

Campbell and Murdoch followed suit, genuflecting toward Azrael and Yael.

What the fuck?

Yael turned slowly.

Lucifer stood on top of the van behind him, shadowy wings of magic blocking out the inky night sky, eyes glowing white. Ripples of lightning flickered over his skin, and the scar on his neck was visible to all and sundry, now he wore nothing but low-waisted leather pants.

Fucking get some clothes on.

The Hell-lord dropped the ground, landing with the grace of a hunting cat, the planes of his face stark in anger. Lucifer strode over to Yael, who fought the urge to back up. He'd never been this close to an enraged archangel before. And for fucking good reason. They were even scarier up close and furious.

Okay, I haven't gotten over my fear. Especially not now Lucifer looked like a Tesla ball gone wrong.

"Where is Rowan?" the Hell-lord ground out, eyes sweeping over the gore-laden ground.

"Dru took her somewhere safe," Azrael replied, as cool and calm as if he spoke to lightning-cloaked archangels on a regular basis.

"Where?"

"I don't know," the dark-haired angel said. "But hopefully the compound."

"*Hopefully* the compound?" Incredulity dropped Lucifer's anger a few notches.

Thank the skies.

Yael might needle and bait the Hell-lord, but even he wasn't stupid enough to take on an archangel who was ready to kill.

"Dru's teleportation skills are somewhat unreliable. But she would have taken her somewhere safe."

Lucifer rubbed a hand over his face. "I didn't know Mortus demons *could* teleport."

Azrael shrugged. "She's a cambion."

So, Azrael wasn't about to admit to the Hell-lord that Dru herself couldn't teleport, she just wore a magical ring that *could*. And the piece of fucked-up jewelry didn't always take you to where you wanted to go.

"Yes," Lucifer said. "Her skin tone did give away the

fact she wasn't pure-blooded. And cambion's powers are often unpredictable." Then the Hell-lord sighed. "This was Satan's work, no doubt. He arrived unannounced in the Tower of Tortures to distract me, just as you were attacked."

The steaming mess of body parts and visceral spray vanished.

"Now that's what I call cleanup," Yael muttered.

Lucifer showed his teeth in a pseudo-smile. "I just sent all of that to Satan's office. I expect to hear from him in three, two, one...gotta go!"

He disappeared.

"I wished he'd removed the stuff from us, too," Kayla said, wincing at the dark blood on her arms.

Murdoch just shrugged. "I don't mind a bit every now and then. Different species' blood tends to have a different flavor."

Yael grimaced. *Gross.*

But what else did he expect from demons?

Murdoch patted the car with a sad sigh. "Well, the van is ruined."

Its white panels were scratched and clawed, while the roof had completely caved in. It wasn't going anywhere fast, that was for sure.

"Let's get back to the compound," Yael said. "We should make sure Dru and Rowan made it there."

"You think they were coming for her?" Azrael asked quietly.

Yael fished out a bag of Devilsgate powder from one of his pockets. Luckily, he'd stored it in plastic, or it would be a blood-sodden mess in the bottom of his pants by now. "They went straight for her at the start."

And they had. One second they'd been on their own, the next, three Envios had been coming for them, making a beeline for Rowan.

Satan must want to know why Lucifer is interested in a human.

At least, he hoped that was the case, otherwise some other faction was after her and they were in a lot more trouble.

Throwing a pinch of dust in the air, Yael muttered the compound's address and stepped through, Azrael and the others hot on his heels.

The parking lot of the compound was empty, and the area quiet. In fact, everything was as peaceful as always.

"Doesn't look like they tried to break in here," Azrael commented.

"No." It made him appreciate the power used to create the wards.

Kayla approached them. "I'm going to have a shower. Let me know if you need any help."

"We're good."

She turned to walk away.

"Kayla," Yael asked, "what kind of demon are you?"

Her bright-green eyes glowed. "Don't you know it's rude to ask a girl what her species is?" Then she sauntered off, hips swinging in a sultry rhythm, despite being covered in gore.

Demons.

Murdoch and Campbell nodded at them before hurrying off to their respective rooms, leaving Azrael and Yael alone. Azrael hurried to Rowan's cabin, beating Yael to knock on the door. It was jerked open, and Dru peered at them from the other side.

"You're back!" She flung herself at Azrael but stopped at the last second, like a puppet being jerked backwards by its strings. "What the Hell happened?"

"Lucifer," Yael ground out.

"That doesn't clarify things."

Azrael made an exploding noise, throwing his hands out at the same time.

Dru's eyes went wide. "Oh, really? Tell me all about it." She stepped out onto the porch, turned her attention to Yael. "Rowan's inside and okay. She fainted, but I've never teleported a human before, so I didn't know that was a potential side-effect. I gave her some wine, it calmed her down."

Azrael eyed Dru up and down. "We're going to steal your room and shower," he told Yael.

Then they were gone.

He didn't have time to tell them he had to share the bathroom.

Yael clenched his fist. *I conjured a sword.* He hadn't been able to do that as an angel—Azrael, Dina and Raze could—but it seemed that he could now he was fallen. Go figure.

Gingerly, Yael stepped inside Rowan's room, only to find it empty. He shut the door behind him. "Rowan?"

The bathroom door swung open, and she tumbled out, stumbling to sit on her bed. Her little black dress had been replaced with a nightgown that had somehow ridden up to show far more of her thigh than he was comfortable with.

She stared at him. "You're dirty."

"Uh—" Was it that obvious he was checking out her legs?

"Use my shower."

"Right. Yes, thanks." His backpack was in the corner where he'd left it earlier, so he retrieved it and headed for the bathroom. He paused in the threshold, looked her over. Her eyes were still a little wild and she was pale and drawn. "Are you okay?"

She nodded, a little too enthusiastically, so that she wobbled on the bed. "I'm fine."

"I'll be quick."

And he was. Well, as fast as he could be considering he had to wash his hair twice, and scrub blood out from places it shouldn't have been able to get. By the time he was done, Rowan was lying on her side on top of the bed, her damp hair spread out like spilled wine.

She rolled over to face him as he placed his backpack next to the door. "Can you come here?"

"Why?"

"Can you?"

Sighing, he complied. It wasn't like she was asking him to go over there and jump her bones. He just really didn't like having the image of her loose-limbed and relaxed, ready to welcome him with open arms.

Whoa. Get your head out of your pants.

He sat on the edge of her bed, as far away from her as possible. "What do you need?"

"Can you, I dunno..." She ran a hand through her hair. "This is so awkward."

Oh Hell no. She is not hitting on me, she is not—

"Give me a hug?"

CHAPTER 28

Rowan felt sick to her stomach, and dirty. And hollow. And just…gross.

Her head throbbed, and she was tipsy as hell, courtesy of Dru shoving a glass of wine at her to 'calm her nerves'. *And* she felt like she'd been to the worst immersive theater production ever. Plus, she'd lost time. Had she suffered a head injury? She felt her skull. No, there were no wounds. But she didn't even remember the drive back to the compound.

I just saw a man get his arm cut off.

Cut.

Off.

Yael—her Yael—had done it without even blinking. She'd known he had military experience, but she hadn't expected him to be so calm about slicing off someone's limb. And that was only the bits she'd seen. Dru had tried to tell her more, but Rowan hadn't been in the frame of mind to listen. She didn't want to know about all the needless death or mutilation.

Or how awesome Dru's knife-throwing skills were.

And the man that had tried to harm her, he had to have been in some sort of cult or something; it was the only thing that could explain the odd markings on his skin. The poor guy had probably been brainwashed into believing he needed to attack them.

No way am I telling Gran about this.

At least everyone is okay.

Not that she'd been told that, but she just *knew* everyone had survived. She'd check with Yael once he got out of the shower. Her head swam suddenly, and she lay back on the bed, curling in on herself. She had no idea what kind of wine she'd drunk—Dru hadn't been all that forthcoming when she'd asked.

It was white. And it had bubbles. That was about all she knew.

But she definitely felt drunker than she should after one glass.

And I fainted earlier.

For someone who'd never passed out in their life, it had been embarrassing to wake up in her room, a concerned Dru by her side. The white-haired woman had even been on the phone talking to someone called Peony, asking for medical advice.

Maybe that's why I have some memory loss? Fainting had caused her to lose some time?

The sound of the shower stopped, and Yael emerged a few minutes later from the bathroom, his hair wet and T-shirt sticking to his barely dry abs. For a moment, the drunken part of her roared to the surface, demanding she strip that T-shirt off and lick her way down his stomach to his waistband.

She clenched her teeth and rolled over to face him as

he dropped his bag by the door. She was not going to do anything to his stomach, no matter that she could see he had an eight-pack.

Memories of the severed arm reached her again and she shivered. Every time she closed her eyes, she could see it, feel the blood spraying against her face. "Can you come here?"

He narrowed his eyes, like she was laying a trap for him. "Why?"

"Can you?"

With a loud sigh, he sat on the edge of her bed. "What do you need?"

"Can you, I dunno...." God, this was even more embarrassing than she'd thought it would be. "This is so awkward."

He looked like a deer in headlights.

"Give me a hug?" she blurted.

He scowled. "A hug?"

She looked at him darkly. "I'm not asking you to strip naked and dance for me. Just a hug."

"But—"

"I need one, okay. I don't feel good."

With a few cuss words, Yael lay on the bed next to her, his feet dangling over the end. He wasn't exactly welcoming, but she didn't care. Snuggling up to his side, she grabbed his arm and pulled it down so she could use it as a pillow, and then draped her forearm over his chest.

Mmmm.

He was so warm.

And he smelled of soap and clean things, not blood and horror.

She lay there for a few minutes in silence, taking solace

in the presence of another person; just listening to him breathe. She'd never had this before, this silent communion between individuals, where she could take comfort without anything else being expected of her.

Eric had always wanted something.

Sex, someone to talk to, entertainment…he hadn't really been good at listening. Or at just being quiet.

She bit the inside of her cheek.

I am such an asshole.

But it didn't change the fact that she and Eric hadn't been the perfect couple she'd imagined. The perfect couple she'd *wanted* them to be.

Tears burned her eyes, so she shut them, not wanting to cry, not wanting to give in to her weakness. But the tears, they weren't for Eric, or for his loss. They were for her. For *her* loss: for her loss of innocence, for her learning about death firsthand, for her witnessing the end of something precious and precarious.

And for *not* missing Eric like she should. For not wishing he was here right now to comfort her, but for being glad that it was Yael instead. Because he didn't try and talk to her, to tell her that everything was going to be okay, that she would be strong and survive. For making her pain an inconvenience—like Eric would have.

He just let her be.

And for that, for those few minutes of silence and acceptance, she would be forever grateful.

Yael's hand came up and he stroked her hair. It calmed her, his touch, despite the tingles it spread over her scalp. It reminded her she was alive, that she was here, and that she was damaged but okay.

Eventually, the tightness in her throat eased enough

for her to speak. "Was everyone unhurt?"

His hand stilled. "Yes, we all made it out."

So, her instincts had been correct.

"Did Luke come back?"

"Just at the end. He was fine."

"Who were those men?" she asked, but she didn't really want to know. Knowing would mean learning of their lives, their cause, what they had thought to gain by attacking them.

Yael rested his chin on her head. "No one good."

"It will be all over the news..."

He snorted, the sound making his chest move, pressing his side against her more firmly. "I doubt it."

"But there were bodies, and blood..."

"Trust me, you won't be seeing this on T.V. or the Internet or anywhere."

She wanted to argue that he was wrong, but she knew he wasn't. In this part of the world—hell, anywhere—they wouldn't want to publicize that a strange cult was attacking foreigners. It wouldn't look good. It would all be handled quietly.

She just wished she hadn't had to see it.

"Tell me a story." She clenched her hand into a fist, so her wayward fingers wouldn't start rubbing circles on his chest.

"What kind of a story?"

She liked the feel of his voice. "I don't know. Something entertaining." She paused. "And not violent."

"Well, that limits my repertoire." He chuckled, and she could feel it in her bones. "I could tell you an erotic tale—"

"No sexy stuff." She had enough dreams of that kind

of thing.

"Maybe you should tell the story, since you're the one with the rules."

She jabbed him.

"Okay, okay. Miss-I-Don't-Want-A-Violent-Story-But-Will-Harm-You-When-I-Don't-Get-What-I-Want."

"Did you even breathe through that?"

"No, I have excellent lung capacity. Now, once upon a time, there was nothing."

"Nothing?" She propped her head up, narrowing her eyes at him. "This had better not be a boring story."

"Hush." He had an amused expression. "You wanted a story, so you're getting one. Too many smartass comments from you and I'll stop."

Grumbling, she laid her head back on his chest.

"So, there was nothing. Until suddenly, the universe burst into life."

"That's called the Big Bang. Are you telling me a story about physics?"

"What did I say about interrupting?"

She sniffed. "Fine."

"At the time of creation, the primordial gods were born. They were raw power, without thought or reason. They journeyed through the universe for millennia upon millennia, some causing destruction, others creation."

"You're saying there was balance."

"Yes." He nodded. "There must always be balance. Eventually, a handful of primordial deities banded together to create something unique, something special. Earth. With it, they crafted Heaven and Hell, and they left the world to evolve, watched over by guardians of good and evil.

"Eventually, humans evolved, and the primordial gods' ultimate creation was achieved. But with humanity came another host of problems. They were complex—and they were neither good nor evil, but a combination of both. They could be swayed to one extreme or another."

It was a creation story. One she'd never heard before; and she'd studied enough ancient cultures to know that it was unique. "You're talking about the development of free will."

"Yes. Heaven and Hell—no one is truly destined for one or the other. It is the choices that are made throughout life that lead you to your doom—or your reward."

"So, you're saying fate isn't predetermined."

He tightened his arm around her briefly. "I sure as Hell hope not."

She pursed her lips. "When you say Heaven, do you mean angels and God?"

"Yep."

"And Hell…fire and brimstone and Satan?"

"Satan only rules one circle of Hell."

"One circle?"

"Yeah, the three circles of Hell: Inferno, Sheol, and Tartarus."

She frowned. "You're mixing up your mythologies." Jewish, Canaanite, and Greek mythologies to be exact, with a little of Dante Alighieri's poetry thrown in.

"Or maybe mythology got it wrong."

"So, which one does Satan rule, then? In this story you are telling me." Although, she was feeling it was more than just a story—like maybe Yael actually believed it.

He doesn't strike me as religious. Although Azrael said their parents were, so who knows?

"Inferno," Yael replied. "Lucifer rules Sheol and Hades rules Tartarus."

At the mention of Hades, an image of a muscular man with a partially shaved head and piercing yellow eyes filled her vision. She blinked and it vanished.

What was that?

She shook her head a little. "That's not the story I was expecting, but thank you." She gave him a quick kiss on the cheek. He stiffened. But when she didn't try anything more, his muscles slowly relaxed.

She closed her eyes, but this time, she didn't see the severed arm or the blood, she saw the wonder of creation, and had the knowledge that every individual could create their own destiny, and that some paths were redeemable.

And some weren't.

CHAPTER 29

A week had passed since the attack, and everyone had fallen back into their normal holding pattern. Dru and Azrael had stayed on, though, to give Yael a break from time to time. He hadn't taken one. He didn't like the idea of leaving Rowan, but he knew that it was the smart thing to do. At some point.

Currently, Rowan was on the opposite side of the pathway to the tomb, staring into the cliff wall like it could explain the meaning of life. She'd been distracted ever since it had been opened and was convinced they should excavate elsewhere, even though the radar-thingy had said there was nothing where she was proposing to dig.

For someone who is so logical, she has great lapses of it.

Like coming to him for comfort after the attack.

Yael didn't know why he'd told her the true story of creation, but he'd wanted to let her know that life was what she'd make it; that she had a choice. And not working for Lucifer would be a good start, although he couldn't say that part out loud.

Not when somehow, she still didn't believe in magic.

His phone vibrated in his pocket. He fished it out and answered without checking the screen. "Yo."

"Yael, it's Raze."

Like he wouldn't be able to recognize the deep voice. "What's up?"

"I found the reference."

His mind went blank. "What reference?"

"To Twosret."

His fingers squeezed the handset. "You did?"

"Yes, in the Mortus den photographs."

"You found a reference to an Egyptian pharaoh in the Mortus den?" Maybe he needed to get his ears checked.

"Yes. The author was quite the megalomaniac, and narcissistic—I still have to work out her identity—but she mentions the stones of Heaven."

Stones of Heaven.

He snorted.

Like Heaven had balls.

When Raze remained quiet, Yael said, "I'm not following."

A long-suffering sigh came down the line. "She documents that there are three stones; one for the angels, one for the humans, and one for the demons."

Three pieces.

Heaven's Heart was apparently comprised of three components, and they had to find all of them in order to win their way back into Heaven.

Yael walked to the edge of camp, out of hearing range of the archaeologists and the guards. "You're saying the stones of Heaven are actually Heaven's Heart?"

"Yes. I might not have put this together, except that

we now know that Z's piece of the Heart is of mineral composition."

Yeah, Z had a dirty big rock stuck in his abdomen, courtesy of the Infernus demons who had kidnapped him. They'd stored it there for 'safe-keeping'—after they'd stolen it from the Holy Sanctum—except now it had fused with the angel's body. The Infernus had come to retrieve it, and they'd died.

Z still hadn't told the archangels that he had it.

So that would be the angelic component…

"But what has this got to do with Twosret?"

"We know the other two pieces of Heaven's Heart have been missing for millennia. But they weren't meant to be stored away in a chamber, they were meant to be used."

"Okay." He figured Raze would get to the point. Eventually.

"The markings in the Mortus den prophesize that the good god, daughter of the sun, last of her dynasty, witness of Troy, will lie undisturbed for millennia. She was supposedly buried with the stone that was gifted to her by Amun. It says she is the catalyst; the discovery of her tomb will either stop or start the end of days."

The end of days?

Yael needed a drink.

Were they talking Armageddon now? Because *damn*. They were only meant to be on a quest to find some stupid rocks. Get back into Heaven. That sort of thing. Not save the bloody world.

"How do you know the reference means Twosret, or even an Egyptian?" Yael asked. They had to be sure this was the right information. Especially if there was doom and gloom to be had.

"She was the last king of the Eighteenth Dynasty. Her title was Daughter of Re—the sun—and one of the words for pharaoh—*neter nefer*—translates to the good god."

He knew that. Well, the good god bit, anyway. He could read Egyptian, after all. But he was still skeptical. "I'm sure plenty of female pharaohs had the title 'Daughter of Re'." He knew Hatshepsut had; he'd been doing some 'light' reading.

"Cleopatra, Twosret, and Sobekneferu all ruled the last of their dynasties," Raze said. "But Troy fell around 1200 BCE. That was near the time of Twosret's rule."

Well, there you go then. That was more convincing.

"So, you think Lucifer is after Twosret because she might have been buried with the Heart?"

"It's as good a theory as anything else. And to be fair, this would work to our advantage if she's in the tomb you're working on."

"She isn't. And Lucifer went in first, so if her body had been there, he would have found the Heart."

"It may be hidden in the chamber itself."

"Quite possible. But it's growing more and more likely that the tomb we found belongs to Nefertiti."

"Fascinating."

Yael swore he could hear the cogs spinning in Raze's mind. "Yeah, archaeological find of the century blah blah. But if the Heart is with Twosret, we *have* to find her."

He'd come back and look for her himself if he had to. He'd just need to be armed with a whole bunch of concealment spells.

He ended the call. Mind spinning, he stayed quiet when Rowan approached.

"I just can't let it go," she said, voice soft.

He glanced at her, then tucked his cell away. "Let what go?"

"The place where I think we need to dig. I can't explain it." She ran a hand over her head, clearly frustrated with herself.

"Then ask for permission."

"We only have the permit—"

"Dr. Mustafa seems pretty pissed at Starre at the moment. He might pull some strings for you, just to see you fail."

"To see me *fail*?"

"Yes, you're Starre's pet archaeologist. The co-director who was forced on him. You want to dig where everyone says there's nothing. You dig, you find nothing, he looks good."

"I'm not sure why he'd stick his head out for that. It's rather petty."

"Humans are petty."

She gave him an odd look, then with a deep breath, turned on her heel and walked purposefully toward the marquee.

He had no idea, of course, whether Mustafa really was that small-minded. But if she didn't ask, she wouldn't get. And Hell, maybe the Egyptian director wanted to dig a bit more of the valley up. His helping her might entirely be altruistic.

His phone rang again.

For fuck's sake.

He checked the caller I.D. this time: Dora.

Great. Just what I need. Rowan's gran checking in on them to see what had been going on.

"Afternoon, Dora."

"It's morning here." He swore he could hear a cane being stamped on the ground.

"How nice for you."

"You haven't given me an update for a while. Actually, ever."

"One, you didn't ask for updates. And two, I thought you had spies to let you know what was going on."

Her voice turned icy. "And those spies told me you were attacked by a militia of Envio demons."

"I wouldn't use the term 'militia'. More like a group?" He hadn't meant that to be a question.

Thankfully, she left it alone. "I take it you all made it out alive."

"Yes."

"How was Rowan?"

"She seems to have bounced back." Remarkably well, for someone who had had her first taste of violence.

"She has a wonderful ability to forget things that don't fit with her worldview."

That he could believe. She had ignored the fact she was teleported back to the compound. She hadn't even brought it up.

Then again, wouldn't most humans?

Which reminded him... "How accurate are Rowan's 'gut feelings'?"

There was silence for a few heartbeats. "She has never been wrong."

"Is that a latent magical ability?"

"I think so. But she'll just tell you she's lucky."

Yael turned back to the marquee. Mustafa was on his cell, and Rowan was pacing back and forth next to him.

So, the co-director had decided to make the call? Go along with her idea?

"I've got to go."

"Don't forget to update me."

"Sure thing, Gran." He hung up on her swearing.

CHAPTER 30

Yael had been right.

Within two days, Dr. Mustafa had managed to wrangle some changes to their permit and convinced the government to grant Rowan permission to excavate on the other side of the visitor's walkway. She didn't know if he'd done it out of spite or out of curiosity. At this point, she'd didn't care.

The downside—and there was always a downside—was that she'd only been given two workers, and she was only allowed to excavate one three-meter by three-meter trench. She'd been traipsing up and down the area for the past two hours, trying to decide where best to place her single excavation pit.

"Is this some kind of ritual?" Kayla's voice made Rowan jump.

"What?"

"The pacing and the muttering and the staring." Kayla watched her curiously. She was wearing her usual khaki pants and shirt, with no hat. If Rowan neglected her headgear, she'd turn into a peeling lobster. Kayla didn't seem to get sunburned at all.

Rowan's cheeks flushed. "No, it's simply me being indecisive."

She should just pick a place and be done with it. She bit the inside of her cheek. But what if she got it wrong? She only had one chance. And she didn't want to waste it, nor make herself look like a fool.

She scanned the beige sand, the orange cliff, as if they could tell her the answers.

Where? Where? Where?

Yael strode up beside her. "Just close your eyes and point."

She drew herself up to her full height. "That is not very scientific."

He folded his arms. "Well, the radar-thingy says there's nothing here. Everyone else says there's nothing here. Your entire argument to dig here is not based on science; it's based on gut instinct. So, close your eyes, raise your hand and point somewhere."

She wanted to argue that he was wrong, that she was cool and logical and that she never made a decision without weighing all the facts. But he was right. She *was* acting crazy, insisting that there was something here when all evidence pointed to the contrary.

But for some reason she couldn't explain, she couldn't let it go.

Then again, she'd never been able to let anything go. It was a fault of hers, one she hadn't been able to override.

Maybe it's worse because Eric is gone, you just witnessed someone get their arm chopped off, and you're missing time. Again.

The first occasion had only been a few minutes, but it

had happened about a week or so after she'd first met Luke. Occasionally, she'd remember a man with black hair and yellow eyes, but the memory was slippery and she couldn't hold on to it.

Yael and Kayla were staring at her expectantly.

"Fine." She blew out a steady stream of air and closed her eyes.

Now what?

You point at something, idiot.

It seemed so silly.

But she didn't have a better idea.

Raising her arm, she moved it from side to side, and thought, *Twosret, where are you?*

Her arm cramped suddenly, and she fought the urge to cry out in pain. But as she moved it, the discomfort lessened, until there was no ache at all. She stilled.

"There."

Opening her eyes, she realized she was pointing directly at her feet.

Great.

"Maybe I should do it again—"

"No take-backs." Yael shook his head. "You've chosen."

"Perfect." Kayla bent down and shoved a tiny wire flag into the ground between Rowan's hiking boots. "X marks the spot."

"It's a flag."

Kayla smirked. "Don't be so pedantic. Go get your stuff and mark out your trench."

Laughing huffily, Rowan walked back to the marquee for her kit. She rubbed her arm absently, wondering if she'd imagined the cramp. *I probably haven't been drinking enough water.* A lack of magnesium could cause cramps, too. She should probably start taking multivitamins.

Her small kit in hand, she went back to the lonely little wire flag. Yael stood over it, as if he was protecting it from harm. It was kind of sweet.

No, don't think that.

It was a slippery road, that one. A month and a half ago, she would have said his proximity, or his occasional acts of kindness meant nothing. That she would never view him as anything more than eye-candy. But that was before she'd changed, before she'd realized that she only had herself to rely on, and that she liked him.

Oh god.

She squeezed her eyes shut against that thought.

"Yo, Rowan. You gonna put your stuff down or just stand there staring at the flag?"

She opened her eyes, leaning back when Yael waved a hand in front of her face. *He can also be an asshole when he wants to.* But that didn't change the fact he was also always just…him. Eric had been more reserved. She had liked it at first, considering the havoc her family represented. But now she realized she needed someone more down-to-earth.

Yael was waiting for her to speak. "I was contemplating my next move."

He tucked his hands in his pockets. "Uh, dig the hole?"

She laughed. "No." It was going to be a while before she could put trowel—or more accurately, hand axe—to the ground.

"But you need to dig a hole." Yael glared at the tiny flag like it had suddenly grown horns.

"I do. But I have to measure it out, make sure it's square, record it with the survey equipment and take a dumpy level—"

"You have to take a *what*?" Both his eyebrows flew up.

"Dumpy level."

Dru appeared then, from God-knew-where. She had a habit of sneaking up on people. Rowan looked around for Azrael and spotted his dark silhouette in the distance. "You're taking a dump on the site? Is this a ritual thing?"

What was with all the questions about rituals? Like *Rowan* was the one under the microscope. "I am not taking a dump on the site. I am measuring its height above the valley floor. The equipment you use to measure it is called a dumpy level."

"Ohhh."

Both Dru and Yael seemed relieved. Like, *really* relieved.

Hanging her head, she tugged her hat down low over her face.

I can't believe they thought I would…poop…on the site before I excavated it. If they'd been joking, they were good actors to look so confused and concerned.

"Here." She shoved a tape measure at Yael. "Hold this."

He grabbed it out of reflex.

Time to get to work.

CHAPTER 31

Now that Yael was paying more attention to the tasks Rowan was performing—rather than wandering the site and ensuring her safety—he was coming to realize that archaeology was boring.

There was a lot of notetaking, a lot of standing around holding stuff, and a lot of laborious digging. Sure, he'd gotten behind the pickaxe a time or dozen himself, purely because he thought he'd go crazy watching Rowan swing a tool almost as tall as she was. She was competent enough with it—she hadn't taken her foot off, at any rate—but it had also felt good to let some steam off.

Plus, he was the fastest at it.

And he needed a distraction, because sharing a room with Rowan was killing him, one hard-on at a time.

It was all because she'd asked for that damned hug. He knew he shouldn't have given in, but he had, and now whenever he stayed with her at night—on the floor—he knew what it was like to feel her body pressed up against him. How her breasts felt against his chest, her legs against his…

Damnit.

He quickly adjusted himself, pretending to bend down and tie his shoelace.

This was becoming a nightmare.

What's more, she clearly had not been sleeping well lately — despite the fact that, in his arms, she'd slept like a baby. She had even called out *his name* in her sleep. Not Lucifer's or her dead boyfriend's. *His*. And not in a sexy way; in a frightened-please-save-me-way. He'd sat on her bed at one point and held her hand until she stopped thrashing and calmed down.

He'd held her fucking hand.

He, who didn't believe in comfort or helping people unless he had to, had gone over to Rowan at her most vulnerable and tried to calm her back to sleep.

He straightened and noticed Kayla leering at him. The demon had slowly grown on him, which was annoying. But he liked her attitude, and the fact that she seemed to have really tried to bond with Rowan, who appeared to enjoy their friendship.

When did I start caring what Rowan likes and doesn't like?

It wasn't a good sign.

He was growing attached.

And that is why I do wet work, and not close protection.

Although, if she hadn't been clever, driven and assertive, he probably would have been able to maintain his distance.

Sighing, he grabbed the pickaxe from where it rested upright against the trench wall. Time to do some more hard labor so his mind wouldn't focus on stupid shit.

Like how it would be to actually kiss her.

He swung the axe down hard. It slammed to a stop,

jolting back up through his arm. "What the fuck?" He let go of the handle and rotated his shoulder. It was tough digging, working through the compact dirt of the valley, but it wasn't usually so resistant.

That had *hurt*.

"What is it?" Rowan stood near the edge of the pit—which was already six feet deep—and peered down at him from under the shade of her hat. Her face and shirt were covered in beige smudges from where she'd been sieving the dirt. He was beginning to wonder at the sanity of archaeologists, but she looked rather charming despite the stains.

No more cute shit.

"The axe met some resistance," he replied.

"Really?" She clambered down the ladder and met him in the middle of the trench. The two workers stopped what they were doing and came over too. It was pretty crowded, huddled together like that. But he made it work.

Rowan crouched down next to the embedded axe and pulled her trowel out of the little holster she kept it in. Until he'd seen it, he'd only thought holsters were for weapons. Who knew?

Rowan troweled around the axe point. "It shouldn't have lodged like this unless it's embedded in rock."

The three of them stood around for her for another fifteen minutes while she laboriously scraped around the tool. It was boring. And exciting. And also boring.

"There!" Rowan sat back on her heels and they peered over her shoulder.

"It's more dirt?" Yael asked, scanning the ground for something, anything. If this was the entry to Twosret's tomb…

"No, it's stone." She twisted her neck to glance up at him. "I think it might be a stair."

The workers talked excitedly amongst themselves and hurried to grab trowels out of the equipment box. They weren't trained archaeologists, but they seemed to know what to with the equipment better than Murdoch and Campbell did. And certainly better than Yael.

He was hustled out of the way a few minutes later, so he propped himself up against the trench wall. Bits of broken pebbles and cracked rock dug into his arm, but it was better to look like he was supervising rather than standing around clueless.

"Here." Kayla ambled over, a notepad in one hand and a trowel in the other. She shoved the tool at him. "Go join the fun."

"I don't know how." Normally, he would have felt embarrassed at such an admission—being ignorant had been a shameful thing in his family—but honestly, when would he have ever used one?

It's not like Mother or Father ever thought to train me in bricklaying or excavation work. The only two things people used trowels for, apparently.

"It's not rocket science. Go." Kayla turned and walked away, ass swaying in her dust-covered pants. Too bad he preferred to watch Rowan's ass, now in a perfect viewing position as she bent down low to check out the pickaxe.

Ugh. Not again.

Maybe he should just have sex with her and get it out of his system. He had no idea if she felt the same damnable attraction, but he'd caught her staring at him a time or two. *You're an angel, she is bound to stare at you. You*

*are one hundred percent more handsome than any human male
she's ever seen.* And that wasn't his ego talking—it was just
fact.

But when had he gone from admiring her body to
wanting to fuck her?

Yael hadn't had sex with anyone who wasn't an angel,
well, ever. And he wasn't about to break that rule now.

"I'm going to check something." Rowan climbed up
the ladder, giving him an excellent view of her ass again.

Just go dig some dirt.

He was starting to feel an inkling of pity for Azrael.
How had the angel managed to handle being attracted to
a psychopathic cambion after being one of Heaven's most
prized warriors? It would have gone against everything
he believed in.

Hell, lusting after a human was putting a serious
strain on Yael's fortitude.

Just get to work. He kneeled on the ground and gingerly
scraped the surface with the trowel's edge.

"Here." One of the workers pointed at the tool and
then showed Yael how to angle it just right. "Like this.
This much at a time." The worker held his fingers a half-
inch apart.

He met the guy's earnest brown eyes and nodded.
"Thanks." Not one to snub instruction, Yael copied the
worker and moved a decent amount of soil that way.

Nice. I rock at this.

Naturally. He was pretty much awesome at
everything, except making friends. Or keeping his
parents happy. But who needed them anyway?

"You suck at bodyguard duty," a voice called out.

He sighed.

Dru.

He stood and shaded his eyes from the sun's glare with a hand. "What?"

"You're meant to be guarding her and she's over by that sieve-thing." Dru pointed to her right, where Rowan stood next to a wire and metal sieve, shoving it from side to side with all she was worth. Clouds of dust coated the air around her.

"Aren't you and Azrael both on duty?" he asked.

"Yeah, but we didn't agree to come here so you can scrape the ground away one inch at a time."

"Pfft, as if I take off that much dirt." The other two workers looked askance at him. Okay, sure, he was a bit more enthusiastic than that.

He'd be here for the next forty years if he went that slow.

And if this really was the start of a staircase, then they had to find out fast. If this was Twosret's tomb, and she was the last human to wear Heaven's Heart…

They had to beat Lucifer.

Time was everything.

"How's progress?" Rowan had returned, even dustier than before. She stood next to Dru, whose white hair gleamed in the sunlight.

"Getting there," he replied. He had certainly mounded up a pile of soil near his knees, anyway.

"Aren't you hot?" Rowan asked him.

"I like to think so."

Dru snorted. "Man, you are so hard up for compliments you will jump at anything."

"It's not my fault if I happen to be ridiculously good looking."

"You're ridiculous, all right," Dru snapped.

Rowan flushed. "No. You're dressed in black. Both of you are." She pointed at Dru as well. "Don't you feel the heat?"

"Not really, no." He barely even sweated.

"*'iinah huna!*" shouted one of the workers.

Yael spun to look. "What did you find?"

The worker pointed to a creamy stone slab, Yael's pickaxe embedded within the surface. The human had traced its position through the trench. It was only three feet long and one foot wide.

Rowan climbed back into the trench. "I think it's a stair. But let's keep going."

First thing's first; he stepped up to yank that pickaxe out.

He had just ripped it free when his phone buzzed. "Excuse me." He hurried over to the edge of the trench, but when he saw the caller I.D., he decided he needed more distance.

He jammed the cell between his shoulder and ear so he could climb up the ladder. "Raze, what's up?" At the top of the trench, he headed for a vacant patch of land around a hundred yards away.

Raze's voice emerged in a rush, like he'd been breathing hard. "Dina was just here."

"*What?*" Dina? *The* Dina who had told him to back off, and that she was done with the Darts?

Has she changed her mind?

"I left the library to get a drink, and came back to see her rifling through my research. She was looking at the Mortus pictures." Raze sounded uncharacteristically ruffled.

"Are you hurt?" Yael asked. Raze was old and powerful, but Dina was stronger.

"No, she saw me and just vanished."

"She can teleport?"

"Apparently."

Seemed like that was a new skill she'd gained since being stolen from Heaven. "Do you think she saw enough of your research to know Twosret had the Heart?"

"I can't say. Let's hope not."

"How did she get in, anyway?"

"I had the wards keyed to all the Darts, in case she and Z found their way back to us. I never thought Dina would come here after she told you she was done with us."

"Change them."

"I'm already on it." Raze ended the call.

Great. So now Dina may know where the second piece of Heaven's Heart was. Or she may not. He'd have to watch both his and Rowan's backs if she was coming for them.

Yael turned to face the trench. Finding the tomb was even more important now than it had been before.

Twosret, here we come.

CHAPTER 32

Rowan was bone tired. She'd been working almost non-stop for days since they found the top of the staircase. When she wasn't on the sieve, she was in the trench evening the walls out with her trowel or helping move soil with a small hand axe.

Yael and the workers had moved a lot of earth since they'd discovered the first stair, and they were nearing what she hoped was the bottom of the flight. So far, her sieving had turned up nothing. Not even a single bead. She hoped that was a sign that the tomb was untouched, rather than this was a stairway to nowhere.

Because no one had seemed too excited by her find. Dr. Mustafa had just grunted when she'd shown him the discovery, then promptly returned to Nefertiti's tomb like nothing had happened. Even Luke hadn't replied to any of the text messages she'd sent, and she'd been sending daily updates.

No one cares.

No one except her, the workers, and Yael. But even the workers had to be reminded each morning to come to

Rowan's trench, rather than head off for the opened tomb, like they'd forgotten what they were supposed to be doing.

Maybe it was because the G.P.R. had said there weren't any chambers here; the other archaeologists probably though it was an unfinished staircase to a tomb that had never been built. But she tried to stay more positive. She had to.

She was risking her reputation on this.

No doubt Gran would have an opinion on the matter, but it wasn't like Rowan was keeping her grandparent up to date. She was still annoyed that Gran had foisted Yael on her without even asking her first—even though she now liked, even appreciated, Yael's presence.

I probably wouldn't have agreed had she asked.

But that wasn't the point.

Rowan wasn't a child anymore, and she didn't need to answer to her grandparent for every life decision she made.

Like running off to the other side of the world and working on an excavation with little to no notice. There was no argument that she'd been running away from Eric's death and his mother's nasty words; she'd needed something to take her mind away, to focus on other things. But it wasn't like she'd gone off to backpack around Antarctica or something equally stupid and impossible. She'd gone to *work*.

But it was strange, how it felt like Eric had been gone over a year, when it had only been a month and a half. She didn't think of him quite as often now, and she'd changed her lock screen image to one of a stray cat sunbathing on the dig site. It had felt callous at the time, but she hadn't been able to stand the guilt she felt every time she looked at her phone. At his face.

Guilt for what, though? Finding Yael attractive?

No, it wasn't that simple. Watching Azrael and Dru, she'd come to realize that her relationship with Eric had been…practical. There hadn't been the bursts of human, the sizzling looks, the simple desire to be in each other's company.

It had been bland.

She winced and wished she was a better person. If she'd been able to replace the image of Eric on her phone so soon after he'd died, and she'd snuggled up next to Yael for an entire night, had she truly loved her boyfriend?

Don't be ridiculous. Of course you loved him.

But sometimes, during the dark nights when she lay awake in her room, Yael resting on her floor, she questioned if she had loved the *idea* of Eric and what he represented, more than Eric himself. How he supported her career, how considerate he was, and how his goals complimented her own. He would give her the stable family she had always dreamed of; no talk of magic, no money-making schemes.

Plus, Gran had never approved of him, either.

Perhaps that was also part of the attraction. That she'd chosen a perfectly *good* man who no one could realistically object to, but her Gran had still found a way to be unhappy with the match. *He's not like us. He's not like you. You are too good for him.*

She'd only said those words once, but they'd stuck in Rowan's mind. Mostly because she had hated the idea of she and Gran being 'us'. Like Rowan wasn't normal.

I am not a witch.

It had become a mantra during her teenage years, surrounded by fun-loving and happy-go-lucky cousins who'd discussed the spells they'd cast, the supposed results that couldn't be empirically measured, and the next magics they had planned.

She'd loved them—still did. Her cousins had been the siblings she'd never had, but she'd thought they'd grow out of their mistaken beliefs, that they'd come to understand science was the answer. They hadn't. They'd become lawyers, doctors, detectives, administration officers, but they'd all maintained their beliefs, even if they'd hidden them to the public. It had created a distance between them, one that she hadn't been able to bridge in their adult years.

And despite her irritation at their ways, she too had buckled to tradition. She'd helped the family business as well, out of a sense of obligation. Gran had raised her, and Rowan owed her.

That was it.

She flinched. Put in those terms, *Rowan* had been the asshole. Not her family. *She* hadn't been able to accept them; *she* had wanted them to be something else. They'd just loved her and taken her for who she was, had smiled through her rants that they should stop the charade, and hugged her after.

Perhaps they really do *believe in magic.*

And she'd been the one naysaying their belief system, like it was trivial and it meant nothing. God, she should understand now—especially after the attack by those strange cult members—that belief was a powerful thing. It motivated people like nothing else could, bar love.

Just because you don't believe in God or magic or whatever doesn't mean you have to force your ideals on those who do.

She wanted freedom to not believe in religion, and they wanted the freedom to follow their spirituality. She was as bad as a religious zealot who'd brook no dissent, just the other way around.

I need to say sorry to them. It wouldn't be easy; Rowan wasn't good at apologies. But she'd suck up her pride and do it. As for her gran, that would be harder, because Rowan honestly thought Gran didn't believe everything she sold, and that she did it to make money.

I've probably still been a brat to her.

Of course, her gran wasn't exempt from bad behavior; it was just Rowan was coming to see that the only thing she could rely on was her family.

And Yael.

Yeah, well, she could rely on him for as long as her grandmother paid his bill. Once that was done, he'd leave her. She rubbed her sternum. The idea of his walking away actually caused a pang in her chest.

What am I doing?

Standing there daydreaming about her life and mistakes when she should be watching her workers and Yael, as they labored to reveal the final stair. She moved to the edge of her trench—which she'd labeled T1 in the hope it led to Twosret's tomb entrance. Already they had discovered the top of a vertical stone slab that might be a doorway, but they needed to clear all the debris in front of it before they could be sure.

Since it was only noon, they might be able to clear the trench out around the frame by the evening. Tomorrow, they may even be able to open the tomb door, if there was one.

Why don't I feel more excited?

This could be it—everything she'd been working for, and what Luke had been so keen to find. Instead, she felt a strange trepidation, like the discovery *was* going to change everything, but in a bad way.

Maybe it isn't Twosret at all. It could be a completely undocumented monarch, which challenges the King Lists and Egypt's entire chronology.

It would be career-changing, that was for sure, especially because introducing new concepts to her peers was often met with scorn and derision. There was a certain subset of archaeologists who did not like the established status quo to be challenged. And this would be a challenge.

"We've probably got another three more hours of digging, and we'll expose the door." Yael said from within the trench.

She stepped back. "Only three hours?"

"We made good time today." He wiped a hand over his brow—even though he hadn't sweated a drop—and left a smear of dirt behind.

She turned back into the trench; the staircase was exposed, all but for a small section of unexcavated soil next to it. They had already exposed eighty percent of a stone slab that could serve as a potential doorway.

KV65. They'd found it.

Rowan hurried to the ladder and clambered down into the pit.

At the base of the staircase, there was only just enough room for her to stand, with the unexcavated dirt coming to her knees. Leaning over it, she peered at the stone slab, and the very faint hieroglyphs apparent there.

She didn't remember seeing any the previous day, and she'd checked.

Frowning, her eyes traced the symbols. There was no royal cartouche, so it didn't indicate who was buried in the tomb. Although it *did* say the beloved of the gods and child of *A'aru* was housed within.

Child of A'aru?

"This doesn't make sense," Rowan whispered.

"What doesn't?"

Yael stood near her, on the stair above hers, peering over her shoulder.

"That the tomb belongs to the child of *A'aru*."

"The Field of Reeds."

She blinked. And she'd done it again. Forgotten he could read ancient Egyptian. *Any why the hell can he read hieroglyphics?* It was a question he had yet to answer.

"How can there be a child of *A'aru*?" A child of the gods, yes. That was a common phrase. But this didn't make sense.

"Wasn't *A'aru* the Egyptian equivalent of Heaven?" Yael asked.

"Yes, but—"

"So, someone who is beloved of the gods and a child of Heaven lies within." Something like excitement burned in his eyes.

"That is a bit of a stretch, to assume that."

"Not all things can be translated literally," he replied. "Context is key."

Normally she'd be the one arguing the same. *But it doesn't make sense.*

Shaking her head, she turned to the next group of text.

It just got even stranger. There was an Old Kingdom curse here. The Egyptians had stopped leaving curses on tombs by the seventeenth dynasty. Instead, they left warnings—which people mistook for spells or prayers.

Yael gave a low whistle. "Check it out. If you enter the tomb unapproved, you'll be killed by crocodiles, attacked by hippos, torn apart by hyenas and be bitten by snakes."

That wasn't the literal translation, but his summary was accurate.

Not something to actually be worried about, but it concerned her that this may not be Twosret's tomb. There was nothing here that identified it as hers, but they wouldn't necessarily advertise the person's identity, especially since this wasn't Twosret's original resting place, but her relocated tomb. Her followers would have wanted her identity to remain a secret, to prevent her successor from defacing the burial site.

"Let's get rid of the rest of this dirt, and I can record it in preparation for tomorrow," Rowan said, a strange kind of worry-slash-excitement building within her.

Because she fully intended to open this door.

She had to know.

Was this Twosret, or something—someone— else entirely?

CHAPTER 33

There is definitely something hinky going on with the tomb, Yael thought.

Each night, the two workers assigned to their trench forget they'd spent the day excavating there—rather they remembered being on site, but thought they'd spent the day shoveling dirt to clear out parts of Nefertiti's tomb, which didn't have any soil to shovel.

Only Yael and Rowan seemed to remember the time with any accuracy.

As for the demon archaeologists, they would come over, get an update, and disappear again, like nothing had happened. Considering the excitement that had pulsed through the site at the discovery of the first tomb, it was surprising they weren't more interested in the second. Especially since this might actually be Twosret's burial chamber, whereas the first clearly wasn't.

"So, what do you think?" Yael asked Rowan. He was sitting at her desk, going over the emails on his Mac. *Need to kill a Goram demon; Want stolen artifact stolen back; Ex needs murdering.* Same shit, day in, day out. Usually Raze dealt with the admin crap of the Falling Star guild, but he was knee-deep in books getting his nerd on.

"I honestly don't know." Rowan emerged from the bathroom, fully dressed and with damp hair. She picked up a brush and attacked her head with it; that was the best way to describe the vigorous movements. No gentle brushing here. Despite her contained violence, it felt intimate, this moment, where he would wait for her like a lover would, at the end of a long day.

Stop thinking like that.

Yeah, he realized that was a losing battle.

He was coming to understand that Rowan had somehow gotten under his skin—an itch he couldn't scratch. Even after he finished the job, he knew he wasn't about to forget her any time soon, even if he did regain his wings through some miracle.

And you won't be able to have sex with her then.

Unions between angels and humans were forbidden.

Just like unions between angels and demons, but look at Azrael and Dru, Z and Peony, Seraphina and Trick.

That last one made him scowl. They were a different case. Plus, he thought Trick should have been dropped in the bottom of a Hell-chasm, not rewarded for being an ass.

He closed his laptop and turned the chair to face her. "What are you unsure about?"

She dragged the brush through a knot, screwing up her face in the process. "The curse. It's wrong."

"How is it wrong? It's a curse." And it had blazed with magic under the Clear Sight spell. It was one hundred percent still active. He was going to have to try and convince Campbell to come and check it out before

Rowan opened the damned door, because he had no idea if she would be classified as 'approved' by the enchantment. It wasn't like there'd been a list of criteria.

"It's from the wrong era," she replied. "We might be looking at a pharaoh from the Middle Kingdom, or earlier, rather than Twosret."

He folded his hands over his stomach and fought a grin when her gaze followed his movement, lingering there. So, she wasn't unaffected by him. It was nice to know it went both ways. "But they didn't start burying people in the valley until the Late Kingdom."

She looked impressed. "I always forget how much you know."

"Like to believe I don't read books because I'm hot?"

She blushed.

He smirked.

"So *how* do you know ancient Egyptian?"

She'd asked him this more than once, and he finally had an answer that wasn't a lie. "My parents were very *keen* on my education. They wanted me to learn a number of dead languages, specifically Latin, Ancient Greek and so on. I picked ancient Egyptian to annoy them."

"You learned hieroglyphics just to *annoy* them?" She dropped her hairbrush on the bed.

He shrugged. "Languages like Latin and Ancient Greek find correlations in modern dialects. Egyptian tends to stand on its own. It's not that useful."

"And they wanted you to learn something useful."

"Yes."

"But you said you speak over thirty languages."

"I do." He read a lot more, but she seemed to think thirty was a big deal, so he didn't bother to correct her.

She'd have a conniption if she knew how many Raze could understand.

"So, you learned Latin in the end?"

He nodded. "I did. My parents are hard to refuse."

Narcissists, the both of them. Not that they would identify themselves as such, but then, no narcissist ever did.

Yael was simply a tool that had been birthed to increase their power and prestige in Heaven. When he had failed them—which he had, regularly—it brought shame on *them*. His feelings and thoughts on the matter were irrelevant. Even his grandfather had turned away from him, no doubt due to the vitriol spewed by his parents. He had probably wanted to distance himself from the mess.

Yael had long thought he'd stopped caring for their opinions, but he'd been lying to himself. When he'd made the Darts, he'd figured that would finally prove himself to them and to his favorite grandparent, but it hadn't. He hadn't been given the rank of captain, and therefore he had failed his parents yet again. Grandfather had had no comment.

He'd finally—*really*—stopped trying after that.

That's why he'd approached Gabriel. He wanted to be the master of his own future; his parents be damned. They'd never done anything positive for him anyway, just bemoan his lack of everything.

They no doubt have publicly denounced me.

He would expect no less.

"Yael?" Rowan waved a hand in front of his face.

He grabbed her wrist out of reflex, and the familiar tingle spread through his palm at the contact. Originally, it had annoyed him, but now he was beginning to enjoy it, despite the fact it sent a message straight to his dick.

"What?"

She turned her hand in his grip and he released it. "You zoned out."

"Sorry."

"What were you thinking about?" She rubbed her wrist, and he worried that he'd hurt her, but there weren't any marks left behind.

Maybe she feels it, too.

"My parents."

"You don't get along?"

"That's a polite way to phrase it."

"I'm sorry." Her eyes turned sad.

"Why? It's not your fault." He stood. No, the only people responsible for his relationship with his parents were his parents.

He opened the door and she grabbed a light sweater. They headed out into the night together.

She hugged her arms around her torso. "My parents died when I was young. I was raised by my grandmother."

He knew he was meant to feel sorry for her, but he would have been nothing but thankful if his parents had had an unfortunate accident when he was younger.

Yeah, because that's a healthy thought process.

He opted for humor. "Raised by Dora. That would have been a challenge."

Rowan shot him a look. "She lets you call her Dora?"

"Is that a thing?"

"It means she likes you."

Why did he feel like that was more a burden rather

than a blessing?

They reached the mess hall to find Azrael and Dru leaving. "Good guard work," Yael muttered to Dru. Shoving her face full of food when she was meant to be patrolling.

"What?" The cambion rolled her eyes. "She is super-safe here. This place is like a damned fortress. And I know: Yael and I broke into one not long ago."

Rowan's eyes went wide. "You broke into a *fortress*?"

Yael lifted an eyebrow and shot Azrael a telepathic message. *Dru really needs to watch her mouth.*

Azrael gave a mental shrug. *Dru is Dru. And Rowan will learn the truth one day. It's inevitable, with her background.*

"It was for a job," Dru explained. "I don't just go around breaking into stuff. Or killing people for fun. It's a lot of hard work."

"Hard work?" Rowan echoed.

"Yeah, there were mon—" Dru caught Yael's cut-it-out look. "Money launderers and booby traps. Horrifying stuff."

Money launderers? He asked Azrael.

Be glad that's what she came out with.

"Gotta go. Bye." Dru waggled her fingers and slid past them. Azrael followed.

Rowan turned to Yael. "Money laundering made breaking into a fortress difficult?"

"I try not to ask too many questions when it comes to Dru. It's a recipe for a headache." He went straight for the food, serving up a huge plate of everything and heading for one of the long tables. He sat down and was joined soon after by Kayla and a thoughtful-looking Rowan.

"How's the digging going?" Kayla asked, nudging Rowan in the shoulder, like there was a joke to be made.

"Excellent." Rowan bit into some pita bread, then scooped up some lentil stuff with a fork.

"Really? Have you found anything?"

Rowan lowered her cutlery to the plate. "Yes, I told you at lunch we've reached the bottom of the staircase."

"You did?" Kayla rubbed her forehead, her bright green eyes dimming slightly. "I must have forgotten."

Yep. There was definitely something funny about that tomb, and he had a feeling he knew what it was.

CHAPTER 34

The severed arm flew at her face, hot blood pouring from the wound, spraying her clothing, her hair, her skin. Rowan gagged as some trickled into her mouth. Rotten meat and dirt and dust permeating her tongue; this was how death would taste, she knew.

No. I don't want to die.

She threw her arms up over her eyes, trying to avoid being splattered with more gore. But then she was drenched again, covered in dark, sticky fluid. She looked over her shoulder at the source of it, and saw Eric, an empty bucket held in his arms, blood drip-drip-dripping onto the grass below.

She screamed, *"NO!"*

"Rowan!"

Strong hands gripped her shoulders and shook, jerking her awake. Rowan gasped desperately for clean, untainted air, and breathed deep. The scent of lavender and bay rum reached her.

Yael.

She threw her body into his arms, wrapping around

him like a limpet. He went rigid, arms held out
awkwardly to the sides, but she didn't care. His heart beat
strongly against her ear, as she pressed her face into his
chest. The familiar electrical zap shot through her, but she
welcomed it. It meant she was alive, that this was real.
Her whole body sang with it, but that sensation paled in
comparison to the overriding feeling of safety that his
embrace gave her.

"Want to talk about it?" he asked

She shook her head. "Not really." She didn't want to
have relive the dream, or Eric's part in it.

"Okay."

She stayed wrapped in his arms until her heartbeat
slowed down, and her mind grew foggy with sleep. She
pulled away and crawled back under the blankets, facing
Yael, who sat on the edge of her bed, barely visible in the
dim light.

"Can you stay here?"

"I won't leave the room."

"No, here." She patted the bed.

For a moment, a pained expressed crossed his face,
like he would refuse. Her eyes burned at the idea she
would have to sleep alone, that she might fall back into
the nightmare. She would be safe from the dark dreams
if Yael stayed with her.

Something in her expression must have registered,
because he sighed. "All right." A few seconds later, he
was lying on his side next to her. "Turn over."

She did. His left arm wrapped over her waist, and she
snuggled back into him. His warmth was luxurious; she
hadn't noticed how cold she was—both inside and out.
She pressed more firmly against him and blushed in the

darkness. *He's got an erection.* Heat burned through her, and she had to fight the urge to press her butt more firmly against it. Until now, she'd thought the electricity between them only affected her. *Maybe he feels it, too?*

Or maybe, the more rational part of her brain snapped, *he got hard because he's lying in bed next to a woman who begged him to be there.*

Sleep claimed her in a sudden wave.

The next morning, Rowan figured she should feel embarrassed about how she'd used Yael for comfort. But she'd slept the best she had since she'd arrived in Egypt— hell, since she'd learned about Eric's death. She wasn't about to apologize for that.

Although he had been a little crankier than usual this morning.

Probably because you slept and he didn't.

She couldn't be one hundred percent sure of that, but she knew he rarely slept at night, and he'd already been awake and ready when she rolled out of bed this morning. She hated to think about how little sleep he would have had in the past month and a bit.

All because of her.

He seemed to tolerate it well enough, except for when he'd left and gotten Dru and Azrael to watch over her for that short period of time. She figured they'd decided to stay because of the cult's attack, even though there'd been no sign of violence since.

Azrael and Yael don't seem to talk much.

When he'd opened up about his parents, he hadn't

even mentioned Azrael in the conversation. Perhaps his brother had been treated differently? Or did they have a strained relationship, too?

She could ask, but she had the feeling today was not the day. Yael's posture was ramrod straight, and his black mood was infecting the other archaeologists.

The blue van—their white one had been too damaged by the cult—pulled up at the valley and they all climbed out. Dr. Murdoch stretched his long limbs before he loped away, toward the marquee, which was still standing despite the blustery weather.

They followed at a slower pace.

"I have no idea how he is a morning person. He hasn't even had a coffee." Kayla took a sip out of her stainless-steel travel mug, holding it with both hands like it was the one ring to rule them all.

"What number coffee is that this morning?" Rowan asked, pulling her hat down lower as the wind swept over them. She shivered. *It hasn't been this cold since we've been here.* It was like the weather had decided to throw in the towel for the day.

"Four." Kayla shot her a look. "Don't judge me. I can see you judging me. This isn't even an addiction. It's a *need.*"

Rowan laughed, and it felt good, free. She was so lucky that Kayla had been assigned to the excavation as well. Dr. Murdoch was nice, in his own way, but Campbell and Mustafa ignored her unless absolutely necessary. It was fine when Dr. Campbell chose to do that, but she was meant to be co-directing with the Egyptian archaeologist.

To be fair, she'd kind of given up on that since she

started working on her trench.

He didn't want her help, and she was too busy keeping an eye on everything in T1 to worry about what they were doing in KV64—Nefertiti's tomb. Yes, yes, they hadn't determined if it *was* hers yet, but Rowan was pretty sure she was right.

They reached the marquee and Kayla finished her coffee in one huge gulp, before she set the mug aside and headed off in the direction of the opened tomb. Dr. Campbell and Dr. Mustafa were already near the entrance.

"I just need to ask Campbell something," Yael said, and hurried after them.

Rowan was left with Dru and Azrael. "Do you know what he needs from Dr. Campbell?"

"Nope." Azrael shook his head.

"Maybe he needs a blow—"

Azrael shot his lover a chastising look. "Dru."

Dru sighed. "Fine. Anyway, it's not as much fun to pick on him when he can't hear it."

Almost at the tomb's door, Yael raised his arm and flipped them the bird.

"He *heard* that?" Rowan asked.

"Lucky guess," Dru muttered darkly.

"Have fun patrolling the site." Rowan gave them a small wave and walked off toward T1. Her two workers were nowhere in sight—probably over by the main tomb—but that was okay. They had managed to clear out the remaining dirt, and Rowan had recorded all the survey stuff yesterday.

Now she just needed to photograph it all and have another read of the hieroglyphs on the door. At the edge of the trench, she pulled out her cell and texted Luke again, but there was no immediate response. With a shrug, she shoved the phone in her pocket and climbed down the ladder. She then descended the ten steps to the door.

Nothing had changed. She read the sections of text that stated the person interred was a child of *A'aru* and that set out the curse. A very faint smear of color was apparent on the curse, and Rowan pulled on some gloves, before reaching out to touch the carvings.

She'd just made contact when Yael jerked her hand away. "What are you doing?"

"There was some color here..." She turned and was taken aback by the anger that burned in his eyes.

"I am allowed to touch it. I was wearing gloves." She held up her free hand.

His expression didn't ease.

"What do I have to come and see?" Dr. Campbell asked, puffing as he climbed down the ladder and into the trench. Irritation was etched into every line of the man's body. "Everyone knows there's nothing here—" The archaeologist's eyes widened as he took in the door. "There's something here?"

Yael let go of her arm. "There's something here."

"Move outta the way." Kayla practically jumped down the ladder into the trench, shoving Dr. Campbell to the side with her shoulder. Confusion darkened her face for a few moments before it cleared into excitement. "There's a door!"

"There's a door," Rowan repeated, smiling.

She stepped around them and up a few stairs as Dr. Campbell and Kayla hurried to the stone slab. The two of them stood close together and read over the engravings.

"That's a strong curse," Dr. Campbell eventually muttered.

"Don't you think it's unusual?" Rowan asked from the top of the staircase.

"In what way?" The portly man rubbed his nose.

"It's an Old Kingdom curse."

"Yes, yes. Very powerful those." He turned back to the door.

"Powerful?" Rowan mouthed to Yael.

"We will need to cancel this out before we enter." Dr. Campbell dug around in his pockets.

"You need to do *what*?" Rowan demanded.

"Neutralize the spell. Won't take too long."

"But there's no spell. There's nothing to worry about. I just need to finish taking photos."

Dr. Campbell threw a handful of dust at the slab just as Kayla reached out and touched the hieroglyphs. A bright light blasted through the trench, and Rowan had to blink a number of times before her vision cleared.

What the hell? Did he throw gunpowder or something on the door?

But the stone slab was unharmed.

"What did you do?" Dr. Campbell demanded, spinning to face Kayla.

A low wail sounded. "My hand." She held her wrist tightly, hand open and palm raised to the sky, like it was diseased.

"What happened? Did you hurt yourself?" Rowan stepped forward, but Yael grabbed her bicep to hold her back.

Dr. Campbell frowned, worry stark on his face. "I

need to have a look at it."

"No, no, it hurts."

Dr. Campbell ushered Kayla up the stairs at to the ladder, where he and Yael helped her out of the trench.

"What happened?" Rowan asked.

Yael crossed his arms over his chest and glared. "The curse."

CHAPTER 35

It was plain to see that Rowan thought the fuss about the curse was hysterical nonsense. But Kayla was growing paler and paler the longer she sat there, staring at her hand as if it had betrayed her. And Yael couldn't blame her. The flash of light that had accompanied her brief stroking of the doorway meant the curse had been activated seconds before Campbell had neutralized it. Unless they did some serious magic mojo, the little demon was doomed.

He'd never heard of a curse reversing itself once it had found a target.

"I couldn't stop myself," Kayla whispered to Campbell, her head bowed.

The curse-breaking demon tsked. "You should have known better. I had almost deactivated it."

"It was like it was calling to me, 'Touch me, touch me'. I couldn't resist."

A seductive whisper would have been hard for a Succubus to refuse, even one as deadly as Kayla.

Kayla was sat in one of the portable chairs, in the

shadiest part of the shelter. On the other side of the
marquee, Rowan paced, watching her friend with
concern. The wind continued to pick up strength,
whipping Kayla's loose hair around her face, and
constantly plucking at Rowan's hat. Good thing Yael
didn't need any headgear.

"Here, drink this." Campbell handed Kayla a
steaming cup.

"What is it?"

"Coffee."

It had an odd odor to it, but Yael wasn't about to
comment on that.

The Succubus took it, sipped gingerly at the liquid and
pulled a face. "This isn't coffee."

"It's coffee laced with something stronger." Campbell
gave her a stern glare and she drank the liquid down
without further protest.

Yael grabbed his backpack from the marquee floor
and rummaged through it, keeping an eye on Kayla. He
had no idea how long the curse would take to work, and
consequently no idea how much time they had to break
it.

Rowan crouched down next to him, her lemongrass
scent rich in the dusty air. "This is ridiculous. They are
worried about something that isn't real. We should just
get back to work. It would take their mind off things."

Yael's hand closed on a plastic bag of puke-colored
powder, keeping it hidden from her gaze. "Do they look
like they don't think it's real?"

"There is no scientific basis to support the theory that
curses are—"

"Don't be a jerk." He shut his backpack and Rowan

wheeled away from him, shock and hurt clear on her face.

Normally, Yael loved Rowan's sharp mind. But this...blindness...to the life around her, it was grating. The spell he held had been made by her vey own grandmother. He was an angel. The comrade she condescended about was a demon.

Maybe she believed none of that was real, but it was getting harder not to be convinced.

She threw her shoulders back. "I am not being a jerk."

"Kayla is clearly upset about touching the curse. She thinks it's real enough to worry about. And you want to tell her it's nonsense and to get over it?"

He could see the struggle in her mind: be the good friend and be supportive, or potentially enable a dangerous thought pattern that was based on nothing more than fantasy.

Rowan sat on the ground. "It's not healthy to play into someone's delusions."

"No, but when nothing happens and the curse doesn't eventuate, she'll realize that it *wasn't real*. Until then, you could help her by being supportive rather than condescending."

Of course, it only wouldn't become active if they managed to neutralize it.

"I am not condescending!" Rowan glared at him then sighed. "Even though that sounded super-condescending. Fine. You're right. This is a problem I've had with my family my entire life. I need to respect people's beliefs more. It's just hard when they're so wrong, you know?"

She stood and went over to Kayla, squatting down next to her and chatting, trying to draw her attention away from her hand.

Rowan had no idea about the real world, but Yael knew that was largely due to the thorough job angels did at keeping their existence on the down-low. There were stories and religions and what not, but they required belief, not hard proof. For some reason, it was how God had wanted it, and so that was how it was done. But it didn't make his kind any less real, or the demons that lived in Hell less vile.

"So, I heard someone touched the curse." Azrael's deep voice was quiet, and Yael half-turned to his fellow Dart. The damned fallen angel was too good at sneaking up on people.

Yael nodded in the direction of the two huddled archeologists. "Kayla."

"She is pretty handsy," Dru muttered.

Azrael elbowed her.

"What?" Dru scowled and rubbed her ribs. "She's a Succubus. They like to have sex. So they're handsy. Get it?"

"Too soon." Azrael shook his head.

Yael was surprised. The dark-haired angel usually let Dru get away with murder. Literally.

For a demon, Kayla isn't too bad, Azrael telepathed him. *And what if Rowan had touched the curse instead of her?*

Yael grimaced. Rowan *had* touched the curse; he'd caught her doing it. But there had been no flash of light, no sense of impending doom. *Nada.*

Maybe it will accept her.

"Don't you think it's funny that the only people who remember that the tomb has been exposed are you, me, and Rowan?" Yael asked.

"What tomb?" Dru demanded. "The first one?"

"The second."

"There is no second tomb."

"Where did Kayla touch the curse, then?" Yael asked.

Dru frowned so hard he thought her eyes would cross. "The first tomb."

Yael crossed his arms over his chest. "My point exactly."

"So, you think only angels and humans can remember the tomb because there's a warding spell on it?"

"It has some pretty strong concealment spells in place—ones even modern technology can't penetrate. But not all humans do remember: Mustafa and the workers forget about it as well."

Azrael looked thoughtful.

"What tomb?' Dru asked again. "Seriously guys."

Normally he loved to rile the cambion, but now wasn't the time. "The one Rowan and I have been working on."

"You mean the empty trench?" Dru withdrew a knife and played with it. Yael had noticed she did that whenever she thought things through. Or was angry. Or amused. Or just because.

Yael stood, bag of powder still in hand. "Yes, but it's not empty."

"That's—"

"One Hell of a concealment spell," Azrael murmured. Dru nodded.

So she believes him and not me.

Well, he was her lover and Yael had made his dislike of her clear.

"Campbell," he said, drawing the portly archaeologist's attention.

"Yes, Mr. Death?" Ahh, the polite formality of someone who hates you, but doesn't want to offend you. Yael was well versed in it from his childhood.

"Here." He covertly handed the baggie to the demon, like they were doing a drug deal.

"What is it?" Campbell clutched it out of reflex.

"It's a curse-neutralization spell, courtesy of Theodora Broome."

"How did you get it so quickly?"

"I already had it."

"So, it wasn't made specifically for a demon?"

"No, I'd say a human."

"I may be able to work with this," Campbell said.

"Good." Yael turned away, only for Campbell to grab his forearm. He took a deep breath as the sudden urge to rip the demon's limb off swamped him. *He is not the enemy.*

Not right now, anyway.

Funny how he thought he'd come to accept working with the demons, but apparently he was still ready to destroy them at the slightest provocation.

Campbell let go of his arm, as if he could sense the fallen angel's seething anger. "Why are you helping her?"

He thought about that. Why was he?

And it was simple, really.

"Because, Rowan won't take it well if she dies."

CHAPTER 36

Poor Kayla had looked terrible last night. Her normally tan skin had been pale, and her irrepressible zest for life had gone. She really had been worried by the curse. And that made Rowan worried, too.

Psychosomatic illness. Where one believed they were sick and so they became sick.

Her gran had said people came into the shop with it all the time, and it was about relieving the mental stress, so that the physical symptoms went away. It's part of why Rowan had believed her grandparent to be a charlatan, selling people placebos. But right now, she would have happily shoved a dozen sugar pills down Kayla's throat if it meant her friend would feel better.

She'd checked on Kayla at least three times last night, much to Yael's irritation at having to re-check everything in the room again and again. Now it was morning, Kayla had decided to stay back at the compound to get a little more rest. Surprisingly, Dr. Campbell had decided to stay with her, and that had seemed to help her friend more than anything else.

Maybe they have a thing going on?

It was hard to picture, bright and bubbly Kayla with the portly and whiskered Campbell, but who knew what direction attraction could take?

It's time to get your head in the game.

Yes. Kayla would be fine. She was being cared for and there was a hospital nearby if she was truly sick.

Plus, Rowan had important work to do, like opening the tomb.

She reached over to the edge of the trench and grabbed a small crowbar she'd placed there. She grunted at the weight of it. Normally, she would have needed another three or four workers to help her pry the slab away, but she didn't want to make anyone else panic about being cursed. No. She'd get the lay of the land first, and when she needed help, she'd ask Yael.

The way he excavated, he was probably as strong as two men, anyway.

Now was the perfect time to open the tomb because he, Dru and Azrael were off doing something with the site's guards. She didn't know why, but she had the feeling he would stop her if he knew what she was up to.

Approaching the stone door—*Who am I kidding? I am not going to budge this at all*—she spotted at a tiny gap between the slab and the tomb wall.

Had someone broken in here overnight?

No one even thinks we found anything...

There were no other signs of chipped rock or forced entry. Maybe she had just missed the fact that the slab had not been flush against the wall when she recorded it earlier. She wedged the crowbar into the small gap and pushed. With barely a groan, the door swung outward, as if on well-oiled hinges, and she jumped out of the way, to avoid being clobbered by it.

The scent of dust, decay and ozone hit her in the face, a tomb's version of halitosis.

She waved a hand in front of her face, as if that would disperse the stench.

That was too easy.

No tomb she'd worked on had ever opened so smoothly; at best, her effort ought to have shifted the rock an inch or so. *Something strange is going on.* The fine hairs on the back of her neck stood on end, and she traded the crowbar for a flashlight. Switching it on, she swept the beam into the tomb's maw, illuminating a darkened corridor, shredded cobwebs, and flickering motes of dust.

This is it.

She went to step inside, but paused. If that door had swung open so easily…she grabbed the crowbar and jammed it into the soil, pinning it against the open door. *There.* That should hold it.

Stepping inside, her skin came alive, like she was being bitten all over by tiny mosquitoes. She rubbed at her forearm, then her legs. Was there a light on up ahead?

Fully inside now, she tripped over, landing hard on her knees. The flashlight flew from her hands, lighting the walls up in a crazy spiral disco. Flashes of blank stone, flaring streams of smoke, and the silent scream of an abandoned skull blurred together as she tried to make sense of what had happened.

"What—?"

The grating sound of metal against stone made her spin on protesting knees, and she screamed as the door swung shut.

No.

How had that even happened?

She lurched to her feet and slammed into the back of the door, pushing as hard as she could. Nothing.

For something that had opened so easily before...

It was jammed shut.

She took a deep breath of the musty air and turned back to the passageway. *There.* Her flashlight lay by...a skull.

A skull? It was unusual to find non-mummified remains within a tomb. She walked down the sand-covered passageway and crouched next to the flashlight. Her knees throbbed; she must have skinned them when she spun round. The light shone on her legs, revealing patches of wet blood.

Great.

She turned the beam to the human remains, then reeled backwards, dropping the flashlight again and landing on her butt with a thud.

No. Not possible. Nope. That thing was not real.

She scurried forward and picked up the cranium, turning it over in her gloved hands, unable to process what she saw.

It was human, but it wasn't.

There were the typical skull components; mandible, maxilla, zygomatic bones, but things got weird around the suture line between the parietal and frontal bones.

There were horns. And they didn't look glued on. Also, the incisor teeth were far too long for a normal human's, and the nasal bones were wider than average.

It has to be a fake. But in the glow of the flashlight, the bone appeared real.

She returned the skull to its position on the ground. The papery sound of stone moving over stone made her turn to the doorway, as dust rained from the ceiling. Coughing, Rowan bent forward, trying to get the sand out of her mouth.

Opening watery eyes, she grabbed the flashlight, spotting a strange rock as she did so. With her free hand, she picked up the stone.

Rose quartz.

It was attached to a broken leather necklace, which snaked over her hand as she handled the rock up. She bit the inside of her cheek, amazed at the stone's size—it barely fit in her fist—and her hand vibrated, like she had the tremors. Where had it come from?

The stone door gave an almighty screech, and more dust rained down on her, a cool and gritty shower. The floor shook, like there was an earthquake. Rowan folded in on herself, the stone clenched in her fist. A sharp flash of pain seared through her palm, but she ignored it, gritting her teeth and hoping the ceiling wouldn't cave in on her. When the shaking finally subsided, she sat back, staring at the open doorway.

Yael glared back at her from the opening. "Get out of there."

She didn't need to be told twice. Scrambling to her feet, she fumbled her way out the passageway, sucking in the fresh air outside the tomb. "I just found—" But when she opened her hand, there was nothing there.

I dropped it. Damnit! That piece of quartz was no doubt an artifact of some importance.

Yael grabbed her shoulders, his eyes dark. "You found

what?"

"Nothing, I must have dropped it. There was a strange skull in there, and the door closed, even though I jammed it open, and I'd only just stepped inside—" Her voice cut off at the look on his face.

He was *furious*.

"You went inside the tomb *on your own*. We couldn't find you anywhere. No one knew where you were. It took Azrael, me and Dru to pry open that door. If you hadn't been there…" He was breathing heavy, and his body was rigid.

"I just opened the door and stepped in—everything was fine until the door swung shut."

Her answer didn't appease him. If anything, he seemed even angrier. "You. Are. An. Idiot." He shook her shoulders with each word, making her head rattle.

"Me? But—"

"Kayla's dead." His words came out harshly.

Rowan swayed, shock slamming into her. "What? When?"

"She died this morning."

No. That wasn't possible. Rowan had seen her this morning. "But *how*?"

"She drowned."

Back at the compound, Rowan stared at the white-shrouded gurney that was being wheeled out of Kayla's room. A woman she didn't recognize, wearing a black business suit, followed the trolley. Not the doctor she would have expected.

Rowan turned to Yael, who was a silent, angry presence at her side. "I have to see her."

"No, you don't."

Rowan ignored him and strode toward the gurney. Yael moved to grab her arm, but she slid away from him before he could make contact. Then she ran to her friend, faster than she'd ever run before in her life.

Kayla wasn't dead.

She couldn't be.

And Rowan was going to prove it.

But as she skidded to a stop next to the trolley, her gut heaved. She was wrong. Kayla was definitely gone.

Her skin was a strange blue-white color, and her eyes, a weird green they hadn't been previously, stared toward the sky. Her brown hair was plastered to her bloated face, and blood had soaked into the white shroud around her legs. Her face was contorted in a terrified scream, fixed there by rigor mortis.

The spark, the essence that had been her friend, was gone.

"What happened?" Rowan blurted. "Where did the blood come from? You said she drowned! We're not even near the Nile!"

The suited woman lifted a single blonde eyebrow. "Her wounds indicate she was mauled by a crocodile."

"A *crocodile*?" Rowan repeated. "But her body was found here?"

"Yes." The woman shoved past her, pushed the gurney and Kayla away to a black van that waited in the parking lot.

"Where are they taking her?" Rowan demanded, trying to follow. Yael grabbed her arm.

"She needs to be examined properly," Dr. Campbell said. "There's nothing more we can do for her here."

"But—"

"She's gone, Rowan," Yael said, voice surprisingly gentle. "They need to examine her body. Let her go."

But she couldn't.

Somehow, with a strength she didn't know she had, she wrenched herself out of Yael's grip and ran to where Kayla's body was about to be loaded into the van. She pressed a finger to Kayla's throat, where her pulse would have once thundered. Now there was nothing. Her finger burned cold where they touched. "If I could give you your life back, I would. I will miss you."

Tears clouded her vision, and sadness poured from her. Kayla had been afraid to die. Had been terrified of the curse.

And now she was dead.

Yael pulled her away from the van. She let him. There was nothing more she could do for her friend. She was gone, like Eric, like her parents.

Just gone.

CHAPTER 37

The Celestial City, Heaven

"I have heard that the fallen angel Raziel knows where the human piece of Heaven's Heart is." The archangel Aurora's voice floated through Uriel's study, delicate and smooth as honey. Funny, how it grated against Michael's ears, as if it were a storm of angry bees.

"Raziel?" Uriel asked, elbows on his walnut desk, fingers steepled together. "He always was an excellent scholar." There was almost a note of regret in the archangel's voice.

As if casting that particular angel out of Heaven had been a loss.

No angel is worthy of regret.

"Do you know where he suspects it to be?" Michael asked, getting to the point. If left to their own devices, Uriel and Aurora would dance around the matter for an age. They were schemers and bureaucrats, the both of them. And it didn't really matter how good or bad a scholar the fallen angel was; it only mattered if he had discovered something of use.

"No," Aurora replied, her golden eyes sending him an invitation to bed, even while Uriel watched, oblivious. "We have an agent looking into it though."

Aurora had asked Michael numerous times to engage in coitus with her, and each time he refused. Her carnality disgusted him. His body was a vessel for his impending divinity, and he would not pollute it with her lust for power.

It was one element of his brother's nature he had never been able to understand.

"Make sure your agent is successful, then," Michael said. "We cannot have those fallen angels finding Heaven's Heart." The first piece of the Heart—the one that had been stolen from Heaven—was still missing, although the Infernus demons that had taken it were dead. Unfortunately. "If they do find it, we shall be obliged to allow them back into Heaven, and it is bad enough that Cassiel was returned."

Cassiel's crime had been to save the life of a demon who had been raped by another angel, although that detail was of little importance in the greater scheme of things. He had gone against tradition, against the rules, and he had been ultimately rewarded for it.

It just demonstrated how their system had become...tainted.

"Why is Gabriel not here?" Aurora asked.

"His loyalty is in question," Michael replied.

"Why is that?" Aurora ran her hands over her body, straightening clothing that didn't require it.

Michael shook his head scornfully. "He told Nanael about Cassiel. If he hadn't, we may have succeeded in removing the traitor's wings before he ascended."

"Gabriel plays by the rules," Uriel murmured. "It is worth remembering that."

Yes, Michael thought. *He plays by the rules. But those rules are broken.*

And only he could fix them.

Chapter 38

The Valley of the Kings, Egypt

Yael didn't know whether he wanted to strangle Rowan or kiss her senseless. The moment he'd learned she'd gone missing, rage and fear had flooded him, turning his mind into a white-hot blaze of fury. It was only when he had figured out she was in the tomb that he'd calmed slightly.

And to then find her, shaken and bleeding after being trapped...he had barely even registered her statement about the strange skull. He'd wanted to grab her and pull her to him, to feel that she was alive and okay. But he'd still been so angry that she'd deliberately snuck off, put her life in danger.

Especially after he'd just learned of Kayla's death, and the effectiveness of the curse.

Yet, here they were, back at site even though someone was dead.

"Do you really think we should be here?" he asked, studying Rowan.

"Yes." She was pale, her body radiating tension. Hell, even he had to admit he was a bit shaken. That curse had been nasty and it had been quick. Campbell had been plying Kayla with neutralizer spells since she'd touched it, and Yael had donated two more curse-breakers in addition to the first one.

But none of them had worked.

Kayla had drowned, her neck had snapped, and her legs had been shredded by animal teeth. The curse had said that the crocodile would strike in the water; it just hadn't specified what kind of water. She'd been drowned and mauled to death *in her fucking shower*.

He hadn't told Rowan that bit.

But he wasn't coming unprepared this time. Azrael and Dru would be along too, and Azrael could see magic without help. Plus, that first curse *had* been neutralized by Campbell after Kayla touched it. So, the magic could be broken prior to activation, at any rate. To assist in that, Yael had brought an arsenal of spells with him, and he had put an extra-thick layer of Clear Sight on his eyelids—he looked like he was wearing makeup, but he didn't care.

He needed to know what they were up against.

He'd also roped Campbell into coming back, even though the demon thought they were going to the first tomb. The curse-breaker was currently reviewing his stock of spells, before being brought to the trench by Azrael.

It was the best Yael could do to protect Rowan. He doubted anyone could stop her going back into the tomb. He'd been guarding her for weeks, for free, because Z owed Dora. Yet she'd run off and put her life in danger.

If she was at risk from anyone, it was from herself. At least if he went in there with her, this time, then they could avoid any nasty magics, and hopefully beat Lucifer to the Heart.

Stop trying to rationalize the fact you're using her.

The only reason you're doing this is because of Raze's intel.

He winced.

Why was his conscience suddenly kicking in?

If there was no link between Heaven's Heart and Twosret, you would never have allowed her back here, not until all the magic in the tomb had been destroyed.

So, he was doing this for himself.

And Azrael, Z, and Raze. And maybe Seraphina, although she seemed happy enough in Hell with her new lover.

Bitter much?

The thought made him pause. Was he…jealous…of Seraphina? He had always admired her, thought her calm and logical and skilled. He may have even had a slight crush on her at one point. But not anymore. No. His entire body had grown attuned to a single person, and that person was someone so inappropriate it was laughable.

Trick had also been inappropriate.

And there it was.

Seraphina had thrown caution to the wind and had hooked up with the master of an assassination guild. And sure, she had accidentally made herself a true fallen angel in the process, but she was now ensconced in Tartarus with her lover and they were starting their happily ever after.

There was no way he could ever have that with Rowan.

For starters, she was mortal. She'd die. And it was all too clear how fragile she was when faced with spells and magics she didn't understand and refused to believe in.

"Okay. Here is where I pressed the last time." Rowan's voice drew him back to the moment. She stood, pointing at the side of the stone door.

Right.

Break into tomb, steal Heart.

Got it.

His plan was so simple it had to work.

"Okay." He grabbed a small crowbar and wedged it in the tiny gap she'd indicated. He then threw all his weight against the tool, leaping out of the way as the door swung open, smooth and quiet, almost colliding with him on the way past.

"That was much easier than how we did it." And wasn't it funny, how they'd ripped the door open and away, and yet it had been magically sealed again when they returned?

"How *did* you do it?"

"Never mind." She wouldn't be happy to hear they'd pried it open using brute force, uncaring about the damage caused to the stone. Then again, it *had* magically fixed itself.

"Here!" Dru appeared at the side of the trench, an enormous boulder in her arms. She wavered a little, then dropped the rock on Yael.

He managed to catch it, arms spread wide and ribs aching from the sudden collision. "Thanks for the warning."

Dru dusted off her hands. "I said 'here'."

Yael hurried over and dumped the rock on the ground

in front of the open door. He turned to find Rowan staring at him, wide-eyed and incredulous. "How heavy is that?"

"I don't know." He shrugged. "Two hundred pounds?"

"How are you ribs not caved in?"

"I'm strong?" He hadn't meant that to sound like a question, damnit. But he forgot that normal humans couldn't throw rocks around as if they were golf balls or footballs or whatever.

She shot him a skeptical look and kicked the rock. He turned to signal Dru to get Azrael. The cambion flipped him off in response. Typical. He pretended not to notice Rowan frowning down at her foot. "Ready to go inside?" he asked.

Hopefully Dru would grab Azrael and Campbell, and meet them back here before they'd gone too far into the tomb. Yael was confident he could ensure they stayed safe for that long, at least. *Hopefully longer.*

It all depended on how well Rowan would listen to his warnings.

She grabbed a flashlight and walked toward the door. He hurried after her.

She probably won't listen at all.

Damnit.

Stepping over the threshold, he hissed. It was like his skin was being pricked by thousands of needles, all at once.

"Did you feel it, too?" Rowan stood a little further in, shining the flashlight on the ground in front of her.

"Feel what?"

"Like you were being eaten alive by mosquitoes."

"Yes."

She turned around and angled the beam of light at the threshold. But there was nothing visible, not even to his Clear Sight spell. He had no idea what magic was at play here, but he hoped Azrael and Campbell would be able to navigate it.

A few steps into the passageway, Rowan was searching the floor with her flashlight.

"I thought I found something here before," she said, "but I must have imagined it in all the chaos." Her green eyes were shadowed in the dim light. "There. The skull."

He looked down at it. It was demonic, that was for damned sure.

Rowan reached down to pick it up, but he shook his head. "Leave it. You can record it later."

"But have you seen the deformities? It has to be some kind of fake, perhaps to warn people away."

"Egyptians did have gods with animal body parts," Yael commented, more to distract her than anything else. He didn't want a debate about the skull—he needed to find Twosret and determine if she still had the Heart or not.

"True." Rowan nodded resolutely to herself. "Let's do some reconnaissance before we decide the next steps."

Thank the skies. He didn't want to have to drag her through the tomb.

They walked down the passageway, Rowan illuminating the path ahead, while Yael scanned the walls, floor and ceiling for any spells. There were few to no inscriptions on the walls, so at least there wouldn't be many curses to worry about. There were spells, but most of them aimed at demonic entities, which was lucky.

Every now and then, he would touch Rowan's arm, indicating she should move a little to the left or the right to avoid any magical traps. She shot him annoyed glances, but shifted without her usual protests. Maybe she was worried about booby traps; after all she had been caught in the tomb earlier.

They had barely walked fifty feet before the passageway turned into a chamber, maybe twenty feet square. It had four pillars and was packed with artifacts around the edges. Half-finished paintings and inscriptions lined the walls, and to his Clear Sight spell, the room blazed with magic. It was almost blindingly bright in the center, where a sarcophagus sat.

Please be Twosret, please be Twosret.

Adrenalin pulsed through him, his heartbeat increasing and his breath short. This was it. They were going to find the second piece of Heaven's Heart and he was going to be one step closer to returning to Heaven.

He pulled on a pair of sunglasses so he could look at the sarcophagus in greater detail. It was stone—something shiny and soapy—with engravings all over it. On the arms were the wings of a bird, while a royal cartouche had been carved over the sternum.

"Twosret," he read aloud.

Rowan turned to him, her eyes alight with excitement. "It's her." She paused. "Why are you wearing sunglasses?"

"Uhh—" He thought quickly, but his mind was blank.

Rowan took a step back and swung her backpack off her shoulder to dig around inside it. As she moved, she bumped into a jackal-headed statue of Anubis behind her. Yael saw the blaze of a spell and leaped toward her, his hand closing over her wrist as a magical flash lit up the entire chamber like the fourth of July.

"What the fuck just happened?" Yael let go of her hand and rubbed his eyes. They *hurt*, like he'd just been hit with a stun grenade.

"I can't see!" Rowan cried.

Blinking quickly, trying to get everything back into focus, Yael dug around in his backpack for his first aid kit. He had just pulled out the tube of saline when Rowan let out a huge sigh. "It's okay. I can see again. Did you know that was going to happen? Is that why you put the sunglasses on? What was it?"

"I have no idea," Yael replied. "And no, that wasn't why I put the shades on." He took the glasses off. For some reason, everything was clear now—like the sun was shining right into the room, even though there was no light source aside from Rowan's flashlight. The place certainly hadn't been this well-lit a few minutes ago.

Rowan lowered her backpack to the ground and took out her camera. She took a few photographs of the sarcophagus, her forehead wrinkling when she looked into the viewfinder.

"What is it?"

"My camera just shows me a black screen."

"Maybe there's not enough light?" What did he know about cameras?

"No..." She closed the distance to the sarcophagus and a placed gloved hand on top. "What the—?"

She fell through the center of the coffin with a scream.

Yael leaped forward...and stepped right into the sarcophagus like was it was a hologram.

"What the fuck?!"

CHAPTER 39

Rowan was sitting in the sarcophagus. Sitting. In. The. Sarcophagus. She was afraid to look around, in case she was in the middle of the mummy's body.

A moment later, Yael stepped into the sarcophagus next to her.

"What's happening?" she asked. Had Yael shoved some virtual reality equipment on her without her knowing? Or was she hallucinating after inhaling some bad spores?

"I don't know." Yael's voice came from above her and outside the stone coffin. He held out a hand, and she took it.

He pulled her to her feet, and they both stepped back out of the sarcophagus. Yael rubbed his chin for a few moments, examining the room. Then he began touching things. Or trying to, anyway. His hand simple swiped through objects like they were illusions.

"I don't understand." She shook her head and wrapped her arms around her torso.

Yael strode to the door back into the passageway. His

image flickered for a second, before he turned back to her. "I think we've been trapped."

"Trapped? How?"

He returned to his bag and rummaged through it. "With magic."

Rowan laughed. "You can't be serious."

"You just fell *through* a stone coffin. Explain that to me." He raised an eyebrow at her, like *she* was the one coming out with the insane answers.

"I'm hallucinating."

She had to be. What was she really doing? Standing in the room staring at a wall? When would the vision stop?

"Then we're both hallucinating, cos I am trapped right here with you."

"You could just be a figment of my imagination."

He stood, his hands filled with little plastic bags of colorful powder. "If I am, why am I wearing clothes?"

She blushed. "Because I don't imagine all the guys around me naked."

She would never admit to him that he had been one of the guys she did.

"Sure, sure." He opened a bag and threw its contents into the air, the powder sparkling in the light. "Cat on a Broomstick, Manhattan."

The glitter rained onto the floor. Nothing else happened.

"What are you doing?" she asked. How would they ever get that stuff out the tomb? People thought mummies were forever, but it wasn't true. Glitter was.

"Trying to open a Devilsgate to your grandmother's store."

"A Devilsgate." She may have heard her gran use the

term before, but she'd never paid too much attention to her gran's products, not unless she was ringing them through the till.

"Yes, it's a magical portal."

"You've gone nuts. Or I am dreaming. Yes, I'm dreaming." She nodded. That had to be it.

Yael pinched her.

"Ow!" She glared at him. "Why did you *do* that?"

"When you think you're dreaming, you're meant to be pinched."

"You're meant to pinch *yourself*. Not have someone pinch you." She rubbed her injured bicep.

"Oops," he said, but he didn't appear exactly remorseful.

"What are you doing now?" she demanded, following him. Yael stopped in front the Anubis statue Rowan had touched just before the flash, and threw some dark purple powder on it.

"Why did you do that? You'll have contaminated..."

The dust fell *through* the figurine onto the floor.

"You aren't dreaming, and you aren't hallucinating. You're trapped in a magical bubble."

"That's ridiculous."

"Then leave."

"I will." She grabbed her backpack and flashlight and stormed to the doorway. Without pausing to look back, she hurried through into the passageway.

She was still inside the tomb's main chamber.

Again, she tried to leave the room, only to feel her body waver for a second, before she found herself facing the doorway again, *from inside the main chamber*. The backpack fell from her shoulder, the thud loud in the quiet tomb.

There has to be a way to explain this, she thought. *Other than magic.*

But as she stood there for seconds, which turned to minutes, she couldn't find a single rational explanation.

She turned slowly back to Yael, tiredness a heavy cloak on her shoulders. "It won't let me go."

He nodded, face grim. "I don't think we're leaving here anytime soon."

She walked over to the wall opposite the door and sat, staring at the side of the sarcophagus. Twosret. They'd found her.

Yay.

"I can lean against this," Rowan said, realizing she hadn't fallen through the wall.

"Probably because it's the boundary of the trap. A spell like this would have limits."

Rowan wanted to refute him, say he was wrong, but she'd tried leaving, and she couldn't. And the pinch he'd given her, well, it had *hurt*. So, the only thing she could conclude was that she *was* awake, and if this was a hallucination, it was so believable she'd be hard-pressed trying to come to terms with 'reality' after.

How many people are diagnosed with mental illnesses because this has happened to them?

Well, not the tomb and the mummy and the...*spell*, but something that couldn't be made clear with logic and science, something that was so inexplicable they had to just *believe* in the evidence before them.

She pulled her knees up to her chest and rested her forehead on them. What were they going to do?

You have a cellphone.

Desperately, she wiggled around until she could reach her handset in her pocket, and pulled it out, triumphant. Triumphant until she spotted the lack of signal, at least. She tried dialing the international number for search and rescue—which was supposed to work without reception—nothing.

Was this really magic, she wondered. If all this was real, how much must her family have laughed at her over the years? The only one in their huge, widespread network who refused to believe. The only one who insisted science had all the answers, the only one who'd sit at a huge Beltane feast thinking it was all a sham.

"You're quiet," Yael said, sitting down next to her.

"Just reevaluating my life." She stared out over the tomb. "So, you believe in magic? Is that why Gran hired you, cos you're in on it?" The picture of a severed arm oozing blood flashed before her eyes and she shuddered. "Were those people who attacked us at the restaurant even part of a cult?"

He shook his head slowly. "They weren't part of a cult, no. They were demons."

"*Demons*?" Rowan's voice grew high pitched. "You expect me to suddenly accept magic is real and now you want me to believe in *demons*?"

Yael's voice cut through her growing hysteria. "Your entire family thinks magic is real, so it isn't a new concept. And yes, demons. They weren't human. And that skull in the passage? Demon."

That skull *was* strange, she couldn't deny it.

"So how did you come to believe in magic, then?" Rowan demanded. She took three deep breaths, to calm herself down, to not shout he was crazy and she was even crazier for listening to him.

"Because I'm not human."

"*What?*"

"I'm not human. I never was."

He's always been too handsome to be real. So were his friends. So was Luke. But... "What are you then?"

"An angel."

She laughed. She couldn't help it. She laughed until she cried, and all the while, Yael sat against the wall next to her, a silent presence. It reminded her of the dream she'd had; Yael had told her he was an angel then, too. "You're not serious, are you?" She shook her head, wiping tears from her cheeks.

"I am very serious."

Her eyesight no longer blurred, she took in his expression. Tight mouth, slitted eyes; he was insulted, deeply so. She blanched.

"I—I thought you were joking." His jaw tightened at her comment. "You don't have wings," she blurted.

"They were cut off."

"Cut off?" she echoed. This was creepily familiar.

He turned away from her and pulled up his black T-shirt, exposing the smooth lines of his back, the taut skin, the bronzed muscles...and the two scars that ran vertically on either side of his spine.

She gasped. "What happened?"

He flicked the shirt down. "A precious artifact was stolen from Heaven. And I was blamed for it."

Wait. Heaven? As in actual Heaven?

"Why you?"

"You don't think I'd be responsible?" He quirked an eyebrow at her.

"No." Yael was a lot of things, but no thief.

He sighed. "I was part of an elite squadron of soldiers who were set to guard Heaven's Heart—"

"Wait." Rowan held up a hand. It was getting too much. "I've dreamed about this. It's a squat building in the middle of a long hall."

Yael turned to her. "You dreamed it, too?"

"Yes."

They stared at each other.

"We shared a dream?" she asked eventually.

He told her his dream: it had been the same. She'd woken up with a split lip she couldn't explain, and it was this, more than anything else, that convinced her. She could be hallucinating everything around her, but she *remembered* that dream. Plus, he'd offered his version first, which matched hers. It was far too much of a coincidence for it to be natural.

"So," she said into the tomb. "You're really an angel."

"I really am."

CHAPTER 40

Yael still didn't think that Rowan believed him entirely, but her views had been shaken, that he could guarantee.

Pretty hard to pretend that magic doesn't exist when you're sitting in a chamber you can't escape and where you can't touch anything.

"Surely Azrael and Dru will come for us soon," Rowan said into the silence.

"How long has it been?"

Rowan checked her watch. "One hour."

Yael ran a hand over his hair. "An hour?" Dru liked to make his life difficult just because she could, but she had been excited about entering the tomb, even though she'd been banned from taking any 'goodies'. He couldn't see her waiting for so long, especially when their goal was to get Campbell inside to neutralize any nasty spells.

"Maybe the door closed again?"

"That rock I put there to block it weighed two hundred pounds." The magic on the door surely wasn't that strong.

Rowan choked. "I thought you were exaggerating."

"I'm an angel, remember."

"But Dru threw it to you...wait. Is she an angel, too?"

"Dru is half-demon, half-human. It means she's a cambion."

Rowan's brow furrowed. "So, humans and demons can mate? And if Azrael is an angel and Dru is a demon..."

"That's generally not allowed. But Azrael is also fallen."

"You said you lost your wings with your comrades. But Azrael is your brother—"

"He's not my true brother," he said, although that tasted like a lie. "We were part of the Darts."

"When you told me he was, it sounded so truthful."

"It's part of being an angel. We can sense truth, and some humans can feel it when we speak it."

"So, he's not your brother..."

"Biologically. Since falling we've created a family."

He hadn't really thought of it like that before, but it was true. That's what they had become. Azrael, Seraphina, Raze and him. Z was included as well, yet more like a cousin than a sibling, because he'd spent most of his time in Hell since being rescued. But still family.

Maybe that's why Dina's rejection hurt.

He hadn't acknowledged it at the time, but he had been pissed when she'd told the Darts to take a hike. They only had each other, and she had turned her backs on them.

She could be a traitor.

Yeah, well, he needed more evidence before he came to that decision.

"I'm going to study the tomb." Rowan stood, notepad

in hand, and wandered around the room, starting near the doorway.

He should probably help her, but he was feeling jittery. He started doing pushups instead. At least it would burn off some of his excess energy.

He'd moved on to burpees by the time Rowan called out his name. "Yael! It's Dr. Campbell!"

Looking up, sweat dripping in his eyes, he grinned. Help was here.

"Dr. Campbell!" Rowan approached the other archaeologist and touched his arm.

Her hand swiped through him. He didn't even blink.

She tried again and again to get his attention, but he barely even moved.

Yael gently touched her on the shoulder. "He can't see or hear us."

"But *how*?"

"Ma—"

"Don't you dare say it."

"—gic."

She crumpled. Right there in front of Campbell's feet. Huge sobs shook her shoulders, and Yael stood like an idiot, unsure of what to do. Comforting people wasn't really his thing.

Last time she was upset she wanted a hug.

He could do that.

He picked her up, and she fought him, kicking and flailing, but he ignored it. He dumped her over his shoulder, fireman style, and carried her over to the other side of the tomb. He lowered her to the ground and sat next to her, an arm over her shoulders.

"Don't cry," he said after she'd sobbed for another few

minutes.

"I'm not crying." She wiped tear-stained cheeks with her fists.

"Uhh—"

"I'm angry."

"You're angry-crying?" He didn't even know that was a thing. She blew her nose on a tissue and then shoved it back into her pocket. Eww.

"Just give me a second." She took a couple of ragged breaths and then closed her eyes. But there were no more tears.

"I—"

She held up a finger, indicating she wanted silence.

He turned back to Campbell. The guy had moved four step.

Four. Steps.

That isn't good.

He hugged Rowan closer, and she let him.

"Sorry for that." Her voice was croaky. "I don't normally do that, but I just got so overwhelmed. Kayla's dead, we're trapped here. But I am back in control now."

"It was an outlet?" Her face was blotchy, her nose red, and her eyes burned green.

"Yes. It helped."

"Good."

It wasn't how he would have handled things, but he wasn't human. And he wasn't her. If she needed to cry to sort through her emotions, then so be it. He'd just done a thousand pushups and around two hundred burpees. They had different ways of dealing with things.

"Thanks." She gave him a small kiss on the cheek.

It should have meant nothing, but his whole body

came alive, his cock hard, and his blood thundering through his veins. He wanted to throw her on the floor and taste every inch of her.

He shut his eyes.

This isn't good.

In fact, his desire for her was just was getting worse.

I've never wanted anyone like I do her.

And there she sat, snuggled up to him like a trusting kitten, unaware that he was using all of his willpower not to beg her to kiss him again.

But then he saw it.

She was breathing quicker too, and her pupils were huge.

She wants me as well.

Wonderful. The two of them lusting after each other and trapped in a tomb with nowhere to go. This was going to end badly.

Hopefully Azrael finds us quickly.

Because he wasn't sure how long he would be able to resist her.

"Campbell just reached the center of the tomb," Rowan said, her voice distracting him.

Thank fuck.

"It's been around ten minutes."

"Time dilation," Yael whispered.

"What?"

"Time is moving slower in here than it is out there."

"That's not possible."

"Actually, according to physics it is. But how…" He stood and strode over to the Anubis statue, scanning its engravings in the hope they'd give them a clue. "Any who touch this statue will know unending torture; hour watchers beware."

"The statue is the trigger," Rowan said. "Hour watches...they were the timekeepers in Egypt."

He was about to make a Captain Obvious gag when Azrael appeared in the doorway. "We need to know how fast time is moving here."

"Well, it would have taken no more than a minute for Campbell to get to the sarcophagus, even going slowly."

"And Azrael wouldn't have been far behind."

"How long has it been?"

"Around fifteen minutes."

Yael tapped his fingers against his thigh. "Egyptians had a base ten numeric system, didn't they?"

"Yes." She was now studying the statue, too.

"So, if we divide an hour by ten we get six minutes."

"I'm not following."

"Maybe for every six minutes that passes in the real world, an hour passes for us."

"Can you be sure? It doesn't say anything like that on the statue."

It was true, all Yael's Clear Sight powder showed him was the spell itself, and the statue had no details of how it worked. Raze probably could have identified the design of the magic. It looked like star constellations.

Yael pointed at Campbell and Azrael. "See how far they've moved and how long it's been for us."

He returned to the wall and sat, watching the scene play out before him. Rowan eventually joined him.

"It's been an hour."

"They had a conversation and Azrael left." Once the Dart had entered the passage, Yael hadn't been able to keep track of him. "It might not be six minutes, but this whole scene appears like it would have taken place in under ten."

"Let's say it is six minutes." She withdrew a calculator from her bag. He'd seen her using it before when she'd been measuring out her trench. "That means that for every day that happens in the real world, we're trapped here for ten."

"Well then, let's hope they work out we're missing soon."

CHAPTER 41

Rowan had to accept it.

Magic was real.

It was the only explanation for what was happening to them. And she wasn't about to deny what was going on right before her own eyes. She'd always said, if she could see it, she'd believe it.

Well, she'd certainly seen it.

For hours.

Dr. Campbell had been slowly—as in, super-slow—moving around the tomb and Rowan had watched, occasionally trying to direct him toward the Anubis statue. Instead, he'd gone to a random selection of items, said some words, sometimes thrown some powder on them, and moved on.

"What's he doing?" Rowan asked. They'd fallen into a companionable silence, while she studied the tomb's objects and Yael either worked out or helped her. She'd tried not to watch the way his body moved when he exercised, but it had been difficult. Too difficult. She'd nearly bitten her tongue off a time or two trying to distract herself.

"Removing any curses."

"You mean spells?"

"I mean curses. Campbell is a Cornak demon, they specialize in curses. It energizes them."

"But he looks human."

Yael grabbed a locket from under his shirt—why hadn't she noticed that he kept it there? She'd certainly been eyeing off his chest a lot—and opened it. A dull gray powder sat within. "Rub some of this over your eyelids."

"Isn't this your eye cream?" But she complied when he gave her a don't-be-an-idiot look.

Eye-cream. How stupid am I?

Suddenly, all the in-jokes she hadn't understood— between Yael and the other archaeologists, and between Yael and Azrael and Dru—were making a lot more sense.

Money-launderers. She snorted. Dru must have been going to say 'monsters', but stopped when she'd remembered Rowan didn't believe in magic. It had all seemed so silly at the time.

After she wiped the dust off her fingers, she opened her eyes. "Whoa." The entire room was a *lot* brighter, with white light glimmering over objects and text, some in shapes she could identify, others not. And when she turned to Dr. Campbell... "What the—?"

He still appeared human, but there was a dull red glow under his skin, and his hair was a lot shaggier, almost like fur in places.

"His glamor is strong, so you can only see partially through it, but you've got a glimpse of what he really looks like."

"So were Kayla and Dr. Murdoch human?" But she

knew they weren't. No human could down fifteen cups of coffee a day and not resemble a squirrel on cocaine. If anything, the beverage had calmed the other woman down.

"No. Kayla was a Succubus, and Murdoch is an Anguis demon, like a praying mantis with scales."

"Huh." She was surprised at Kayla, but Murdoch had always reminded her of an insect; long and spindly.

"Don't you want to know what Luke is?" Yael asked, a taunting note in his voice.

"Luke?" He was too handsome to be human, she had to admit it. But, a demon?

"His name is Luke M. Starre."

"Yes?"

"You don't see it?" Yael was incredulous.

"Don't see what?"

"He's Lucifer. 'Luke' is short for Lucifer. 'M. Starre' is short for Morning Star. You know, the King of Hell. Well, King of Sheol. Hades and Satan rule the other two circles."

"Wait—wait. That story you told me about the circles of Hell is *true*?"

"Yes. But *that's* what you're worried about? Not the fact you've been working for *Lucifer*?"

"Luke is not Lucifer. That's—"

"Wait, let me guess. Crazy. Or ridiculous. You were going to go with one of those two."

She folded her arms. "You can be a real smart ass, you know that?"

"Yes, I pride myself on it, really."

Rowan laughed, but the sound was cut short when Luke suddenly appeared in the tomb.

One moment it had just been Dr. Campbell and the next, her boss stood next to the archeologist, dressed in a designer suit, his long hair loose around his face. He wasn't wearing glasses, although she could see they were tucked into a pocket.

"Can he see us?" Rowan asked. She stood, and approached them, but Luke didn't bat an eyelid. "I can't hear them, can you?"

Yael shook his head. "And their mouths are moving too slow for me to lip-read. We may as well sit back and watch the show."

"What do you mean?"

"This is going to take a while."

And it did. For ages, the pair just stood there; it was the most irritating thing she'd ever had to witness.

"This is taking forever." She let her head fall back against the wall.

Sometime later, as she was drawing sketches of the artifacts, Yael called out, "There it goes!"

Rowan quickly turned back, mouth opening as she saw Luke lift the alabaster sarcophagus lid ever-so-slowly, eventually placing it on the ground. "That would be several hundred pounds of stone!"

"I told you he wasn't human." Yael looked smug.

"I didn't say I didn't think he wasn't human. But King of Hell?"

"That's a lot of double negatives there. But I think I follow. He's the King of Sheol. He's the first fallen angel. And he's still an archangel, despite the fact his wings were removed. But most of all, he's a total asshole and not to be trusted."

She watched as Luke peered into the coffin, his face

slowly morphing into a mask of anger. He turned to Dr. Campbell, who grew visibly worried.

Rowan was beside them as Luke pulled on a pair of gloves and removed the lid of the second, nested sarcophagus. There were usually two or three nested coffins protecting a significant mummy. She peered inside. There, wrapped in bandages, was Twosret. Her shrouded body was covered in amulets and jewelry, and four canopic jars were nestled at her feet. Each jar contained Twosret's internal organs: liver, lungs, intestines and stomach. They weren't normally placed within the sarcophagus, but this had been a quick reburial, so things weren't standard.

The lack of protocol didn't bother her, though. Rowan's heart thumped at the significance of the find.

Luke ran his gloved hands over the bandages shrouding the mummy, and picked up each amulet, studying it before replacing it exactly where it had been.

Don't do it. Don't touch them.

But he couldn't hear her thoughts, and even if he could, she doubted he'd pay attention.

"What's he searching for?" she asked.

"Heaven's Heart."

"But you said it was stolen."

"There were three pieces. Heaven only had one. Apparently, one was kept in the human realm, and one in Hell."

"And you think Twosret had it?"

"Not just me; apparently Lucifer thinks it as well. It's why he wanted to find her."

"So that's why you helped me with the trench and the tomb." She frowned. "But what does it do?"

"I don't know. It was never used in Heaven."

"It must be powerful if Luke wants it—if he really is Lucifer."

"My thoughts exactly."

They stood side by side as Lucifer rifled through the grave goods covering Twosret's body; he even unwound the wrapping at her throat, exposing a severed neck. Rowan's mind was screaming against the sacrilege. He was unwrapping a mummy, exposing it to the air, before it had been properly studied.

There was nothing there.

Luke growled, and shadow-like wings erupted from his back, while lightning danced over his flesh. She could hear the echo of the sound even here. Primal fear danced through her, and she knew that she should never have seen this, never have known what he was.

He really is *Lucifer.*

His moment of rage over, the wings vanished, and Luke returned to his normal, too-handsome self.

Then, over the next several hours—for Rowan and Yael, at least—Dr. Campbell and Luke returned the sarcophagus to its prior condition. If she hadn't seen it with her own eyes, she never would have guessed the tomb had been disturbed.

Her skin crawled at the idea that any number of tombs or bodies could have been manhandled in this way, their final resting places desecrated by treasure hunters, regular archaeologists and historians never knowing what had happened. What had been stolen.

"That would have taken them all of one to two hours," Yael said, when Luke disappeared.

"How long has it been for us?" Rowan asked.

"Twenty."

She didn't even feel tired. "I think your theory was right."

"For once, being right isn't that much of a good thing."

"But it's odd. I don't feel hungry, or tired, or any of the usual things that being awake for over twenty hours would do to me."

"It must be part of the spell. To ensure that whoever gets trapped lives a *long* time in this place. It is meant to be torture, after all."

CHAPTER 42

Five days.

Five whole mother-fucking days had passed, and Yael was going to go postal. He hated this, being trapped with no way out. He'd tried dozens more spell-breaking charms and had zero luck. And he'd gone over that damned jackal-headed Anubis statue a hundred times, all to no avail. He had no idea how to break them out.

Having Dru's teleportation ring would be handy right about now.

Even then there was no guarantee it would work; they'd been taken out of the current reality, or timeline, or whatever. He needed to watch more *Star Trek* to get up on the lingo.

In all that time, though, Rowan hadn't needed to sleep; she'd spent a large majority of it cataloguing the tomb's contents. He helped her, when the boredom threatened to get to him, but he'd tried to keep his distance, when he could. Being near her, knowing no one else could interrupt them, that they were alone...

It was dangerous.

She was human. Mortal.

His initial objections—not wanting to risk being kicked out of Heaven forever for sleeping with a human—had vanished. It was inevitable, their joining. But he worried now that he was too attached, that he would crave her for years, for centuries, and that one taste wouldn't be enough.

She's going to die.

Kayla's demise had just driven the point home earlier than he would have liked. Yael would live for millennia more, provided he didn't meet with an untimely beheading or angel-killing Cushiel. Was it worth it, to love for a human lifetime, knowing he may never find the same thing again with one of his own kind?

Two months ago, he would have straight up said 'no'. Then again, he would have thought the idea of his falling in love with a human was—as Rowan would say it—ridiculous.

But now, now he thought it might be worth it.

You're only thinking this because you're trapped…

Maybe.

But he'd spent five days continuously with Rowan. And weeks before that. Never, not in his entire life, had he ever been able to tolerate spending that much time with another person. Not even the Darts, and he'd adopted them as family.

He enjoyed his and Rowan's banter; her quick wit, and her ability to admit she was wrong. She hadn't formally apologized to him or her family yet for thinking they were cray cray, but she'd accepted that magic was real, and had admitted as much.

It took a Hell of a lot of resilience to do that.

To learn that a whole new world was real, one you thought was nothing more than nonsense and legend, and to roll with it, showed she was of stronger character than he or her family had thought. Hell, then even *she'd* thought.

"Why are you staring at me like that?" Rowan asked. She stood near the sarcophagus, notepad in hand, her red hair a wild nimbus around her face. She'd never appeared sexier, not even in that black dress of hers.

"Like what?"

She gulped. "Like you want to...devour me."

"Maybe because I do?" He stepped right up to her, so she had to tilt her head back to look at him.

"Are you ill?" She tucked her pencil into a pocket and felt his forehead.

He was feverish all right, but not from illness. "No."

"You're hot."

"Thank you."

"That's not what I meant, and you know it." She rolled her eyes, a smile tugging on the corner of her lips. He wanted to kiss it away until she couldn't smile, couldn't laugh, could only gasp his name.

"I'll take what compliments I can. You're so forthcoming with them, after all."

"What do you mean by that—?"

He claimed her mouth in a searing kiss.

The tingles that accompanied their usual touches flared in an explosion of heat, racing through his body, making his skin come alive. Every touch, every faint stroke of air, it electrified him, made him hungry for more.

He cupped her jaw and tilted her head to the side, so

he could gain better access to her mouth. She moaned, low and needy, against his lips. His cock, already hard, jerked.

"Fuck." He pulled away for a moment, resting his forehead against hers. Electrical tingles pulsed through him, making him hotter, harder. "This feels too good."

Way too good.

Kissing had never gotten him so worked up before.

"More." Rowan grabbed his face, stood on her tiptoes and kissed him, her passion re-igniting his own into an inferno.

His hands developed a mind of their own, and they caressed her neck, her back, her waist. One swept up over her ribcage, coming to a stop so it could stroke the underside of a breast. The weight against his hand made him groan, plunge his tongue into her mouth to plunder, take everything she had to offer.

She pressed closer to him, and his hand closed over her breast. They both gasped, then he pulled away as his fingers stroked over her nipple, felt it harden beneath his touch. He would kiss her there, touch her…taste her.

"Yael?"

He glanced down to find her lips trembling, but not from desire. No, her burning gaze was sad, guilty even.

Had he just totally misread the situation?

"Yes?"

"I'm not sure I'm ready…Eric died…and Kayla died…"

He stumbled back, numb. *She didn't want him?* All that fire and passion and she *didn't want him?*

"I see."

"No." She closed the distance between them, grabbing

onto his arm. "I want this, I want you, I'm just not ready."

He couldn't look at her. Her words were true, so she believed them, but he couldn't see past the rejection. *Not good enough. Again.*

"Okay."

"Yael?"

He turned to face the wall. "I need some time alone."

"I—"

"Alone."

She hesitated, as if she expected him to turn back around, to make peace with her, but he couldn't. He would have made love to her then and there, had she let him. As a fallen, he wasn't forbidden from being with a human, but he would still potentially risk giving up his ticket back into Heaven by being with her.

And Rowan?

She'd been so consumed with guilt for wanting to fuck him, that she'd stopped.

Goes to show he was always second best.

Even to a human.

CHAPTER 43

Azrael gripped his cellphone. For hours, he'd been debating whether to call in help. Yael was gone, as was Rowan. They'd been missing for half a day. There was no sign of them in the tomb, nor at the site or the compound. They could be dead.

Or they could have been trapped by a spell.

It was the latter, he suspected, especially since he and Dru had been caught by something like that once before. It was how they'd bonded. Kind of. How they'd learned not to kill each other, anyway.

The bonding and the sex had come later.

Dru was prowling under the marquee, her white hair whipping around her face whenever she turned. "Lucifer was in there before," she said. "I spied on him. He couldn't find the Heart."

He sighed. He'd told her not to go sneaking around, but Dru was Dru. It was why he loved her, after all. "That means Lucifer didn't see them, either. Angelic help probably won't be of any use, then."

That crossed Seraphina and Trick off the list. He

disliked Trick anyway—asshole had tried to seduce Dru about a million times—but he did trust Seraphina.

"But who else is there?" Dru came to a stop and tapped her lip.

"Well, we do know an Egyptian god."

"Set?" She screwed her face up. "We kind of cut off his head. Plus, he has a hit out on us; that's why we've been playing babysitter. He won't want to help us."

"No, the *other* Egyptian god."

"Ooohh." A sly look swept into her eyes, and he had to stop himself from pinning her to the ground and kissing her senseless. She grinned, as if she could sense his desire. "Hold that thought. Let me make a quick call to my sister."

CHAPTER 44

Yael hadn't talked to her for a day.

He'd needed space, he said. She'd given him space. But now she felt like an asshole. Kissing him had been the most amazing moment in her life. She'd never felt so alive, so sexy, so wanted.

And she'd ruined it.

Because for a split second, Eric had popped into her mind.

He'd never kissed her that, like he if he didn't, he'd die. He had never truly been passionate with her, and that solidified her belief that their union had been one of practicality.

And her guilt had spiraled out of control. There she was, enjoying herself, making out with another man, just two months after Eric had died.

She'd loved Eric, she had.

But maybe she hadn't loved him like she should have.

And she'd stopped Yael, stopped him right about when things were going to get hotter and even more fantastic, because she'd been scared. Scared and guilty.

She'd already been falling for Yael; what if having sex with him pushed her over the edge, into love? Did that make her fickle? Not worthy of a second chance?

Argh.

She clenched her hands into fists, pressing them against her temples. She hated this, this second-guessing, this not knowing.

Yael was an angel.

She'd never get another chance at being with him, not if he gained his wings again. And once their business transaction was over...sure, he might have feelings for her. But he was going to live forever, maybe, and she wasn't.

Life is too short to be afraid.

It was something her cousin, Juliette, had once said on the phone to her. Right before she'd jumped out of an airplane, skydiving somewhere in Peru.

She'd been right.

Yael was back over by the Anubis statue, staring at it like he could intimidate it into freeing them. "Yael?"

He turned to her, his eyes flat and hard. He'd never looked at her like that, not even the day they'd first met back in the mansion.

"I'm sorry," she blurted.

"Excuse me?"

"I said I'm sorry."

"For what?"

She didn't like this cold stranger he'd become; like he'd shut himself off from her, so she couldn't reject him anymore.

"For being afraid. For not believing. For laughing when you said you were an angel. Need I go on?"

"Please do."

Ugh. Why was he punishing her? "I'm also sorry for stopping the other day. I didn't lie. I do want you."

"Just not enough." His voice was laced with bitterness.

"Trust me, it's enough."

"Not compared to how you feel about your boyfriend."

A lump formed in her throat. "No."

Hurt lashed across Yael's face, and he turned away from her. *He cares.* It wasn't just some ego-thing about being rejected. He thought she hadn't wanted him, and it hurt, because he wanted *her.* She reached out, placing a gentle hand on his shoulder. "I want to be with you more than I've ever wanted to be with *anyone.* That's why I stopped."

He spun back. "*What?*"

"I loved Eric; I loved the idea of him. He was my first boyfriend. I thought we'd get married and I'd have the normal family I'd always dreamed of. But that wasn't real. And for a moment, I felt guilty. How dare I enjoy myself, how dare I let myself want another man, when Eric was barely in the grave? It's only been two months, even though it feels like it was a lifetime ago."

Old Rowan, the Rowan who had been happily wearing blinkers and living within the careful parameters she'd selected—she'd chosen Eric. But the new Rowan, the Rowan who was finally beginning to see the world as it really was, she wanted Yael. Had wanted him from the moment she'd met him, even though she hadn't acknowledged it then, because it meant betraying Eric.

Yael raised a hand and caressed her cheek. "I don't expect you to love me more than him, but for you to not want me at all because of him..."

She gave a watery chuckle. "Trust me. That's not it at all."

"I don't like being rejected." His gaze softened.

"Oh, really? I wouldn't have guessed."

His gaze dimmed. "It's me who should apologize. I was acting like an ass. I shouldn't have made you say sorry. My whole life, I've been a failure to my parents. Never good enough. And so when I wasn't enough for you—"

"You didn't take it well."

"No." He let out a deep breath. "I was a jerk. And I won't take my frustration out on you again."

Rowan reached out and placed both hands on Yael's shoulders. "I know your parents are angels. But they're idiots. *They* aren't good enough for *you*. You were an elite soldier. You can speak over thirty languages. You learned one of them just to piss them off! You're clever and quick-witted. And handsome. Why wouldn't they be proud of you?"

"Because I'm not an archangel. Because I wasn't first in my class. Because I wasn't captain of the Darts. And because I'm not very good at self-sacrificing. Seraphina— one of the Darts—went into Hell to save one of our comrades. I could have done it, but I refused. Kept looking for another way. But she just did it. Even when she asked me to return the favor your grandmother was owed, I didn't want to. Just wanted to keep hunting for the Heart, favor be damned."

"But you did it in the end."

"Out of guilt." He took her wrist in his hand. "I am not good at putting others first. I am not good at bending to what other people want. And I want to get back into Heaven."

She glanced down. "And being with me—"

"Will be worth it. Even if we find all three pieces of the Heart, I can wait to return."

"Wait for what? Me to die?"

He met her stare, his cool and calm. She stepped back. "But I will grow old and you won't."

"We could find a way to make you immortal. Your grandmother already thinks you're something special. There might be a way."

"And then what? What if I become immortal? What if they ban you from Heaven because you chose to be with a human?"

"Then I will deal with it at the time. But here's the one thing in my life I have always craved: choice. I want to be able to choose my destiny, not have it foisted upon me like an unwanted mantle."

Choice.

He made it sound so easy, but she knew it wouldn't be.

However, they only had the now; potentially, it was all they were ever going to have. So why not enjoy it? They may never get rescued, may be trapped here for eternity. It was time to take advantage of the situation, rather than fight it.

"Fine." She threw her hair back over her shoulder. "I choose you. Right now."

"Right now?"

"You got it." She closed the distance, all but leaping on him. Her mouth pressed against his, urgent, hungry, while her hands clenched on his shoulders, the muscle underneath firm. She wanted to explore that muscle, feel his heat without any restriction between them.

One hand snaked up under his shirt, while the other tugged at his sleeve. He got the message. A moment later, his T-shirt was gone, and there was nothing but firm, masculine flesh before her eyes.

She kissed his pec, right over his heart, before returning to his mouth, feeling the zap of awareness between them. His mouth left hers, trailing wet kisses down her neck, onto her collar bone. She wrapped one leg around his waist, bringing her core into contact with his erection. She rubbed herself against him, growing wetter and wetter as the friction sent lightning bolts of ecstasy through her.

She gasped, and threw her head back, giving him better access to her neck, and her chest.

"Ahem." A cough echoed through the chamber.

Rowan and Yael sprang apart, her body on fire, her core aching, her limbs weak from trembling.

I needed to finish that.

"*You!*" Yael lunged forward, kicking out at the intruder who stood next to Twosret's sarcophagus. His foot flew through the man's torso, failing to make contact.

"Have we met?" the newcomer asked, staring at his chest, amused. He appeared Egyptian, with slightly tilted eyes and sun-kissed skin, but his English was perfect. He was handsome, but she was beginning to think that most non-humans were.

And he was wearing surgical scrubs.

That's odd, even for magical stuff, right?

"You can see and hear us?" Rowan asked, leaning forward. Yael wrapped an arm around her torso, pulling her back.

Yael jabbed a finger at the stranger. "That is Set."

Set the god of chaos? He's real, too?

"Set? Oh. I see." The newcomer shook his head. "No, I'm Osiris, his brother."

Yael glowered. "You look exactly like him."

Osiris threw his shoulders back. "My eyes are yellow, and his are red. We're very different. Although we are twins."

"So, uh, why can you see and hear us and other people can't?" Rowan asked, trying to diffuse the tension. If this guy was their ticket out of here, she wasn't about to quibble about his identity; if he was a bad guy, they could no doubt try to escape him later. Yael was a pretty badass fighter, and she knew Azrael and Dru would be, too.

"Because I am a *god*."

"A deposed god. Lucifer was here before and he couldn't see us."

Osiris' lips curved in a secretive smile. He raised his hands. "But I am an Egyptian deity, and this is my domain."

Yael didn't hide his skepticism.

"In one legend, Anubis was thought to be Osiris' son," Rowan murmured. "And Osiris is the god of death. And we're in a tomb."

Osiris rubbed his hands together. "Very good."

"Well, can you get us out of here?" Yael demanded.

"Are you sure you want to leave?" He waved at them. She blushed. How much had he seen?

"We've been stuck here for days. Yes, we want to leave." Yael let go of her. He looked about ready to strangle the deity.

"It won't take long. Wait a second." Osiris touched the Anubis statue and wavered, like his body had just been plucked out of the real world and dumped into theirs.

"What are you doing? Why are you joining us?"

"There. Time will pass as normal now." He stroked his chin. "We're about to have a visitor."

The ceiling exploded.

Chapter 45

Stone shattered as something shot down through the ceiling of the tomb. When the dust cleared, a figure with ink-dark wings hovered effortlessly over the sarcophagus. Yael walked around the pillars, so he could discover the identity of their visitor. "They still won't be able to see us?"

Osiris shook his head.

"Dina," Yael whispered.

Harshly beautiful, her golden hair was pinned back from her face, while her clear blue eyes rapidly searched the tomb. She landed next to the sarcophagus and cleared away debris that had fallen on the stone coffin.

She lifted the lid and pushed it aside.

"Stop her!" Rowan shouted at Osiris.

But the god shook his head. "I may be a god, but the power she wields…"

Dina had been on the brink of ascension for centuries. Osiris wasn't a fool, hesitating to do battle with her. Even Yael thought twice.

"There are three of us—"

While they debated the issue, Dina pulled off the second nested coffin's lid, and stared at the mummy. She rifled through the amulets that Lucifer had so carefully handled, and then punched her fist through the mummy's chest. Yael couldn't hear it, but he imagined the sound of dry cracking ribs, of old flesh torn asunder. He flinched.

Rowan yelled, "What is she *doing*—?"

Dina threw her head back and opened her mouth in an unheard scream of rage. Then she launched herself up through the hole she'd created in the ceiling, and vanished.

"You let her do this." Rowan was panting in anger, her fists clenched at her sides as she faced off against Osiris. "She just desecrated Twosret's resting place! She desecrated *Twosret*!"

Osiris walked away, back to the Anubis statue. He touched it, and Yael felt dizzy for a heartbeat. Rowan's legs buckled beneath her. He caught her, and gently lowered her to the ground, careful to avoid sharp rocks that had fallen from the ceiling.

"You're back in normal time," Osiris said. He turned melancholic eyes on the opened coffin, approached it and held his hand over Twosret's chest. He closed his eyes, and a golden glow emanated from his palm, filtering down to the mummy below.

Rowan stood and hurried over, her mouth dropping in awe. Yael watched, too, as the damage done to Twosret was repaired.

"What was she searching for?" Osiris asked.

"Heaven's Heart." Yael and the god shared a meaningful look.

"And she thought Twosret had it?"

"So did Lucifer."

The god held up both his hands. "I fixed the damage to her. But this is now officially above my pay grade. As you say, I am merely a *deposed* god."

"Oz!" Dru's voice reached them, before she and Azrael appeared in the doorway. She fist-pumped the air. "They're back!"

Rowan gave a wan smile. "We're back."

Then she collapsed.

Swearing, Yael caught the redhead. Panic thumped through him. What was wrong with her? Had the spell's release affected her because she was human?

Osiris got in his face. "Let me have a look at her."

"You're a death god, you're not touching her." He jerked his torso to the side, Rowan moving with him.

"He's a doctor," Dru said.

"Really?" Yael wasn't buying it, but could tell Dru wasn't lying.

"I'm a pathologist, but yes, I have treated living patients before. Z was one of them."

So, this was the surgeon they'd gotten to check Z and determine if Heaven's Heart had been inserted within his body. "Fine."

Osiris quickly felt her pulse and checked her eyes. "She's just passed out. How long were you trapped here?"

"Around six days. Maybe seven."

"Seven days?" Azrael exclaimed. "You weren't even gone twenty-four hours."

"It's just exhaustion," Osiris said. "She'll be fine."

Relief swamped Yael. She was going to be okay.

He left the tomb without a backward glance. "Can you grab our gear?"

He heard Dru rummaging around while Azrael followed him. "Seven days?"

"There was a time dilation effect or something. Time passed slower for us."

"Ten times slower," Osiris added.

"Well, did you find the Heart?" Azrael asked, when they emerged from the tomb, into the cool air outside.

Yael inhaled deeply, tasting pollution, sand, and old magic. "No."

"*No?*"

"We got trapped before we could search. But Lucifer came, and so did Dina, and they both left empty-handed."

"So, it wasn't there?"

"It doesn't appear so."

Azrael sighed. "Back to the drawing board, then."

Yael shifted Rowan into a fireman's carry and climbed the ladder, careful not to drop her. At the top, he moved aside so Azrael and Osiris could follow, but Azrael reached the top alone.

"Osiris?"

"He vanished."

Gods. Typical.

Rowan stirred against him, and he lowered her to her feet. She opened groggy eyes and leaned against his chest. "What happened?"

"You passed out."

"I'm such a badass."

He chuckled and kissed her, uncaring that Azrael was there, that they were under the open sky where any angel might fly. They were out of that trap, and now they had the rest of her life to find the Heart, cure her of mortality, and have sex.

He planned on them having a lot of sex.

A cold voice lashed through the air. "Isn't this touching?"

Yael turned to face Lucifer, who stood opposite them in a flannel shirt and jeans. Campbell and Murdoch were on either side of him, the lanky Murdoch almost appearing apologetic.

"Well, we're touching, yes." Yael smirked. He'd never been very good at respecting authority.

Lucifer clicked his fingers, and Rowan vanished. Yael growled low in his throat and launched himself at the Hell-lord, garotte in hand, only to stumble as he met no resistance. Raising his head, scanned the area, the taste of sand and blood in his mouth.

He spat out a gritty glob of saliva.

Gone.

They were all gone.

"Mother *fucker!*"

CHAPTER 46

Rowan stumbled and fell onto her butt. The air stank like rotten eggs, and it was hot, like desert hot. Glancing around, she yelped, crab walking over the ground to bump into something hard. Two 'people' stood in front of her, one with dark red skin and a fur pelt, the other, tall and insect-like, and covered in scales.

Dr. Campbell and Dr. Murdoch. It has to be.

Luke strode into view, coming to a stop, hands on hips. A thunderous expression marred the beauty of his face. He was angry, at *her.*

What have I done?

The rattle of a chain accompanied the lowering of a metal grate, separating her from the others.

"What is going on?" She was in a small cell, dark stone lining the walls around her. There was no bed, or toilet, or water. She was trapped.

Again.

Except this time, she was exhausted. And scared.

Where was Yael?

"If you hadn't decided to get so...comfortable with

your angel bodyguard, you wouldn't be here." Luke shook his head, as if disappointed in her. "But I can't trust you anymore. So, enjoy your new room. If you cooperate, you'll graduate to another area of the Tower. If you don't, you'll find yourself in much worse accommodations."

"I don't understand."

There are worse cells?

Luke rolled his eyes. "It was cute, when I first found you, that you didn't believe in magic. But it's annoying now. I am Lucifer, King of Sheol, archangel, and so forth. These are demons." He indicated the archaeologists on either side of him. "And you are a conduit."

"I don't have any powers—"

If she had, she probably would have come to accept magic was real long before now.

"You don't need to. You make yourself available to me, and I can use you to harness magic currently unavailable to me."

"I'm not going to help you."

"Brave words. But time—and torture—can change the strongest of wills."

Then he left her.

He just left.

Dr. Campbell followed the fallen angel down a corridor that vanished into darkness, but Dr. Murdoch lingered for a moment. "For a human, you aren't stupid. If you cooperate, life will certainly be better for you." His mantis-like head tilted to the side. "And he wasn't lying when he said things could get a lot worse."

The demon scurried after the other two, and she was left alone, in a new prison. But this one, this one was going to be a lot harder to break out of.

What do I do now?

CHAPTER 47

"She's gone?" Seraphina paced Raze's study, while Yael looked on, propped up against a bookcase.

He still couldn't believe it.

One click of his fingers, and Lucifer had stolen the most precious thing in Yael's world.

"I thought you might know someone who could get her out. You said you were taken to the Tower of Tortures..." Yael let his voice trail away.

Seraphina stopped moving. She turned to look over her shoulder, at the giant winged bastard who stood near the windows.

Trick.

Fuck, Yael wished that asshole wasn't here. But he had contacts they needed. And when it came to Rowan, he was willing to make a deal with anyone.

"We don't know if she's in the Tower," Azrael said, ever the reasonable one.

Trick rubbed his chin. "It's Lucifer. His fortress is the Tower, it's a good guess."

"I agree with Trick and Yael," Raze said. "It is the most

likely place to start our search."

"But how are we going to break in?" Yael demanded.

"*We* won't," Trick replied.

Yael shoved a hand through his hair. "I don't get it."

"Let me make a call." Trick vanished.

Teleportation. Lucky bastard.

Yael's phone rang. Glancing down at the screen, he cursed, then answered. "Hi, Dora. How are you?"

"My granddaughter is in the goddamned Tower of Tortures and you dare ask how I am?"

"Not well, I assume?"

She screeched.

He held the phone away and rubbed his ear. "Do you have any Siren ancestry in your family tree?"

"You were meant to look after her! You were meant to prevent Lucifer from taking her! And guess what happened? *Lucifer took her!*"

"He teleported her right in front of me. There was nothing I could do." At least, that's what he kept telling himself, because he couldn't live with himself if there'd been something he could have done to prevent her kidnapping.

He had to get her back.

He simply had to.

"She is a conduit of immense potential. Do you know what he could do with her?"

"Bad things," he guessed.

"*Very* bad things. You idiot!"

"We're working on getting her back."

"Don't worry about it. I'll get someone onto it."

Anger scorched through him at her dismissal. "I won't rest until I get Rowan back. And we're getting help right now."

"Oh, and who is on the case?"

"I thought you knew everything."

"Don't get smart with me."

"Trick."

"You're sending Trick after my granddaughter?"

"He has changed a little since you last saw him, but no. Trick is getting hold of someone who can get your granddaughter out of the Tower."

"How do you know it will work?"

"Because they've done it before."

Tension built in the room until it became all but unbearable, then with a *pop* and the scent of ozone, two figures appeared in the library.

Hades and a beautiful Japanese woman.

Trick appeared a second later.

Yael had never met the god before, but he'd seen images. Tall, with a partially shaved head and long black hair, yellow eyes, and an expression that made a resting bitch face look like a fucking smile, Hades was not an entity to mess with.

"You want Asha to break someone out of the Tower of Tortures *again*?" The god's voice boomed through the room, and they all shuffled a little on their feet. Even Dru, who grew up in Hell.

"If she could—" Yael began.

"Absolutely fucking not. Lucifer is already on high alert after Satan fucked with him. Asha could be walking into a trap."

"I can speak for myself, you know," the woman said. Her long dark hair was tied back in a bun, and she wore a blue cheongsam. Her almond-shaped eyes glimmered with amusement.

"Yes, but you're crazy enough to say yes." Hades glared at her.

She turned to them and shrugged. "He's right."

"See?" Hades growled, as if vindicated.

"I like collecting favors," Asha added.

"You mean you like hoarding them."

Yael and the others watched them like this was a tennis match, heads turning between the two.

Asha's hand dug into a bag she had slung over her shoulder. "Hoarding, collecting, it's all a matter of opinion."

"You got away with it last time because he didn't know that Trick and Seraphina were there." Hades growled. "He will realize the human is missing."

"My illusion magic has grown exponentially recently," Asha said. "I should be able to hide that she's gone for a little while. At least until we're out."

Hades looked ready to protest further, when Raze murmured, "Rowan is a conduit."

Hades' head snapped toward the dark-skinned angel. "What kind of conduit?"

"A *true* conduit."

The god rocked back on his heels and whistled. "That's different."

"How so?" Dru asked.

"True conduits are descended from gods," Hades replied. Yael was caught off balance: he didn't think the god would bother with something so trivial as an explanation. "*Primordial* gods. Whoever uses her can tap into the energy of the universe. I can't let Lucifer keep her."

"She is not a thing to be kept," Yael ground out.

"Semantics." Hades waved a hand dismissively. "It would create an uneven power balance, and that can't be allowed."

"So, you'll do it?" Yael asked Asha.

"Yes. I need to sort out a few spells, but I'll do it. You'll owe me, and so will the conduit."

"Two favors?" Yael demanded.

"Two."

He knew he shouldn't decide for Rowan without her consent, but her life was on the line. If she didn't give Lucifer what he wanted, he'd torture her until she did. If she somehow survived that, mind intact, and still refused him, he'd kill her.

Yael couldn't let that happen.

"I'm going with you," Yael demanded.

Asha met his stare, a cloak of shadows and power enveloping her body, leaving just her face free. Her eyes bore into his, black and fathomless, her cheekbones sharp and skull-like. He took an involuntary step back. This woman was *not* the cambion she was rumored to be.

"I work best alone." Her voice echoed with the screams of the dead.

"You're Hades' *personal assistant*," Trick said incredulously.

The aura around her vanished. "Yes, but I am the *only* one."

Yael decided not to delve into the logic behind that. "I have to help save Rowan."

"Not with me, you don't." Asha shook her head.

Hades narrowed his lemon-colored eyes. "No, but you can come with me."

"Go with you where?"

The god grinned, evilly. "To create a distraction."

CHAPTER 48

"Just open yourself up to me." Luke's voice was a hot whisper against her ear.

Rowan rolled over, blinking her eyes open. She jerked upright. She'd been asleep on the rock floor of her cell. Luke stood on the other side of the metal bars, staring at her.

"What were you doing?" she asked, shoving a handful of hair from her face. It had knotted into a bird's nest.

"A little subconscious influencing. Did it work?" He smiled, that beautiful charming smile. She should have known it was fake the first minute she saw it.

"No."

"A shame. You won't like my more conscious methods."

She didn't doubt him. "You aren't wearing glasses."

"No, I don't need them. But they work for my human persona, don't you think? A little like that superhero."

Lucifer had likened himself to *Clark Kent*?

"I hope you're enjoying your accommodations. I put you in one of the nicer cells. Did you like the guards coming by? Still don't believe in magic?"

She ignored his taunting. He was trying to get to her, to make her edgy. Well, she hadn't been raised by the most stubborn woman in existence for nothing. "I won't let you use me."

"That's where you're wrong. You already have." He tucked his hands into his pockets, looking like he'd just stepped off a photoshoot.

"What do you mean?" She shuffled until she could sit, leaning her back against the wall. She hated to think she'd inadvertently helped him. *But what could I have done?*

"I got you to find Twosret for me. Eventually, I'll find what I need."

"You mean Heaven's Heart?"

His pale eyes narrowed. "So, the fallen angel told you about that?"

"He thought it might be what you were searching for."

"He's not wrong. When you first entered the tomb, did you see anything that could be the Heart?"

As if I would tell you, you dirty big snake. Considering she had no idea what it looked like or what it even did, she answered honestly. "No."

Angels can sense the truth.

Yael had taught her that. And Luke—Lucifer—was the first fallen angel. If she lied, he'd sense it. *I have to be very careful in what I say.*

Because she wanted to make it out of this alive.

"No pretty jewels, or fancy stones?" he asked.

A flash of the rose quartz she'd thought she'd found sprang to mind, but she shoved it away. It wasn't what she'd call fancy or a jewel, so she said, "No."

"A pity. There must be a hidden compartment in the

tomb. I'll just have to keep hunting."

She didn't have anything to say to that, and he just watched her, unblinking, like she was an insect he was about to dissect. "You have no idea how powerful you are."

"I can't do magic, I already told you that."

"No, but you can siphon the universe's energy into a magic-user's hands. With the right tutelage, you may even learn to harness it yourself. Don't you want to become powerful? To not fear those stronger than you?"

"Your sales pitch is missing the obvious."

"And what is that?"

"You have already trapped me. You would never teach me enough to escape you, so I would *always* be at the mercy of someone stronger than me."

He laughed, as if delighted by her.

"From the moment I met you, I knew you would not disappoint me. Your will is strong, but you will eventually give in to me. You already have once."

"I agreed to the dig because it was the opportunity of a lifetime." And look what had happened. The tomb had been ransacked by a black-winged angel the day it was opened, she'd been caught in a time warp, and she'd managed to fall for Yael.

It had all been a bit of a disaster, really.

"Yes. But you set aside those precious principles to do it. And we could still do this the nice way."

She pressed herself further into the wall. "The nice way?"

"I was planning on seducing you. Making you my consort. And I'd already made significant progress in that." He glared. "Until that fallen interrupted things."

"Significant progress? I rejected you." And she'd felt bad at the time, as well. Hah! Goes to show what she knew about men.

"Only because you had a lover. Once he was gone, it would have been simple."

"Once he was gone? He died in a car accident."

Lucifer smirked. "Did he?"

Horror washed through her.

No.

No.

"You killed him?"

"Drunk drivers are *so* unpredictable."

He murdered Eric. Because of her. But why? He said she was a conduit thing, but she'd never been capable of channeling magic.

What about those times Gran asked you to be 'open'?

She'd thought it was nonsense, like she had everything else. But maybe there was some truth there.

It was still her fault.

She'd contacted Lucifer because she'd wanted to study the *Amenonuhoko*, a Japanese artifact he'd housed in his collection. *Why had I been so interested in it?* It wasn't her normal area of expertise, but she had been focused on finding it. And she had. He'd flown her to his mansion so she could study it in person.

If she'd never gotten the stupid idea in her head that she had to research the thing, Eric would be alive even now, because she wouldn't have ever met Luke. None of this would have happened.

The tolling of a bell echoed through the Tower, deafening in its intensity. "What now?" Lucifer muttered. "I'll be back." He strode away.

Rowan leaned her head back against the stone wall, closing her eyes. *It's all your fault.*

Perhaps.

But she was going to have to learn to live with it.

"Psst."

How can I be with Yael when I am the reason Eric is dead?

"Pssst."

Rowan's eyes snapped open. She thought she'd heard—

But no one was there.

She stood, approaching the bars.

"You're Rowan?"

Rowan jumped. There, in the shadows outside her cell, was a beautiful woman, with midnight hair. She quickly emerged from the gloom, dressed from neck-to-toe in black, just like Yael did.

"Yes, I'm Rowan."

"Good." The woman appeared Japanese, but her accent was strange. And her eyes weren't pure brown, rather they had flecks of gray and green and other colors hidden within. "Stand back."

Rowan took a step back automatically, just as the woman threw a handful of dust at the bars. She muttered a word Rowan couldn't understand, and the stench of hot metal filled the room, adding to the already pungent odor of rotten eggs.

"Climb out," the woman urged.

Rowan hesitated. "How do I know this isn't a trap?"

"I like how you think, but it isn't. I'm risking my own ass being here."

"And you are?"

"Must we do introductions now?"

"I am not leaving the cell until I know who you are and that you aren't working with Luke—I mean, Lucifer."

"My name is Asha, and I am Hades' P.A. I don't work for assholes. Well, not total assholes."

She wasn't sure what convinced her, but she knew in her gut that Asha wasn't on Lucifer's side. She climbed through the hole in the bars, careful not to touch the red-hot ends.

Outside the cell, Asha drew some Japanese *kunji* on the walls around the entrance. Then she cut her finger and smeared a single drop of blood in the central marking. She gave Rowan a thumbs up. The wound had already healed. "Let's go."

"What were you doing?"

"An illusion spell. It'll hold for about thirty minutes, which is hopefully all we need."

They made it to the end of the corridor, just as a huge demon guard came around the far corner. Asha pressed Rowan against the wall, using the hanging darkness to hide them temporarily. She muttered quickly under her breath. A strange tugging sensation made Rowan itchy. It was coming from where Asha touched her; her skin growing cold. Instead of fighting against the feeling, Rowan opened herself up, just like her gran asked her to.

Shadows coalesced around them, until Rowan could see nothing but black. Footsteps pounded by, but there were no shouts of recognition. Once the footsteps faded into the distance, Asha pulled them free of the gloom. "That was close. What did you do? I can't normally call shadows that well."

"I'm told I am a conduit. I just…opened myself."

Asha stared at her for a few heartbeats. "Don't go advertising that. Ever. Let's move."

They hurried into another corridor and reached a stairwell. They climbed. Rowan was puffing after one flight. The lack of sleep and food had caught up with her. She had to rest on a landing five flights up, and Asha tugged them into a corner, doing her shadow thing again in case someone came by. But there was no one.

"I'm surprised the patrols are so slow," Asha murmured. "Makes me wonder about a trap. But let's go."

Eventually, they emerged out of the top of the stairwell and a small chamber, which had several guards stationed around the room. "Keep out of the light."

Rowan nodded.

Asha grabbed hold of her hand and they skirted the edge of the room, dodging behind oblivious guards. Whatever magic Asha had, it was certainly effective. They passed beneath an archway and entered a wide brick hall, decorated with suits of armor. Rowan gagged involuntarily at the sight of them: she swore skulls stared at her from behind the face plates.

Asha tugged on her hand. "It's the suits. They are fueled by necromancy. Your body knows it's magic that goes against nature."

There was a small alcove up ahead and Asha pulled her into the space. "Time to leave." She waved a hand, and a glowing oval *thing* hung suspended in the air.

"What—?"

"It's a portal. Come on." Asha pulled Rowan through. Her entire body sizzled, like she'd touched an electrical socket.

One step later and their surroundings had changed, a rocky shoreline stretching out before her. Sand glittered in the twilight sky, sparkling like it was made from tiny black diamonds. A dull gray ocean lapped at the shore, and peace sunk into her bones, a sense of serenity dampening the air, which held the mild tang of sulfur.

Asha bent at the waist, grabbing her side as if she had a stitch. "We're out."

I'm free.

For now.

I have to speak to Yael. She grabbed her cellphone out of her pocket, heart sinking when she saw there was no signal. Although… "Where are we?"

"You're in my domain, on the Isle of Himiko," Asha said. "Your cell won't work here, not unless you have had it upgraded for Hell."

"Hell?"

The woman nodded. "We're in a part of Tartarus."

Tartarus. Yael said that Hades ruled Tartarus. So, she was free of Lucifer. But was Hades any better?

Asha said he wasn't a total asshole.

But that meant he could still be a *bit* of an asshole.

Stop worrying. You're free now.

"Thank you. For saving me."

"You're welcome." The woman grinned. "Now, let me let my boss know we're out."

CHAPTER 49

Tower of Terrors, Sheol

It was a new experience, looking like a woman, but Yael knew he rocked it. He was wearing the illusion of Asha, so Hades appeared to be paying an official visit, P.A. in tow. The only downside was that he certainly didn't sound like one, so he had to keep his mouth zipped. Which was cool, because the only thing he wanted to do to Lucifer was rip the guy's head off. Concentrating on keeping his witty one-liners behind his teeth helped distract him.

"Lucy, you've been a bad boy." Hades had condescension down to an art form.

The other Hell-lord stared at the Greek god like he was dirt beneath his shoe. "At least I didn't fuck my niece."

Hades drew back, placing a hand over his heart. "Low blow, Lucy. Low blow." But the god wasn't offended, if anything, he seemed amused.

"And what are you trying to blame me for, this time?" Lucifer sat behind an obsidian desk, while Yael-slash-

Asha and Hades stood in front of it. The fallen angel's office was spartan, with only a handful of decorations, none of his antiquities collection in sight.

"You kidnapped a conduit," Hades accused.

"I did not."

"*Tsk tsk.* I may not be an angel, but I know when someone lies to me."

Lucifer glared. "Who and what I kidnap are none of your concern."

"See, that's where you're wrong. Kidnap a regular human, no big deal. Kidnap a demon, again, not a huge deal. But kidnap a conduit? That changes the balance of power, and you know that isn't allowed."

"What are you going to do? Tell on me?" Lucifer sneered.

"Yes. You have twelve hours to return her, or I'll get Ereshkigal involved."

"I'm so scared."

But something flashed in Lucifer's pale eyes. Fear maybe? Or irritation? It was hard to tell.

Who the fuck is Ereshkigal? It was the name of some old god, that much he knew. But why was she a threat?

Raze may have the answer.

"Twelve hours." Hades waved a hand and they teleported out of the Hell-lord's office, appearing in a small wooden boat, just off the shore of a small island. The scent of brine and sulfur were pungent and not particularly pleasant.

"Where are we?" Yael asked.

"Just outside of Asha's domain." The god clicked his fingers, and Yael's legs morphed from the long, elegant jean-clad ones of Asha, into his familiar black cargos.

"She has a domain?"

"Yes." Hades began rowing. There was a soft tinkling of bells, and moments later the boat beached on a glimmering shoreline.

"*Yael!*" Rowan's voice cut through the air and then she was in his arms. He hugged her to him, burying his face in her hair.

Lemongrass and sweat and her.

Fuck.

His heart kicked hard in his chest. She was here, she was alive, and she was safe.

He stared over her shoulder at Asha, relief and gratitude in his eyes. "You got her out."

"I did. Lucifer hadn't amped up his security since I was last there, which was surprising." Asha turned to Hades. "He's overconfident. That makes me think something else is going on."

Hades nodded. "We will discuss it later." Then he stared at Rowan. "You're different."

Rowan lifted her head and turned to the god. Her green eyes clouded. "I've seen you before, but I don't…"

Hades strode over and touched her gently on the forehead. Rowan's back arched like she'd been electrocuted, and Yael growled low at the god. "What the fuck did you do to her?"

Hades withdrew his finger. "I gave her her memories back. She now knows magic is real, so there's no harm there."

Rowan shuddered in Yael's arms. "I remember you, now. And Seraphina, and Trick. They employed me to find the *Amenonuhoko*. I didn't just go looking for it on my own. That's how I met Luke." She looked at Hades. "They did it for you."

"They did. But everyone lived, so I call it a win."

Rowan didn't seem happy about it, and to be honest, Yael wasn't either. It had sent her straight into Lucifer's sphere. But she was here now. With him. Safe.

Hades turned to go, but stopped. "Oh, and did you happen to touch any strange stones lately?" Hades asked her. "Looks a bit like quartz?"

Rowan bit her lip, then nodded.

Hades clapped Yael on the shoulder. "Guess you just found the second piece of Heaven's Heart."

The god vanished.

CHAPTER 50

I have Heaven's Heart? Rowan wondered.

The piece of rose quartz she'd dropped in the tomb? But where was it? Had it somehow attached itself to her?

"You found it and you didn't tell me?" Yael asked, his expression shuttered.

"I didn't know what it was. I found it in the passageway on the ground. Then I dropped it and couldn't find it again."

He looked thoughtful. "Now we really can't let Lucifer get his hands on you again. Can you show it to me?"

"I don't know where it is." She shook her head, holding her hands out from her sides, boots sparkling with black diamond dust.

"When worn by a human," Asha said, "the Heart is absorbed into the flesh. You could only see it if she dies, or if she's touched by an archangel."

Well, she wasn't going to die any time soon. She hoped. Prayed.

And it wasn't likely that she'd be running into any archangels.

"Are you sure?" Yael demanded.

"Do I look like I don't know what I'm talking about?" Asha replied, her voice sharp as a whip.

"No—"

"Thank you for helping me," Rowan said. She didn't know what Asha was, exactly, but Rowan wasn't about to risk Yael making her angry. The woman could control shadows, and the slightly skeletal mask she wore— visible from time to time—was no doubt the result of some scary origin story.

Asha turned cunning eyes on Rowan "You owe me a favor in the future. Unspecified."

"Okay."

Asha seemed mollified. "Now, this is my domain. No one can enter or leave here without my permission."

"Your domain? But isn't this Tartarus? How can you have a domain?" Yael asked. Rowan wanted to stomp on his foot.

"This is the Isle of Himiko and it's mine because I made it," Asha replied. "But since I answer to Hades, it's under his direct rule, so no issues there. Now, I have a Wayfarer's Hut here. You are welcome to use it for twenty-four hours, after that, you're on your own."

"What's a Wayfarer's Hut?" Rowan asked, before Yael could make another smartass quip. She loved his humor, but she could see not everyone else did.

Asha started walking up the beach. At the edge of the sand, blue spiky grass grew, spreading out into a field beyond. There, nestled in the shadow of a peak, sat a timber hut. A small path of diamond sand led to the front door, which was a bright cherry red.

"Wayfarer's Huts are safe places in Hell. They were

created at its dawn, and they are very rare. I had to lure this one here from Sheol. It wouldn't leave until it laid an egg."

"An egg?" Rowan echoed.

"Yes, turns out they have chicken legs, and can walk when they want to. It didn't want to leave the space vacant. One day, there'll be a new Hut there." Asha shrugged, like it was a little odd, but there you go. "Anyway, they're sentient. So don't piss it off."

It's sentient?

Thankfully, her manners kicked in. "Thank you for letting us stay here."

Asha turned back to them and smirked. "Use your twenty-four hours wisely. Oh, and if you break it, you bought it." Then she waved her hand, created a shimmering portal, and left.

Together, Yael and Rowan walked to the hut. She knocked tentatively on the door, and it swung open, silent and smooth. The scent of cherry blossoms wreathed through the air.

"I've been in a Hut before," Yael said, stepping inside.

"You have?"

The interior had a strong Japanese aesthetic, with rice-paper partitions, and a minimalist interior. But after Rowan crossed the threshold, it morphed, changing into her ideal apartment: soft pink, gold and white tones, with a functional kitchen, large living area, and small dining zone. A gray sofa was positioned in front of a glowing fire.

"This is amazing," she said. The temperature inside the hut warmed, and every surface seemed to glimmer more brightly. "Thank you."

Yael gave her a thumbs up.

The small bit of praise made her heart swell. *I can do this. I can cope with weird.* "I need a shower," she said.

In answer, a door opened to her left, leading into a decadent bathroom. A sunken bath sat in the middle of the tiled expanse, with a huge walk-in shower right near the door. Rowan hurried for it with single-minded focus.

She hadn't showered in a week.

"Need help washing your back?" Yael asked, waggling his eyebrows.

She paused.

You don't deserve him. You are the reason Eric's dead.

No. Lucifer was the reason Eric was dead. And maybe Hades, or Trick and Seraphina. Not her. And yes, if Yael wanted her, she'd have him.

She turned back and held out her hand to him, "Yes."

His mouth crashed down on hers before they made it to the bathroom. The charge between them sparked to life, hot and needy and hungry. She could have kissed him all day. He tasted like mint and spice and all things nice. She barely had enough time to rip off her dirty clothes before Yael crowded her into the shower. He radiated heat; his body smooth planes of warm muscle. She reached behind her to find the faucet, turning it on so that hot water rained down on them from the ceiling.

It felt opulent, like they were standing beneath a warm waterfall.

Yael's hand swept up over her stomach, then up, up, cupping one of her breasts in his palm. *Yes.* God, it felt right. She moaned as he stroked her nipple, and then he bent down, taking the hardened bud into his mouth, licking and sucking on it until she was panting, clutching at him like she'd run a marathon.

Why does it feel so good?

Her fingers dug into his shoulders, and then she lowered them, letting them run wild over the smooth skin she could feel for miles. Over his back, his ass, and then around the front, playing with the hair just above his cock.

He pulled away from her breast for a moment to breathe, "Tease", before taking her other nipple in his mouth. She reached down, running a gentle hand along his length. It jerked against her touch, burning hot and hard. Oh, it was so hard. She looked down, taking in the view of him at her breasts, her hand stroking his cock.

This is so hot.

She'd never felt so aroused in her life.

He stepped forward, pushing her against the tile wall. She gasped at the temperature contrast; freezing cold on her back, burning heat at her front. Yael stood, resting one arm on the tiles behind her, sheltering her from the waterfall. "You are so beautiful."

His gaze was intense, his gold-flecked eyes burning. And for the first time, she truly did feel beautiful. To him.

His free hand swept her body, sliding right down between her legs, cupping her core. She moaned, arching against the tingling sensation. He ran a finger along her sex, then pressed in, finding her so wet and needy it hurt. His finger moved to her clit and started stroking, fast, then slow, fast, then slow. She kissed him, her tongue thrusting into his mouth, demanding more, demanding everything. "And you called me a tease."

He slid two fingers deep within her, and she bit his lip.

He grinned against her mouth.

Yael pulled away, sliding down her body, until he kneeled between her thighs. She mourned the loss of his weight, his heat. Then he lifted her leg up, placing her knee over his shoulder. She was utterly exposed to him, vulnerable. He licked her, one long sweep of his tongue that had her body clenching in ecstasy, on the verge of orgasm.

She grabbed his head. "More!"

"Demanding woman." When his mouth finally latched onto her clit and sucked, she screamed, an orgasm crashing through her, the pleasure so intense, so intimate, she thought she'd die.

Stars fading from her vision, she rested, panting, against the tiles while Yael stood, grinning widely. "That's number one."

Pushing up on her toes, she kissed him, moaning as his arms closed around her. He lifted her up, his cock wedged between them, and she squirmed, trying to get access to it.

His voice was low, rough with need. "Wrap your legs around me."

She did, and it pressed her against his erection. She arched, the friction making her gasp in pleasure. He cupped her butt, titling her pelvis forward. With her free hand, Rowan guided his cock through her folds, then further. "Mmmm."

He thrust home in one slow, burning stroke.

She gasped at the sensation of being filled, being one with him. And then he was moving, each stroke elevating her desire, bonding to her him, tying them together. The pleasure kept building and building, until she screamed, "I'm coming!"

He hiked her legs higher around his waist and pounded into her, out of control. His muscles corded as he kissed her, and she felt a third orgasm crash through her as he came, groaning through his release. She clutched him to her as his essence filled her, hot and intense.

They stayed like that after, pressed together, still joined, heartbeats riding out an exhausted rhythm. He pressed his forehead to hers. "I love you, for as long as I have you."

She hugged him, happy in this moment, with him, her heart full. "I love you, too."

CHAPTER 51

Their twenty-four hours up, and his limbs as limp as overcooked spaghetti, Yael opened a Devilsgate and brought them to Rowan's apartment. She'd wanted to go there first, to grab her essentials before she'd return with him to the mansion.

They were officially making a go of it.

And they'd had sex. A lot of it.

Totally worth it.

Rowan packed some clothing into a suitcase. She was much more methodical than he'd been. "So, what are you going to do, now that you have the second piece of the Heart?"

"Find the third." He leaned against the doorjamb of her bedroom. Inside was all cream modernity, just as the Hut had mimicked.

"And then?" she asked.

"I don't understand."

"They said you'd have to kill me—"

He approached her. "Or get an archangel. They never said we had to unite the stones. They just said we had to find the three pieces, bring them back to Heaven."

She smiled, although it looked strained. "I just—we just found each other. I've just lost two people I cared about. I can't lose a third. And I don't want to die."

She was worried about him, he realized. About *them*. And her fears for her future were totally justified. "I am not giving you up, not while there is breath left in my body. Don't worry." He cupped her cheeks and kissed her.

"Isn't this touching?" The new voice was like a cold slap.

Yael spun around, pushing Rowan behind him for protection. His jaw dropped.

"*Mother?*"

There, just outside the doorway, stood Iliane, her pure white wings rising behind her back in a sweep of arrogance. "You always were a disappointment."

What the fuck is happening?

Had Hell frozen over?

"Why are you here?" he demanded.

"It is shameful to admit, but there is always a bond between mother and child, no matter how much she might wish it would vanish. I used it to find you. Do you know what your fall did to us? If we hadn't already publicly distanced ourselves from you, it would have damaged our reputations. Didn't you think about what it would mean? Your grandfather was speechless."

Considering Yael's grandfather had been meditating for several hundred years, the latter wasn't a surprise.

"You should be ashamed of yourself!" Rowan shouted, scrabbling past him to see Iliane. "Yael is wonderful and you're nothing but a nasty piece of work."

His mother drew herself up, wings splaying out behind her. "You dare talk to me in such a fashion? You *scum*." Scorn burned in her hazel eyes—eyes identical to his own—and then the room vanished around them.

Yael stumbled back as he appeared in Heaven, Rowan behind him. They stood in an open area lined with gold pillars and clouded-filled walls.

We're in the archangels' section of the Celestial City.

"What the—?" His mother had never had that power before.

"So, you found a conduit." Another cool, scornful voice.

Yael jerked around, careful to keep Rowan partially hidden by his body.

He took in the two large forms.

It wasn't Mother's power.

"Michael. Uriel." Yael nodded.

When will this shit just end?

Couldn't they have their happily ever after already?

The two archangels stood side by side, wearing identical expressions of contempt. Gold-threaded wings flared, as if to show their power and his utter lack of it. This wasn't a good sign, not a good sign at all.

"You thought you could use this conduit to try and sneak back into Heaven?" Uriel demanded.

Yael's jaw hung open in shock. "What? No."

He wasn't about to use Rowan for anything. And he had no idea he *could* have.

"Conduits are a danger to the power balance of the world. Lucifer has already taken her once, and Satan tried to before that. She must die." Michael appeared in front of them, hand closing on Rowan's shoulder before Yael could wrench her out of the way.

Yael tried to free Rowan from the archangel's grip, but Michael had stopped dead, his face taut. "I see you found the second piece of Heaven's Heart," he spat. "We will take it now."

Michael pulled Rowan toward him.

Yael growled low and conjured a sword. "Let her go."

Michael flicked a hand, conjuring his own blade of fire. "You can't stop us."

Yael reached out mentally and called to the one person who might step in, who might help. But he had no guarantee.

Grandfather! Help!

Nothing.

His thought had reached the target, but there was no response. Desperate now, he considered calling Trick—the bastard might be able to intervene. Might be able to do *something* as Rowan was slowly pulled from him.

Please, Grandfather. I need you.

Oh, how that had hurt to admit.

A heartbeat later, white light blasted through the room. Yael shielded his eyes, keeping a tight grip around Rowan's arm, all that he had left. When it faded, a gray-haired archangel stood in the center of the room, his wings so threaded with gold there was almost no white left. Power pulsed from him, steady and strong.

Shock flashed over Uriel's face. "Metatron."

The newcomer ignored him. Instead, he turned to Yael. "Grandson."

"They want to take Rowan and kill her."

"She is an abomination," Michael said coldly. "The Heart belongs here. She should not have stolen it."

But Metatron appeared thoughtful. One by one, more archangels appeared in the room, teleporting in. Aurora, Gabriel, Raphael, Nanael, Enlil and others besides. Their presence brought a wave of power, and it was all Yael could do to stay upright. His mother dropped to her knees, unable to take the onslaught. Rowan stood tall, shoulder still in Michael's grip.

"Why did you bring them here?" Uriel demanded.

"Heaven's Heart was broken at the dawn of creation, one part to be worn by an angel, one by a demon, and one by God's children. She has a right to wear the Heart, if it is the Heart meant for the latter. We should all bear witness to this event."

"She *stole* it," Michael snapped.

Metatron approached Michael, indicating he should step aside. He did so, reluctance visible in every line of his body. Metatron placed a hand on Rowan's shoulders and breathed deeply. "She has the right Heart. It chose her. It is done."

Michael stepped forward. "But she's a conduit—"

Bells tolled, and a new presence appeared. *What's with all the bells?* They seemed to sound whenever a Hell-lord appeared in a new realm. "Well, isn't this nice. A reunion."

Lucifer.

What the fuck?

Grandfather...

Metatron ignored him, focused on the Hell-lord, as were all the other archangels.

"Why are you here, Lucifer?" Nanael demanded, her tone haughty and cruel.

The Hell-lord smirked, arrogance seeping from him.

"You have something of mine."

"You were banned from ever setting foot in Heaven again!" Enlil shouted, hot-tempered. "Begone!"

"I will leave, as soon as I take my property with me." Lucifer pointed at Rowan.

"No!" Rowan protested. "I am not yours! I am not anyone's. Let me go!"

Yael wanted to grab her, pull her close to him, but he couldn't. Not yet, anyway. It would be an insult to his grandfather, if he did it now.

So, this is why Lucifer didn't have extra guards posted. He had a backup plan.

"You are, you signed a contract." A piece of paper appeared in Lucifer's hands.

Contract?

"Show me." Metatron held out a palm. Smugly, Lucifer passed it over. Yael could almost see him thinking *checkmate.*

"It is an employment contract." Metatron said, voice cool and calm. "It states that one Rowan Broome agrees to be your employee until you terminate the contract."

"That's not what I agreed to," Rowan said, moving a little closer to Yael.

Lucifer tilted his head. "It was in the fine print."

From Rowan's face, it hadn't been in the fine print of the copy she'd received.

Nanael stepped forward. "Let me see." Metatron handed her the document. The archangel scanned it and passed it back, with a raised eyebrow. "It's invalid."

"Invalid?" Lucifer demanded, face darkening. "Don't bother lying to me. I *was* one of you, remember?"

"This contract is designed for use by Hell-lords with

humans *only*," Nanael chided. "It is in the approved template in accordance with Code four-three-three in the Temptation Codex. Rowan is not human, and so the deal is void."

"Not human?" Lucifer wheeled on Yael. "What did you do to her—?"

Nanael *tsked*. "She is the wearer of Heaven's Heart. It has fundamentally changed her. She is immortal, and therefore, cannot be human."

"*What*?" Lucifer's shadow wings burst from his back, smoke horns crowning his temple as lightning danced over his flesh. Then he calmed. "But she was human at the time the contract was signed. So she must abide by it."

"If you can produce the human," Nanael said. "You can take her."

Lucifer's expression turned crafty, the lightning fading away.

"You may not remove the Heart. It is forbidden for any angel—fallen or not—to kill the Heart's *true* host. A rule some people need to remember." Nanael glared meaningfully at Michael, then Lucifer.

With a curse, the Hell-lord vanished.

But his voice pierced through Yael's mind. *This isn't over.*

No, things were only just beginning.

CHAPTER 52

One by one, the archangels left the cloud room. *I'm standing in a cloud.* It didn't feel real, none of it did. But here Rowan was, in front of an archangel even she'd heard about: Metatron, God's personal scribe.

Eventually, only Yael, she, Metatron, and the female archangel who'd schooled Lucifer on contract law remained. The female archangel was barely five feet tall, with russet-red hair, and eyes of dark brown. She was kind of terrifying.

"Lucifer is up to something," Nanael murmured. "He wants to alter the balance of power."

"Yes." Metatron nodded, stroking his chin. "He has never accepted his fate."

"I will go and discuss this further." Nanael turned to them. "Say hello to my brother and his mate." Then she too, disappeared.

"Brother?" Rowan asked.

Yael sighed, a long-suffering expression. "Trick. And Seraphina is his mate."

She brightened. "They got together?"

"They did."

Metatron placed a hand on Yael's shoulder. "Grandson, it was good you called to me."

"I didn't know if you'd come, but I couldn't let them hurt Rowan. And you have always been the voice of reason."

"My voice has been silent for too long, I fear." The gray-haired angel was handsome, with the faintest of lines forking out from the corner of his eyes. But he was sad, deep down inside, she could sense it.

Yael's grandfather is the scribe of God?

She suddenly needed to sit down. Or have a glass of wine. Probably both.

It was only through sheer willpower she remained upright. She was going to have to get used to these things. Angels, archangels, Hell, Heaven, witches, magic, *gods*.

Metatron winced and tapped his temple. "Your mother has been quite vociferous in her disapproval of my interference. And I must apologize. She did not want me to be around you as a child, because she said I was a bad influence. But now I see she only kept me away because they were jealous. They did not like that you enjoyed spending time with me more than with them. I am sorry I was not there to save you from their selfishness. But I fell into deep meditation, and when I resurfaced, you were an adult, calling for my help."

"They told me you no longer wanted to see me because I was such a failure."

Metatron's eyes darkened. "There will be a reckoning, do not fear. And your wings—"

"They are gone." But Yael didn't seem angry this time, more accepting. She pressed her shoulder against him in silent support.

"Are they?" Metatron's mouth turned up in a secretive smile. He turned to Rowan. "As the wearer of Heaven's Heart, you are now immortal, provided you don't get decapitated or lose the Heart. Guard it well."

"But, where is it?" Rowan asked, bewildered. Everyone said she had it...but how could she lose it if she didn't know where it was?

Metatron waved a hand over Rowan's neck, and a heavy weight suddenly rested against her sternum. "What—?"

She looked down. The rough-cut rose quartz she'd found in the entrance to the tomb rested against her chest. The archangel waved his hand again, and it vanished, but she could feel an echo of the weight that had briefly rested against her skin.

"It is not designed to be worn. The Heart will become part of you, fused with the very essence of your soul. The bond is new, and fragile, so you must guard it."

She frowned. "But if this makes me immortal, then how come Twosret died?"

"The last wearer of the Heart was murdered, and demons tried to steal the stone for themselves. But they could never have worn it, never bonded with it. And the Heart chooses its mate. Humans hid both Twosret and the Heart from angels and demons both."

"But what does it *do*?" Yael asked, taking her free hand in his.

"It depends on the individual. You are a conduit, so who knows. You may become a great and powerful witch."

"But I can't *do* magic, I can just channel it."

"You *couldn't* do magic. Now you may be able to." Metatron smiled, and it was so radiant her breath caught in her throat. "Now, here is my gift to you. I have spoken with the other archangels and we agree, you need a protector, so people like Lucifer can't abduct you and try to tip the balance of power in the universe. It is the only way they will agree to let you leave here."

"A protector? Wait, what happens to other conduits?" She had the feeling it was nothing good.

"It depends on the power of the conduit. But you are strong, and Lucifer has already tried to use you. Some of the archangels would have ruled for your death, others, clemency. But many hold Michael's views."

Rowan bit her lip. So, if she hadn't found the Heart…she'd be dead. Killed by Yael's kind.

Aren't angels meant to be the good guys?

"However, the archangels have ruled that you need a protector, one who will put your safety first above all others. But they must be an angel."

"And I can choose?"

"This is my gift to you."

She felt Yael tense beside her. "Will they have to be a Heavenly angel, or can they be fallen?"

"The others have decreed it must be a Heavenly angel."

"What is the exact phrase they used?" Rowan asked, mind spinning through the possibilities.

"That you must be guarded by one who will put your safety above all others, and who is a member of the Heavenly court of angels. No fallen."

"I am sure they have a list of recommendations?"

Metatron's brown eyes grew amused. "They do."

"Then I pick Yael."

He jerked. "*What?*"

Rowan waved an arm at the archangel. "Make him winged again, or unfallen, or whatever it is."

"But I was given a task—" Yael started.

"Yes, you were. But this is more important. Very important." Metatron smiled kindly. "Your parents always thought you were destined for greatness, because I saw you would one day guard the Heart. They thought you would captain the Darts. But that is not what I saw. You were born to do this. Surely you felt the bond the moment you two first touched? Yes? And your powers have increased since you've been together, even though you lost your wings?"

Yael nodded, speechless for the first time since she'd met him.

Metatron touched Yael on the shoulder, and the angel buckled in agony. "I'd turn away if I was you," the archangel said to her gently, as if she wasn't strong enough for whatever would happen next.

The old Rowan wouldn't have been. But the new Rowan, she watched as bony appendages burst forth from Yael's back, bloody and raw. Watched as they extended, hardened, and as feathers grew, covering his wings until two snowy white wings adorned his back. Watched as he gritted his teeth through the pain, stronger than anyone she knew.

He's whole again.

Funny, how the wings looked *right*.

Yael was breathing heavily as he glanced over his shoulder, eyes widening in joy at the sight. "They're white."

Metatron dipped his head to the side. "You are her protector. You're no longer a soldier."

"I am welcome back in Heaven?"

His grandfather nodded.

Yael let out a whoop and grabbed Rowan, spinning her round and round while laughing. "You did it!"

She smiled, delighted to see him happy. *"We* did it."

CHAPTER 53

Rowan had moved into the mansion with him. Yael may be welcome back in Heaven, but he wanted to live with Rowan in the Human Realm, let her continue her passions, live her life as she saw fit.

After all, they would eventually have plenty of time to live in Heaven, but her family and loved ones only had one lifetime to spend with her. Not that they'd spoken about that yet, but that was immortality for you.

At times, it sucked.

But right now, now Yael waited outside Cat on a Broomstick while Rowan met with her family. She'd wanted to go in alone. A few days ago, he would have thought it was because she was ashamed to be seen with him, but now he knew it was because she needed to do it on her own. To prove she could. She needed to take charge of her life, not have someone run it. And Yael, who'd only ever wanted the freedom to swim in his own lane, could totally understand that.

It had nothing to do with him.

"So, when's the party happening?" Dru asked.

Yael started, and gritted his teeth. "How do you keep doing that?" He scoped the alley and still couldn't work out how she'd snuck up on him.

"It's a secret."

"Of course, it is."

Azrael appeared behind her, grinning. "We heard there was going to be a celebration."

Yael threw his hands up. "I have no idea. I'm just waiting here."

"I heard about it from Seraphina," Raze said, his deep voice added to the mix.

As if called, Seraphina appeared in the alley next to Azrael. "And I got it from Trick."

Trick strode into view, and wrapped his arms around Seraphina's middle, nuzzling at her neck. "And I made it up."

Typical.

The alley behind the Cat on a Broomstick suddenly felt very full. Everyone who meant something to him was here—aside from Metatron. And his adopted family was impressive: Azrael, Seraphina, Raze and Z. Plus, Dru and Trick, although he couldn't say his in-laws excited him.

I'd take Dru over Trick any day.

He'd never tell anyone that, except maybe Rowan.

"Nice wings," Trick said, eyebrow arching.

"Fuck off." Yael flipped him the bird.

"Hey! That's my line!" Dru glared at him.

The back door to the shop opened, and Rowan poked her head out, scowling when she spotted them all lurking there. "What are you all doing out here?"

"We've come for the party," Trick said, holding up a six pack of beer that hadn't been in his hand a moment ago.

"Party?"

"Move aside." Dora's cane shoved at Rowan until she stepped away. The Crone then stood on the stoop, surveying them with narrowed eyes. "Well, come inside then. We'll use the upstairs space."

"Upstairs?" Rowan's mouth opened in surprise. "We never use upstairs."

"And we don't normally host parties at the shop. Go! Now!"

They complied, some of the most powerful people in Hell filing through the door like obedient children. Z was careful to keep his wings tucked close to his body, and Trick made some smartass quip on his way past.

The stench of ozone filled the air, and two new figures appeared.

Yael gulped.

Hades held two bottles of whiskey, and Asha wore a cocktail dress that looked like a piñata had vomited confetti all over her. "We heard there was a party," Asha said.

Dora glared. "It's bad enough there's an archangel, a Mortus cambion, and the mate of the Mortus Queen. Now you two want in?"

"What? I love parties!" Asha gave a little jump then rushed past them, into the shop.

Hades followed more sedately. The god's hair was braided into a complicated style, exposing the side of his shaved head. "Trying to stop Asha is just going to give me a migraine. And I don't get headaches."

He disappeared inside the shop.

Then it was just Rowan, Yael and Dora.

The old woman smirked and patted him on the cheek, hard. "I told you you'd be my grandson-in-law." Then she thumped off toward the staircase, shouting instructions at the partygoers.

"Grandson-in-law?" Rowan murmured, smiling at him.

"Yeah. She knows everything. Blah blah." He closed the distance to Rowan, shutting the door behind him with a decisive click.

"Blah blah?"

"Yeah. You know. We'll get married, live happily ever after, all that shit."

She kissed him, sweet and soft, and the taste of home.

"And all that shit."

Epilogue

Asha Himm, demigoddess extraordinaire, Personal Assistant to Hades, King of Hell, may have had a little bit too much to drink the night before. A Cock-sucking Cowboy, ten mojitos, twelve shots of tequila, and a keg of Djinn spiced mead that Hades had teleported in, had been overkill. She should have refused the Cowboy.

But she couldn't resist a party. And she liked Rowan; the human had spunk. Guts. *Cojones.* Celebrating her and Yael's freedom had been worth it. Plus, she'd liked dancing with the quiet dark-skinned fallen angel, Raze. His stormy gaze had burned through her clothing, stroking over her skin like a psychic touch.

Worth it.

Taking a sip of green tea, she let the warm toasty aroma fill her senses. Then she shuffled the papers on her desk for effect, rather than purpose. Her office was neat and pristine in its orderliness; she had bookshelves filled with the bare necessities to do her job. Unlike her boss, whose office was crammed so full of extraneous crap it gave her hives just staring at it.

A large iMac took up valuable space on her desk, but she loved computers. She even had a machine that ran Windows, tucked away under her desk. Hades said she was fucked up because of it, but she didn't care. Like his sense of interior design was any better. He kept a statue of a cursed gargoyle in the corner of his office.

She met the piercing blue gaze of the black-winged agent who sat opposite her.

"Your name is Dina, right?" Asha asked, sensing the impatience building in the angel.

"Correct."

"And you are unfallen?"

"Also correct."

"Why are your wings black?" Asha leaned forward. That wasn't part of the employment survey she had prepared, but she wanted to know. She was nosy. Sue her.

"I was kidnapped from Heaven, and my wings cut off by Infernus demons. When they grew back, they were black." Her voice was cold and precise.

She's not lying.

Asha had a spell in place to detect that. She tapped her lip with a pencil. "You were formerly a member of an angel squadron called the Darts?"

"Yes. I was their captain."

So dispassionate, like she was reciting facts, and not one of the most devastating events of her life.

Asha could relate.

She checked her survey. "Why do you want this role?"

"Because I don't want to go back to Heaven, and

Hades seems like the least objectionable Hell-lord."

Not exactly the answer she was hoping for.

She ticked the box labelled 'Self-preservation'.

"You could work for an assassination guild. Or one of the larger demon clans."

"I am an angel. That would be like painting 'target' on my forehead and walking into an archery range."

She has a point.

She wrote down, 'Good with metaphors'.

"Do you have any administrative experience?"

"No. I was a solider. I've always been a solider." Dina paused, as if sensing she hadn't said the correct answer. "But I can learn."

"How you feel about the dead?" Asha asked.

"As in dead bodies or ghosts?"

"Both."

"I have no objection to either," Dina replied.

"And killing people?"

"I excel at it."

Asha ticked the box next to 'Psychopath'.

"And finally, what is your allegiance to your other Darts?" Personally, Asha liked them. Hell, she'd partied with them into the wee hours of the morning.

"I have none." Her expression closed off even further.

Wow. Okay. Asha had thought the angel was emotionless to begin with.

So that had been candor.

"Perfect." Asha understood having allegiance to others, but if Dina was going to become her P.A. — what? She was super-busy — then she should be loyal only to her. And Hades.

But mostly to her.

Asha stood, and Dina followed suit, the movement so graceful it reminded her of *kabuki* dancers. She held out a hand for the angel to shake.

Dina took it, her grip cool and dry.

"You're hired."

Author's Note

This is a work of fiction, but I tried to keep the historical and archaeological facts as truthful as possible, without being too boring. Archaeology is a painstakingly slow profession, filled with far more paperwork than is healthy. I should know, I'm an archaeologist.

But the Eighteenth Dynasty in Egypt was one of the most fascinating periods, I think. It had at least three — maybe four female pharaohs — plus Akhenaten (formerly called Amenhotep IV), who is the first person on record to introduce monotheism as a belief system. He and his family worshipped the Aten, the sun disk, and he eventually erased the other gods from worship. After his death, his queen, Nefertiti, is thought to have taken on the role of pharaoh and ruled as Neferneferuaten. Although new research has said Neferneferuaten was potentially one — or more — of her daughters.

Akhenaten revolutionized the Egyptian religion to such an extent, that after his and Neferneferuaten's death, his son, Tutankhaten, changed his name to Tutankhamun (with Amun being a traditional sun god) and returned the religion to its former glory.

And we all know who Tutankhamun is; the boy king with the intact tomb.

However, sadly, Akhenaten and Neferneferuaten were removed from the official king lists, and were later described as 'the enemy'. We know of them simply because his abandoned city, Amarna—the brand-new capital he created to worship the Aten—was discovered by archaeologists, a veritable treasure trove of information.

So, with so many interesting historical figures to pick from, why did I choose Twosret?

And yes, she was a real pharaoh.

I decided on her for two reasons: one, because she is one of the few pharaohs from the Eighteenth Dynasty whose mummy is yet to be identified. And two, because she was a female king.

In ancient Egypt, the pharaoh was not only a king, but a god, *Neter Nefer*. While the role was typically filled by men, the title wasn't gendered. Women took the mantle from time to time, and Twosret was one of them. Her reign was short, all of three years, at the end of the Eighteenth Dynasty, and like Akhenaten, her successors wanted to obliterate her name from history.

Currently, her tomb has yet to be found, although archaeologists suspect they may have discovered her remains in KV14, in the Valley of the Kings. However, her identity is disputed.

As for the two new tombs that were discovered in this novel, they haven't been found yet and are unlikely to exist (but who knows!). There is one unexcavated tomb in the valley—found through G.P.R.—and archaeologists are planning to excavate it when they can. Here's hoping it's Nefertiti!

Acknowledgements

Ascending Passion was a long book to write, done madly during my daughter's naps. As usual, there are plenty of people who deserve thanks. Firstly, I'd like to thank my husband Tom, who gave me the time to write this book. I also want to thank my wonderful beta readers Joanne Danton and Kel Carpenter, and my eagle-eyed editor Pete Kempshall. As always, you are invaluable in the creation of my work. And last, but certainly not least, the real Kayla Perkins. You died well.

Amanda Pillar is an USA TODAY Bestselling Author and award-winning editor who lives in Victoria, Australia, with her husband, daughter, and two cats.

Amanda has had numerous short stories published and has co-edited six fiction anthologies and solo-edited two.

Amanda's first novel, *Graced*, was published by Momentum in 2015. The stories *Captive* and *Survivor* were also released in 2016, followed by *Bitten* and *Ashes* in 2017. She has also just launched the Heaven's Heart series.

In her day job, she works as an archaeologist.